Wish I Were Here
A Novel

Erin Lavan

Copyright © 2016 by Erin Lavan

All rights reserved.

This book or any portion thereof
may not be reproduced or used in any manner whatsoever
without the express written permission of the publisher
except for the use of brief quotations in a book review.

Cover design by Savannah Kodish

Printed in the United States of America

First Printing, 2017

ISBN: 978-1-52-126135-4

DEDICATION

For "Doc" who inspired me to write it.
For Norith Soth who brought it to life.
For my friends and family who read it with fervency.

CONTENTS

Hands	1
Ax Man	12
Drugs	26
Key	31
Murderer	37
Jello	40
Fat Cat	49
Dead Socks	53
Diner	65
Fireworks	75
Alps?	82
iCoffin	91
Ramen	97
The Gang	102
Churros	124
Spiders	139
Beast Master	150

Pierce	164
Nice Jets	174
Ekhard	179
Bully	188
The Lift	197
Stature	205
Brain Surgeon	211
Aliens	221
The Portrait	230
Femme Fatale	239
God's Bosoms	243
Tornado	248
Unicorn	254
Pure Eve	259
Kissing Distance	270

HANDS

"I KNOW WHAT YOU'RE THINKING. Nothing has value," she said, "until it's lost. I see that in *your hands*. I see it in the way they hold things. In one image, the hands drop a ring of keys. In another, they hold onto the petals of a dying flower. That one is holding..."

As usual, Suzanne couldn't shut up. And, I couldn't tell her to shut up because I had made a living off of her analysis of *my* work. When the rest of the world considered me worthless, she saw me as *important*, kind of like the Egyptian princess who saw Moses' basket flowing down the river. I was Moses. Minus the Ten Commandments.

"...a Twix candy bar, I think? It's unwrapped. It's been bitten into. It's already lost. When I was a kid, I was always depressed, halfway into a candy bar. I wanted to go back to when it was whole and still fully wrapped."

The meaning she saw in my paintings was astonishing. Usually, this shit was fun to hear... but not tonight.

"It's so *apropos* of your life. You're turning forty. Forty is a very fatherly age. Fifty is more motherly."

Where did she get this crap? Seriously. SHUT UP! Or the cute guy in the Hawaiian shirt will stop eye-fucking me.

"Forty is when dads go through a profound mid-life crisis. They buy Harleys, Corvettes, Porsches. Their taste in women gets more virginal. They start jogging as they reflect, and realize their youth was completely wasted. Thrown into a fireplace. Gone, whoops! "

Jesus. She was drunk, too. I told Joy, no Chardonnay for Suzanne or she will latch onto me like a poodle without a master.

"Your hands are all men's hands. Each one of them. Not young men's either. This recalls Michelangelo's Sweet Sistine."

When Suzanne calls The Sistine Chapel "Sweet Sistine," she's a ticking time bomb, and you better run for your life.

"This is a great show. I mean, I don't know why you abandoned those delicious lovers' portraits, but the hands are a very, very close second. "

"Hand Maid" was the title of my new exhibit. 23 paintings. All hands. These limbs get to hold things, touch things, break things. In one canvas, sand seeps through fingers; in another, a cigarette burns to the fingertips.

Why did I choose hands? A) Because I miss the yellow pages. B) Because I miss handwriting. C) Because I play with myself too much. D) Because I'd really like to see Hawaiian Shirt's hands if Suzanne would stop cock-blocking me!

"I'm sure you know that you can tell what someone is thinking by the formation of their hands."

Meanwhile, Hawaiian Shirt was still glaring at me, unblinkingly, and I had to start wondering if he had that Japanese businessman disease (where they're lock-jawed into a shit-eating grin for decades). How could this guy keep it up for so long and not make a move? And who wears Hawaiian shirts outside of Hawaii? What's up with him? There were at least two dozen chicks under 35 here with bigger tits than mine. His left hand held his wine glass. His right hand was in his pocket. Alas, I failed to put Suzanne's "mind reading" theorem to the test.

"You can actually tell if someone is lying. You don't even need a lie detector test. They should teach cops to..."

Before she could complete her law enforcement dissertation, Hawaiian Shirt dug up the courage to enter my "force field." My fight or flight instinct did the rest. I whispered to her, "Suzanne, this is a...buyer. Can we talk after?"

She whispered back, "Of course, Savannah. You want me to lubricate the conversation..."

"Oh no, we've already spoken. Thank you so much."

I winked at her. She winked back, nearly ran over a waiter, and got swallowed up in the crowd. I could still hear her squeal from the other side of the room. Through, like, 47 people.

"Hello, Gaspar DeVillier."

He was French. His accent wasn't bad for a Frenchman. *My definition of "wasn't bad" means I understood WTF he was talking about without scowling and recoiling.* We shook hands. His grip was firm. His hand, sort of big. Made me feel a little adolescent. In a good way. He was about 5'11", 205 lbs. Jesus, Savannah, cool it, you're not a cop, you're a painter. You paint hands and shit (alas, fatherly ones).

"Savannah Waters," I offered, smiling back with my pearly whites. It's the least I could do to repay all the smiley faces he'd been sending me throughout the night (live ones, as opposed to texts).

"I know," he said, "I'm your number one fan."

"That is...frightening," I said, jokingly. But, of course, he didn't get it. His oceanic eyes telegraphed concern. That he'd offended me.

"Oh no, don't be afraid. I am a very well-behaved number one fan. I won't stalk you or steal your dirty underwear, or anything like that."

I cackled.

My spinal cord feels like it's being jerked back when I hear my shriek... but men think it's cute. He did anyway. One woman's self-loathing is another man's sunshine.

"I was actually talking about *Misery*," I clarified, "that Stephen King movie. Did you ever see it? The number one fan..."

"Oh, yes! That was the movie of the fat girl and the writer. She made him write her favorite book. She cut off his legs."

Fat girl? Kathy Bates was a grown woman, a widow, in that movie. French guys love to feminize things. Good luck feminizing my fatherly hands.

"That would make you the, uh...fat girl," I joked, "and I'm James Caan."

"Yes, I will keep you in my home in Bretagne," he suggested, "and force you to paint for me against your will. Ha, ha, ha!"

"Best offer I had all night," I said, girlishly...I think.

"So, I overheard your friend; you're...forty?"

Suzanne will be blacklisted from all my shows until the end of time.

"Yes. The great wall of forty."

"You look nothing like forty."

"What, like 39?"

"No, no, no, like 29."

He's full of shit. But I'm blushing anyway.

"Thank you."

"And your body...of work is..."

Ugh, I thought he was going to compliment my physique. But, I'll happily accept a compliment on my work.

"...Intoxicating. I love it. I've always loved it."

Wow. I didn't know a French man could actually pronounce "intoxicating." Very, very impressive. Great jaw muscle range, if you know what I mean.

"I adore the hands. How you paint them. Strong. They remind me of my grandfather's hands."

Great. I went from fatherly to grandfatherly. Next, ancestors?

"Why are you wearing a Hawaiian shirt?" I asked. Now, I was getting drunk on Chardonnay.

"Oh, I like the flowers. In Bretagne, where I am from, we have flowers everywhere. There are contests for who has the best arrangement of flowers in a village... *it eeze* very romantic. I don't see very many flowers in LA, so I wear them."

He was *sweet*.

"And, what provoked you to do paintings of hands?" He leaned in and stared into my eyes.

"I don't know, Gaspar. I miss masculine hands. A man shouldn't only use his hands to text. He should grab things. Lift things."

"Yes, I totally agree. I used to see people in France always reading. Now, they're all looking at their iPhones, using their index fingers to type messages."

"I hate seeing men do that." I actually do. I can't stand it.

"It's so feminine," I added, when I noticed Joy make a face at me. It looked semi-alarmed. She was also talking to a guy who, from behind, didn't look half bad. She was trying to say something, enunciating each syllable as if somehow I could formulate the words. I checked my iPhone to see if she'd texted me, but it was dead. Black. Like a little coffin. I actually caught a glimpse of my own reflection. My left eye looked forty.

"Yes, men should not...do that," Gaspar confirmed (re: men employing texty hands).

"A man should *not* hold his fingers like this," I said, redundantly, waiting for him to switch gears on subjects.

"But the creature that once ruled the Earth had hands like that?"

"Which one?"

"You don't know? The greatest predator on the planet? Everyone was scared of him?"

"The greatest predator on the planet had texty hands?"

"The big dinosaur. The T-Rex. He was giant, scary, and mean… he ate everyone, but had little tiny hands."

I knew there was a reason I don't trust men with small hands.

Gaspar held his hands like a T-Rex, fingers dangling like he had just gotten his nails painted. I smiled and said "That's funny," and then remembered something I had read about Americans having the sort of non-visceral reaction of saying "That's funny," instead of just laughing. So, I kicked it up a notch and let out a good cackle. It was infectious. He cackled too.

"The vampire had them, too," he laughed. "Nosferatu. He would have enjoyed texting."

"Right." I recomposed myself, getting further signals via Joy and her catch of the night. Why do women love gesticulating? Whereas men love to scream? Of course, this depends on what time of the night it is, how many drinks have been consumed...Gaspar noticed my *communiqué*, and pivoted around.

"That is my friend you're looking at," I said protectively.

"Manuel is your friend?"

"No, Joy is my friend."

Her chaperone spun around, too. All four of us were now trading looks. You know him. You know her. I know her. I know him.

"Joy is my cousin. And friend, too," I added.

"Beautiful *cousine*. Wonderful genes. I am so glad your grandparents fornicated."

That's one very French way of looking at it. Glad my grandpa and grandma did it. Because otherwise, my parents and Joy's parents (my Uncle Jim and Aunt Daisy) wouldn't have been spawned, and therefore Joy and I wouldn't have been born. You've gotta hand it to the French.

"Yes, mathematically, it's very romantic."

Before I knew it, we were a foursome, talking over each other like in the British courts. Joy, who is my true number one fan, not just of my career but of my life, kept going, shoving her iPhone in Manuel and Gaspar's faces, showing off pics featuring more of my impressive images.

"This is what Savvy did with a fogged-up window."

Savvy is short for Savannah, in case you haven't caught that. Most people call me "Savvy". Even though I wouldn't categorize myself as "savvy."

"Look at the details."

"Joy, stop it."

But actually, I was enjoying it. Gaspar and Manuel were both glaring at me with mutual amazement.

"How did you draw a house with snowflakes like that? Amazing!"

"Right."

"She's incredible."

"A genius."

"A beautiful genius."

It's no accident I timed this exhibit to occur on this day. Usually, I don't care to celebrate my birthday. This way, I could have a big party without officially celebrating my fortieth. It was a battle, but I had made Joy assure me there would be no cake with forty fucking candles erected on it. Reluctantly, she agreed to my wish.

"Since she was, like, right out of her mother's womb, Savvy was drawing. She drew on the walls, she drew on the stove, in the bathroom..."

"Oh, like Lascaux," said Manuel, "Gaspar and I did some hiking in the Dordogne last summer. We saw many cave drawings."

"It's the first art form," Gaspar said, "drawing and creating images from your head."

"Sure, but I heard that Lascaux is not the real Lascaux," Joy interjected. I sometimes called her "Kill Joy" due to her strange way of being a...well, a killjoy.

"Well, they're really close," Gaspar fought back.

"Yes," Manuel defended Gaspar's country, "they are fairly close. It is done to protect the real caves of Lascaux."

I think Manuel was Spanish. He was tan and had great posture, Matador-like.

"People breathed on the originals and already ruined them permanently, so..."

"Oh," Joy replied, sipping more Chardonnay, "we wouldn't want anything ruined. I was just saying..."

Suddenly, Gaspar and Manuel switched their transaction to French. I don't understand a word of French, except for *Camembert*, *Filet Mignon* and, as you know, *Chardonnay*.

"I didn't mean to insult Lascaux," Joy said, guiltily, "I just meant, they're not the real ones." An awkward silence should have ensued, but French men never feel awkward. Instead, they gracefully distanced themselves from us so we could sort it out.

It doesn't matter if guys speak English or another language, they always have their own language; they get into that faggy huddle and strategize how to get to the end zone.

"Why were you signaling to me earlier?" I asked Joy.

"Oh right," she recoiled. Her tone sounded slightly serious. Meanwhile, Gaspar and Manuel's French conversation was getting more intense, guttural; and I presumed it was about us, since they kept glancing over and smiling.

This probably meant I wouldn't be going home alone tonight. Cool. I liked Gaspar. There was a chemical reaction when he shook my hand. I prefer meeting men in the flesh rather than an iPhone app since you can tell so much by touching his hands. I have judged a good portion of men by the sensation of the hand. Sometimes it's cold and creepy, like a T-Rex hand, but with Gaspar, his hands were warm. And electric. Like an electric blanket.

"Is your phone off?" Joy asked me. "Or maybe you left it in the car or something?" She could never get to the point.

"Are you trying to call me, Joy? I'm right here!" I smiled.

"Mrs. Parsons has been calling and texting me." Joy was not smiling.

"Mrs. Parsons? Axel's mom?" I un-smiled.

Why would she call me? I wondered, perturbed. I didn't really know her, but I hoped she was OK. I hoped Axel was OK. I grabbed Joy's phone, went outside, and looked at the texts.

"This is Mrs. Parsons."

"I need to talk to Savannah."

"It's urgent."

I got chills and my hands began to shake as I hit the call button. While I listened to the phone ring, people waved to me, expressing how much they loved my *hand*s... finally, Mrs. Parsons' very quiet, distant greeting.

"Hello?"

"Hello, Mrs. Parsons. I'm sorry, my phone's battery ran out. Joy said you've been trying to contact me?"

The pause was so long, I thought I'd lost reception. I was about to say "hello" again, when I heard her voice become nasal, and high-pitched.

"You killed him."

"What? I'm sorry, who?"

"You killed him. You killed meeeeaaaawww booooy!!!"

What? Axel was dead?

"You killed him, you killed him, you killed my son!"

"What happened to Axel? Mrs. Parsons? What...?"

But she became more incoherent, and she sounded like she was speaking in tongues. She made sounds I wish I never heard.

... I had to hang up on her. I had to call Axel. But I had Joy's phone, and Axel's number was not programmed in there. I somehow mustered every fiber of memory to recollect his digits; considering I hadn't done this since 2002, it was a pretty amazing task. But, we were not here to admire my cerebral wonders. I was trembling as I dialed his number. His all too familiar voice greeted me, as it had hundreds of other times.

"Leave a voicemail...or a voice female...at the beep..."

I had to hear this a few times before I accepted what was to become my reality. The ground underneath me felt like air, like I had been thrown out of an airplane. My gut felt like it was my throat. Axel was dead. He was my ex (kind of). We were together for just about six months last year, and though I think I loved him during that short time, I never felt so great about dumping someone. Sure, there was guilt, but the security of having made the right decision made me feel like an adult. Like I had made a grown-up decision. Now, I was forty and he was dead. All I knew was that I missed him being alive.

AX MAN

    THERE ARE DEATHS for which you are obligated to feel pain – aunts or uncles in your family that you only see once or twice a year. And *you do*. Right when it happens, but it's mostly out of shock and obligation. You're never really destroyed over it, because you probably haven't seen them in years.
    I had a dog, Benjamin, who died when I was 23. I cried more for that dog than anyone because I had seen him every day for years. He was a family heirloom. When my car died, a Volkswagen Beetle that had been with me since I was 17, I cried. That car was an extension of my body. No matter what kind of work the car needed, I would fork the money over. I was gladly ripped off by mechanics to fix that car. I was close to that machine. Even though Axel and I weren't together very long, our relationship was very deep, very profound. We were kindred spirits. Interlocked. But he was dead. I would never see him again. I would never hear his voice, ride the back of his Harley, smell the weed on his breath. The truth was, he had been dead. But only dead to me. Now, he was completely gone, vanished, dead to everyone. I dumped

him, and now he's dumped everyone in his life. For good. Even his own mother. And when you get dumped, you're looking for someone to blame. I was now appointed that position... *the someone to blame.* Perks of being the last *girlfriend.* Believe it or not, this never happened to me before. Most guys I dumped were dead just to me. Some of them may not be around anymore, but I wouldn't know. They're gone. But Axel was *really gone.*

When you're really close to someone, it's as if you give them a piece of you, and when they die, that piece of you dies with them. I died a little for Axel. My stomach ached and rejected food and pouted away from everyday life. Contrary to what people say, the stomach is where true affection lies, not your heart. Just think of the times when you've been nervous about something. Think of the sensations you've felt when you see the first person you found attractive. And then, of course, there are those memories of wonderful meals. It's no accident that the courting process occurs in restaurants. The way into anyone's heart is through the stomach. Axel made my belly butterflies go wild.

Great, you're thinking. Then, why did I dump him?
I'm getting to that.
About eight months ago, in the summer, I was commissioned to paint the carousels for a festival at the Abbot Kinney Pier. Most modern day carousels use mainly fiberglass horses cast from the molds of the antique originals, but this one had wooden horses dating back to the early 1900s. That alone intrigued me. Plus, local government jobs paid pretty well, and I could always use the extra cash. I had been given a number for the "carousel engineer", so I called to set up a meeting the next day.

"Hello," the voice said. It sounded like a man who was being interrupted.

"Oh, uh...hi, this is, um...I'm looking for the carousel engineer."

"Yep," he said.

"That's you?"

"Yep," he answered.

"Hi, I'm, uh, Savannah Waters."

"Who?"

"The painter commissioned to, um, paint the carousel."

"I don't know anything about that."

"Oh...really? Carl and Tracey said..."

"I'm just kidding."

He had really, really dry humor. Seriously, he told jokes like a doctor that tells you you only have a month to live.

Anyway, he knew who I was. I proposed we meet the next day at 7 a.m. I wake up really early. I feel cheated if I don't get to see the sun come up or go down. I was there at 6:45 a.m. with a double espresso from GJelina. I was sitting in front of the carousel, which was blanketed with a blue tarp, covered in morning dew. The beauty of this side of LA was the occasional fog, and this morning a beautiful gray blanket had claimed the sky.

The silence was peaceful, but as time wore on, I grew impatient. At 7:15, I called the engineer.

"Hello," he sounded like he ate sandpaper.

"Hi, It's Savannah. We're supposed to meet at 7?"

"a.m.?"

Shit, did I not specify a.m. or p.m.? I could have sworn I had, and how could anyone start work at 7 p.m.? Anyway, he got there. At around 9:45. I had taken a walk down the beach at that point, and fought being pissed off by thinking about how lucky I was to get the gig (plus, I was secretly anticipating what the engineer might look like). I was not disappointed.

"You must be Savannah, Georgia," he said. "I'm Axel". I looked up at the man with broad shoulders, chiseled jawline, and oceanic eyes. He looked like a sculpture – a Michelangelo. He called me "Savannah, Georgia," or sometimes just "Georgia." A pet name was established in our first meeting. I called him "Ax Man".

"Could I see the carousels now?" I asked.

"Sure, Georgia," he said, and disappeared inside the tarp. It was as if he'd vanished, the perfect tease. I followed suit. We were together in this whimsical cave and the outside world disappeared. Of course, he could have strangled me to death right there and no one would have known. It was exciting.

I saw the horses for the first time. Their original designs were badly faded, and some of them had very severe-looking teeth, which I thought was fun.

I studied the merry-go-round opposite of Axel. He kept walking toward me, but I kept walking away. He said nothing. Just watched me. I sketched each horse, but kept glancing at Ax Man. He resembled them, actually – wild, with tan, weathered skin and sunlit hair falling loosely out of a wind-blown ponytail. His eyes were a piercing blue, very much like the horses', and I got a little jolt of electricity every time he looked at me. His retinas even bulged cartoonishly, like the mares', and since he didn't blink all that much, the whites of his eyes were startling. Yet thrilling. I'll never forget that first afternoon. He kept following me around and around. Even his nostrils had a horse quality to them, in a good way. It was as if he was absorbing my scent. The chase was established, quietly. It got hot inside the tarp, but I didn't ask him to remove it. I liked it closed. It felt like the moment belonged only to us.

It had to be afternoon by now and the sun was probably shining brightly, but under the tarp, it let in just enough light to sketch all of the wild ponies, including Axel. I couldn't help myself. I outlined his jaw, his hair, his eyes. Then quickly buried it in my sketchpad in case he snuck up behind me.

"Oh my God, what if he'd taken advantage of you?" Joy asked during a later phone conversation.

"That's the idea. But he won't. It's a cat-mouse thing."

"I'm so jealous. You get to paint ponies and have a hot guy chasing you around the merry-go-round. Tell me more about him."

"He has a motorcycle."

"Check."

"Ponytail."

"Check."

"Nice hands."

"Full house."

He never officially made a pass at me. He didn't talk much, except for the occasional dry joke once in a while. He would call "Savannah, Georgia" when he needed to tell me something.

"Savannah, Georgia, you want the white horse closer to you?" The tarp was gone and the sun was out. I was officially working, but it was one of the most exhilarating jobs I have ever had. It was like public art in a way. Different from painting canvases that would be hung on the wall and looked at, these ponies would interact with humans. Small humans mostly, but still. They would create memories. Ax Man was focused too. He became sort of like my assistant. I only had about ten days to complete the job, so we spent a lot of consecutive hours together. We ate lunch without ever formally calling any meal a date. I knew he smoked weed because I could smell it on his fingers. That should have been a red flag; I'm no prude, but you know, these were my last days on *that* side of 40. There were certain things I no longer wanted to do as I entered the second half of my life, like hook up with potheads.

When the ponies were finally complete, I took steps back as Axel operated the merry-go-round slowly to dry them.

"What do you think, Ax Man?" I asked him.

"I think you should take a ride with me!" he hollered from the control center.

"But they're still wet," I teased.

His gaze was serious as he gestured to the Harley parked alongside the carousel. I may have raised one eyebrow, which is something I've never been able to do.

When the sun bled purple across the horizon like only an LA sunset can, that's when we sped across PCH. I was wearing his denim jacket. The ride was dangerous and reckless, but somehow as soothing as the merry-go-round. I felt like we were just going in circles, and I never wanted to get off.

He took me to his favorite beach, off Temescal. We were the only ones there as we watched the sun squeeze itself like a grape on the horizon. That's when he kissed me.

Intoxicating.

"Why did you wait so long?" I asked.

"Well, we were working together. It's forbidden."

The way he said "forbidden" got me really excited, as if I was 14. We're so Pavlovian, it's sick. Men and women just need certain buttons pushed. Whenever I hear someone complain that they can't get laid, I'm baffled. We have "on" buttons just like any machines.

We made out until...I don't know...it was really fucking late. Nothing annihilates time like sex. You can make out for ten minutes and five hours goes by. It's like a wormhole.

"Savannah, Georgia, I like you," he said.

"You never told me what you thought of my work."

"The ponies."

"You don't like..."

"No, no, they're...they're..."

I was sure he would say "nice" or "pleasant" or "fine," but instead he said...

"Ambrosial."

"What?"

"That's what they are."

"That's a word?"

"Yep, like Ambrosia."

"I know what Ambrosia is."

"Your ponies are like Ambrosia."

I was in his bed two hours later. We had sweaty, primal, pastrami sandwich sex. I call it that because the only time I would eat a pastrami sandwich is after *that kind* of sex. And that's what we did. We went to Johnny's Pastrami, which closes, I think, never. The waitresses have been there since, like, 1904. I mauled my French Dip like I'd hunted it down and killed it myself. He ate quietly, staring intently at me the whole time. His mouth moved like a rabbit, and I thought he would never finish, but suddenly the sandwich had vanished.

"Ambrosial, huh?"

"Yep," he said, gazing at me like he had no eyelids (that's how infrequently the man blinked).

"That's the nicest thing anyone has ever said about my work," I said, and I meant it. Maybe the stomach is the way to the heart, but when my belly is full, compliments on my paintings work wonders.

"I have work, too, as you call it."

That's when he mentioned his band, No Way Out, which I think I had heard of before. Axel invited me to check out his show the next day in Silver Lake.

As I watched his hands methodically tickle the guitar, sometimes with gentle strokes, and other times with fierce aggression, I heated up like a lava lamp. I had visions of those same hands all over my body. I was jealous of the guitar. The show was... ambrosial.

That night after the show, it was ambrosial, too.

We engaged in what I call horror movie sex. You think it's over, but it's never over. The boogeyman comes back. We're done. I have my clothes on. I'm out the door. Then, I'm lured back in. He kisses my neck and, before I know it, yep, I'm in bed again (or on the floor, or the closest surface). Like the merry-go-round. It was the same thing over and over again. I didn't want it to end.

Attending No Way Out performances became a regular thing. Afterwards, instead of racing home and fucking until we heard seagulls, we would hang out with his band member buddies and drink for hours. They knew us at the bar, so they'd let us drink there long after they closed.

"You know about the multiverse?" Axel asked during one of these late-night sessions.

"I read about it, I think," I replied. Had I?

"You would know, Georgia," he insisted, glazed-eyed from weed, "trust me. You would know."

"OooOK...why don't you tell me what it is, Ax Man?" I shrugged. I could tell he was irritated, as his bandmates leered at me like I was in trouble. They knew this shit was important to Axel, especially when he was smoking out.

"OK, let me explain it like this. You have regrets, right?"

"Sure," I replied.

"Well, you shouldn't. Do you know why?"

"Why, Ax Man?"

"Because every thought you've ever had exists. The world is made up of every single, fucking version of every scenario ever thought about by yourself and any human who ever lived. Every single one of those thoughts is a version that exists somewhere. You didn't win the lottery, but a version of you did."

I actually had never even considered this scenario, but it seemed really unfair. So, somewhere in the universe, there was a version of me with 50 million dollars. Days later, I actually considered what I would do with all that cash...and I got nervous, thinking long lost relatives would call or text me, asking me to share the wealth.

"Every single, solitary thought exists. Every version of everyone and everything exists. That's the multiverse, where we live. Your life right now is only one out of three sextillion versions. You're a painter here, but somewhere else, you're an accountant, an actress, the President of the United States. There's versions of everything. You are only one version."

This was a subject very dear to him. When he got high. I liked him more when he was quiet and mysterious. The more I was with him, the more he mentioned this "multiverse." He compared it to a giant library, where every page in every book had a sentence, and in each sentence, a collection of letters, and we were just living one letter in one of these books. Every time he got stoned, he'd explain it again. As if I was a fucking idiot. Or he just liked hearing himself talk. Like in many relationships, I started to miss the mystery. The Axel who helped me paint the ponies. The silent one. The one who kept his mouth shut.

One night, while Axel was asleep, I was restless. I looked over at him – so peaceful, so still and statuesque. I was nostalgic for the days at the merry-go-round when I secretly sketched his profile out of intrigue. I tiptoed to my desk drawer and reached for my sketchpad. I fanned out the pages until one single sheet glided to the floor. There he was, my beautiful wild pony. I completed his face and began sketching his sleeping, naked body. I didn't stop until I had mastered every crevice. It was somehow therapeutic for me, and I later used this model to paint a canvas. I loved the painting. It was beautiful and angelic and it reminded me of all the reasons I'd fallen for Axel. I looked at it every time I was alone. I looked at it so much that I started to feel guilty; I was more attracted to the painting than I was to the flesh. It felt secretive, and a bit like betrayal. I had to tell him.

By now, we were frequently hanging out at my place in Marina Del Rey. I existed at the same Mariner's Bay Apartment for 17 years. My dramatic arts roommates had been replaced with rooms full of art. I always complained about the space, but I secretly found comfort in it. It was close to the beach and away from the bustle. I could walk to my favorite places in Venice, and could go days without driving.

"You're going to show him the naked picture?" asked Joy.

"I feel an obligation, Joy."

His face did not move a muscle when I unveiled the painting. He was like a vacuum. He went to my balcony and lit up a joint. I didn't say anything. When he came back into the living room, I had to break the ice.

"I'll burn it, if you want."

"No, it's very nice. It's nice to see me through your eyes."

"Oh, I'm so glad," I said as I approached him and wrapped my arms around his neck, like I always did. But, this time he wasn't hugging back. His hands remained in his pockets.

"Somehow, I feel like what American Indians say about their souls being taken," he said, looking away from me, reeking of weed.

"That's for pictures, not paintings."

"It's for images."

I moved my arms off of him and offered once more, "I'll extinguish it if you want."

"No, it's already done," he said, gazing at me now, "I want you to keep it."

"You sure?"

"Yep. But you owe me one of you now."

"One of me what?"

"Like that. I want one like that."

"I don't do self-portraits," I said with my serious voice. Meaning, non-girlish in any way, straight-up CEO. Joy calls it my "school teacher" voice.

"I won't ask you again," he said calmly, like I imagine a mobster would, and never brought it up again. The request hung there like the barrel of a gun, pointed at my face. The truth was, the painting I'd done of Axel was one of my best. I didn't want to burn it. I didn't want to lose it. I'd done boyfriends lying in bed before, but none of them had really cared until now. It wasn't overtly nude – I mean, sure, you could see his ass and part of his testicles, but you couldn't even really tell it was him unless you had already been there. But the way his ribcage protruded, it was beautiful. The way his spinal cord swiveled down like a snake about to bite his near-perfect ass... I didn't want to give up this painting.

I could rationalize it all I wanted. I captured a private moment without his consent. It wasn't right.

"You're going to paint yourself?" Joy asked.

"I'm going to try," I explained.

"Naked?" she asked, stunned.

"Why, what's wrong with that?" I asked, defensively.

"I don't know," she said. That "I don't know" – for some reason – really pissed me off. Did I have to be a supermodel to be in a nude portrait? Why did I have an embargo on self-portraits in the first place? It's not like I ever spent time reviewing my own *ambrosias*. Suzane Valadon was a model before she was painter. Of course, she was French, but so what, do you have to be French to do anything? Also, I had painted numerous portraits, usually of couples in love, romanticized, holding hands, getting lost in the sea of each other's eyes. I was especially into really old couples. One of my favorite things in life is to paint an old person's skin. A person's aging face tells such a story, with their wrinkles and folds; they tell the story of disappointments. The face represents a wear and tear of existence. I did a couple who were 98 and 85, respectively. That was my favorite. I enjoyed every wrinkle, every evidence of decay... my greatest accomplishment. And I never saw it again. It was sold, immediately.

Darcy, a wealthy woman who collects my paintings like coins, can't get enough of the old couples. I paint one, she buys it, and I never see it (or the old couple) again. The old people are probably dead, unless they're vampires. But, the paintings live on without me. Pretty much, once I created these fantasies, that was it. They were exhibited. People like Suzanne studied them, or Darcy bought them. They didn't belong to me anymore, and I missed them. And then, I was always on to the next one. Like stamping cookies.

I saw this self-nude as a challenge.

I went to Home Depot and bought several mirrors. I propped them up in my bedroom, creating several vantage points. I drew sketches of myself, French Riviera-style.

It was a very odd experience. I'm as narcissistic as the next person, but I've never been a self-stalker (one who glances at the mirror, any chance they get). Sure, I check myself out throughout the day to make sure there isn't a turkey sandwich hanging off my face, but once I confirm I look civilized, I'm back in the zone.

I'm not really sure how to describe this mini-journey, and I'm not sure I ever could. It was essentially like staring directly into my own soul.

I don't know what that means.

I had never gazed at myself so microscopically before. I could see the pores in my nose. I understood the size of my own kneecaps. The size of my toes in relation to my big toe. I understood that one of my breasts is slightly larger than the other one. I understood how my hip bone protrudes and pivots. It was as if I'd opened the hood of my car for the first time and was studying the engine. I learned that I really like my body. I had never been so grateful for it.

At the same time, I was staring at a ticking time bomb. Every female, when she is changing from girl to woman, spends time glued to the mirror watching her body transform. That was the last time I'd spent chunks of hours in front of the mirror – and now it wasn't just one mirror, but four. It soon felt like Savannah was another person (or four), inside the mirror, independent of me. It felt like, at any moment, Savannahs could jump out of the mirrors and grab me. I captured these expressions into one pose. The self-reflection. The glaring into my own soul thing. The nostalgia of me studying myself when I was twelve and growing boobs. The complete misunderstanding of female power. And the decay of my own flesh...the modern day stuff. There I was. Me, sitting on my own bed – you know, naked as the day I was born.

DRUGS

THE PAINTING WAS EVEN BETTER than the one I did of Axel. I felt like I gave birth to it. I literally felt like this giant square thing had been ripped out of me, complete with birth pangs and tears of joy. I felt nauseated. Hungry. I was proud, too. I saw myself and felt a heightened new energy, like I'd come alive from my own vignette. But, I also felt like part of me was trapped in there (you know, the American Indian thing).

This was going to be Axel's Christmas present. But, Christmas couldn't come soon enough.

Things between me and Axel were losing momentum. We had reached the six month mark. The long nights in smoky bars had gotten old. The talk of the multiverse. Old. Even the sex was getting stale. I wanted to care a little more than I did, but the relationship was taking a natural course beyond my control. I had been in too many relationships to feel discouragement when the honeymoon stage wore off. The seduction process is as long as the relationship. "You must keep watering the plant," Joy would say. She's had the same boyfriend for 14 years. She knows, I guess.

But I didn't want to keep watering the plant. Axel knew it too. I worked more than usual, stayed late at my gallery, and rarely went to see his band play anymore.

Joy and I were feasting on ramen as we did every Thursday for as long as I can remember.

"Something is off, Joy. My feelings towards Axel have changed, and he's changed too. He seems distant, distracted." (He did.)

"It's probably for the best, Savvy. I always thought there was something off about him. I can't really put my finger on it, but I knew he wasn't the one for you."

"Why didn't you say something? You told me to water the plant!"

"Well, I'm always on your side Savvy, but I knew you would get tired of him eventually. You always do." Joy smirked.

Was that true?

I went home that afternoon, and laid down on my bed; partly because I was too full of pork broth to do much else, but also because I wanted to meditate on my painting. She was hanging on my bedroom wall. I stared and studied and got lost in every brushstroke. It became a ritual. Every day after work, I did the same thing. And every time, I discovered something new. Kind of like watching Natural Born Killers. Axel and I used to watch that movie over and over again... Shit, Axel. Even though we were hanging on by a thread, I still had to give him the painting. It was only fair. Maybe it would be the spark to reignite us. It was almost Christmas and this was Axel's gift.

I still had keys to his little studio apartment, so one slightly chilly afternoon, I brought the painting over to hang on his wall as a surprise. I glanced around the room and tried to determine which wall I should hammer into. I decided on a good spot across from his window, where the sun would miraculously smile a beam on it every morning. I went to the kitchen hesitantly, to look for a hammer and nails.

Against my will, I hung up the goddess and collapsed on the bed to admire her. I began to sob. Being a painter was like being a domesticated dog. I'd give birth to a litter, only to watch the pups be given away to the neighbors, or total strangers. I'd never see them again.

I reached over to his bedside table where he kept tissues in the drawer. When I opened the drawer, it made a squeal that sounded infant-like. My fingers squeezed on something plasticky. I grabbed it and held it up in front of my face.

"What the fuck is this?" I said out loud to no one. Of course, no one answered. I held it up in my right hand and gave it inquisitive dirty looks, as if maybe it would answer me. It was drugs. Not weed. But *drugs*. The kind of drugs that killed half the musicians in the late 60s. Self-destruction in powder form. Wow. Axel does drugs. Maybe this was what Joy meant when she said something was "off".

I shoved the baggie back in the drawer and ran out of there, leaving the painting alone on the wall.

"I wish I never saw it."
"Are you crazy?" cried Joy. "You are so lucky you saw it. You could have stayed a year with that junkie...you better dump him."

I looked off into the distance, numb to the conversation.

"I don't think I have to."

I was sad. Sad that Axel was a druggie, but even more sad that I had already lost interest. But now I was sad that I was guilty that I'd lost interest. I was confused by my own guilt, sadness, and loss of interest. I was drowning in stomach-turning emotions.

Axel was sad, too. I had really looked forward to spending Christmas with him. I mean, that's why people get into relationships in the first place, right? So that they have a date during the holidays. It's so dreary to be alone.

"Why did you even give me this painting if you don't like me anymore?" he asked in a text.

It broke my heart.

I started to wonder if I'd led him to crack, if maybe doing the nude of him had triggered it. I felt responsible.

Axel called me during New Year's. And a dozen times after that. Each time, he was more and more emotional, almost hysterical, and really acting kind of weird.

There wasn't much left between us, so I didn't really know what he was clinging to. Eventually, in a last attempt to snap him out of it, I said, "Axel, look at it this way, there's a version of you and me somewhere in the multiverse, right? It's just not happening in this dimension."

He was quiet. Really quiet. He didn't say anything for at least a minute – which in phone time is an eternity. Then, shockingly, he said, "You're right." And he no longer called me. He actually, religiously, believed this shit.

Like Kirk Cameron believes in Jesus. Like Tom Cruise believes in Scientology. Like Cat Stevens believes in Allah.

I missed the old Axel, Ax Man, the lead singer of No Way Out.

He was such a perfect stereotype of cool when the merry-go-round was running. I watched him control the levers with such grace and confidence. He was like a rare animal in a zoo that you admire, where you think, "It's a good thing there's bars because that animal would own this neighborhood." His mother watched him with the same respect and admiration.

She was full of life when I met her. She recognized me from – well, I suppose from seeing a picture of me, or the way Axel must have described me. I remember it clearly – she touched my shoulder, I pivoted around, and I just knew she was his mother. They had the same eyes, the same predatory gaze.

"You're Savannah. Axel told me all about you."

"Yes, you're Axel's mother?"

"He's crazy about you," she said. "He already said, 'Mom, I feel like I can't live without her'."

KEY

DRESSING FOR A FUNERAL is not easy. You don't want to look like shit, yet you want to feel appropriately like shit. You don't want to look like you're going to the prom, but you want to look elegant, like it's an event. You want to look decent, yet you want to blend in with everybody else, consumed in the sea of darkness.

I remember when Joy's dad died. He'd asked to be cremated, which is pretty normal, but he'd asked that his family *watch him get cremated.* That was his *dying wish.* He was a compulsive gambler, alcoholic, and God knows what else, but his final act topped every horrible accomplishment in his life. Joy, her mother, and her mother's new husband, Paul, were forced to watch his body as it was fed into a giant oven that made sounds circa turn-of-the-century London. The scorching of his corpse was imprinted in our minds for days. Joy's face twisted into an ugly look of despair as she watched the coffin being fed into a human BBQ-looking thing. You could continue to *see it* getting incinerated on a little black and white screen, like an ultrasound for the dead. Joy was badly shaken up. She'd wanted me in there with her, anticipating the trauma she would have to endure. Paul just comforted Daisy, and you could tell that neither of them wanted to be there, but were there out of obligation, and to support Joy, of course. I was hugging Joy most of the time as she shrieked and blew her nose on my dress.

Today, when I needed Joy to go with me to Axel's funeral, she flatly refused.

"Savvy, that was different. I'm not related to Axel. I barely knew him. It just wouldn't be...*appropriate*."

It made no sense, but Joy was inherently fragile emotionally and it was just too much for her. I know she would have liked to be more supportive, but the truth was, I would probably end up comforting her. Even so, I was honestly terrified to go by myself. I felt like a sheep wandering into the black forest. I had only met Axel's mom once, but since *that* phone call, I feared the worst. The only other people I knew were a couple of the band members from No Way Out. Trent (the bass player, I think?) and I had gotten along well, back when I was an unofficial groupie. After him, I would have no one to talk to. *Come to think of it, I can't even recall one conversation with him.*

Of course, there was also the matter of the painting, my nude selfie, that I wanted back, and I would have to speak to someone about it. I needed Joy there for moral support, but the truth was, she admired me for my strength, not weakness. She couldn't dare to be around me when I was this vulnerable. She worshiped me too much; poor girl had propagandized an image of 'Savannah' that she looked up to. Anything that hurt that image, she separated herself from. "You'll be OK on your own," she said, "you always are."

The procession was way out there, off the 605, where LA became the wasteland that no human being should have colonized, because it's obviously a fucking desert. It was a hot spring afternoon in Whittier, particularly in pitch-black clothes. The rows of cars gleamed like they were also heavily perspiring. Memories of Axel, the man I had sort of fallen in love with, spun in my head as I drove there. His smell, his jean jacket, his obsession with multiverses. But, the images that were chiseled in my brain were of the baggie in my hand...and the way he looked the last time I saw him.

I had taken a walk at Mother's Beach, a tiny little beach in front of my apartment building that was packed with families on the weekends. But it was Tuesday, and it was pretty desolate, aside from a homeless person or two. The fog was thick that day. I sat alone, sketching some drawings and peacefully considering ideas for my upcoming show, when the homeless man with his back to me turned his face in my direction.

With a gasp, I dropped my sketch pad and stared in shock.

He was not a homeless man; he was Axel. It had been months since I had seen him, but when you spend that much time with a person, you recognize them no matter how they metamorphose. He looked awful. He was unshaven and had dark circles under his eyes. I could smell the weed on him even from a distance – or maybe it was petrulli. It smells the same. I hate that shit.

"Axel?"

"Hey Savannah, Georgia."

"God, you look...terrible."

I actually kind of wanted to draw him. That's how disturbing he appeared. I wanted a souvenir of his transformation.

"You look ambrosial," he said.

"Thanks," I said, and quietly remembered how charming it had been the first time he used that word. Now, it was just sad.

We watched the feeble waves wash along the beach for a good ten minutes before the next exchange.

"Axel, I never gave you your key back," I said, standing above him as I unfastened his key from my keychain. He was still looking at the waves, though his head was turning, as if he was saying "no, no." I freed his key, got up, and brought it to him.

As I approached him, he looked up at me with a feeble smile. "Please, keep the key, it's too sad to take it back." I nodded, even though I didn't really want to keep the key to his place. But the symbol of what it meant to him was moving. I looked down at the key and refastened it to the ring. I thought maybe I'd put it in a jar somewhere. But by the time he passed away, procrastination won and the key remained on my keychain.

I stared at his key, which was gleaming with sunlight, as I pulled up to the place where the service would be held. I parked, and walked towards the structure, relieved to see Trent standing outside. I quickened my pace and felt my face soften as I approached him… that is, until I saw the look on his face.

"Savannah, you shouldn't go in there," he said. "For whatever reason, Axel's family doesn't want you here."

I was stunned. Staring at him through my sunglasses, I felt my eyes drowning in my own tears. "What did I do?"

"Mrs. Parsons…" He shook his head and looked down. "God, Savannah, she thinks that you broke his heart and drove him to drugs. I'm sorry."

Did I? Maybe she was right. And it wasn't just Axel's mother; it was the whole family. They all gazed at me venomously from inside the entrance. "I only came to pay my respects, to say goodbye."

"Why did you kill Uncle Axel?" asked a child out of nowhere, a girl who couldn't have been more than seven. She was brainwashed. But she wasn't the only one. Before I could answer her question, people in black seemed to squirt out of the doorway, each one more sinister than the last.

"Savannah, you should probably go," Trent whispered.

"You broke his heart!" Axel's mother accused, pointing a witchy finger and advancing toward me from behind the others.

"Why did you kill Uncle Axel?" asked the little girl again.

I was having a problem accepting reality. Half a dozen people in black were surrounding me like a cult, their eyes boring into me like red hot skewers. The mother beelined for me like a black swan, as a path was formed for her pursuit. I guess asking about the painting wasn't in the cards today.

I retreated. OK, I ran the hell out of there like a witch in Salem.

As I made a three-point turn, I could still see the black figures. From far away, they looked like crows, ready to pounce on me if I decided to come back, and poke my eyes out. There was a man with a salt and pepper ponytail standing by himself just around the corner smoking a cigarette. Keeping my watery gaze down, I asked him for a smoke, and took notice of his rugged, manly hands. I digress. I grabbed the Marlboro light and ran off.

On the 605, I started receiving text messages.

"Killer."

"Murderer."

Then, finally, a text from Trent. "Savannah, are you OK?" then, "People don't die from a broken heart." How did he know? I considered the concept of a broken heart. Did I really "break his heart"? Is such a thing even possible? Maybe I was a murderer. I looked down at his key again and thought about the last time I was in his apartment and found the baggie.

"My painting!" My heart raced as I clung to the one sunny spot in all this gloom. I could get the painting myself. I drove at lightning speed to Axel's apartment, unlocked the door, and swung it open. I ran through the kitchen towards his bedroom alcove and collapsed at the sight of the empty wall. My painting was gone.

MURDERER

I WENT HOME AND DRANK. I needed the numbness of alcohol. Two bottles of Conundrum later, I was still receiving texts, from a variety of unknown numbers. I read a traffic jam of insults. "Selfish bitch". "You abandoned him." "Witch." I missed being called a "bitch". And I started to believe it all. *Selfish whore, evil bitch, murderer. Me.*

The murderer staggered to Abbot Kinney, where only a week ago, she'd been a celebrated painter. Or a respected artist of some sort. Not a 40-year-old narcissistic murderer, staggering from bar to bar.
The murderer sat alone. Drank alone.
Saw time and memory vaporize.
The murderer would blink and wake up below a stranger. The weeks blurred by. M T W Th F S S went by with relentless speed.
"Hi, it's Joy, where are you? Call me back."

Time emulsified like a roulette wheel that never ended (or a merry-go-round with screaming children, reaching out desperately for their parents, not building nice memories).

"Call me back. Where are you?"

The murderer woke up in another strange bed that smelled like mushrooms, as the night before returned to her memory in fragmented images of booze and sex. She ran outside to graffiti a wall of broken hearts, and threw up at the sight of lovers in the park.

"Don't ruin your life over this."

Hearts broke and bled on buildings and benches all over the neighborhood.

"It's not your fault, Savvy. You can't blame yourself."

The murderer was arrested. But not for murder. For destruction of property. She had a hot pink spray-can in her hands. They took her picture. All three angles. They gave her an orange jumpsuit that smelled like cigarettes and Tide, and threw her in a cage. She had one phone call, but her cell had been confiscated. She could only muster up one number as it was still on her prefrontal cortex from the day her life was destroyed.

"What the hell do you want – haven't you done enough?" Mrs. Parson's answered Axel's phone.

"Mrs. Parsons!" She was excited just to hear a voice on the other end. "I'm in jail! Please help…call my cousin, Joy…please…"

"Good. That's where you belong."

The murderer fell against the wall. Mrs. Parsons would be no help in getting her out of there. But, now was her chance.

"I want my painting back."

"Oh, I see," laughed Mrs. Parsons, "I know what painting you mean."

"You do? Please, Mrs. Parsons, that was something I made for Axel. It's all I have left," she wept.

But, Axel's mother just laughed. At first lightly, then maniacally.

The murderer sank to her knees and cried. Not because she'd been thrown back into a cage, but because she – the bitch, the whore, the murderer – was now the prey.

As she sat in the corner of the cage, her matted hair covered her face like she was Medusa (just the ugliness, not the power of turning people into stone, unfortunately); she felt the meat of her flesh, the nerves of her limbs, the orb that sparked her will to live...dissolving.

She wanted to die. But, instead, she existed in a state of near-consciousness, drifting in and out of sleep on the cold, hard floor of the cell. She opened her eyes to find her jail-mates (similarly dressed in orange) huddled together for warmth. They were telling stories and even giggling a little, while another squatted over a toilet made of steel. She closed her eyes and exited the surreal reality until she was jerked back into it by a large, brown hand grabbing her arm. "Savannah Waters?! Get up." Her clothes were thrown at her and she was shoved into yet another, smaller, windowless cell.

I put on my clothes and realized that I would be getting out of there. So, I stood waiting. And waiting. I sat back on the bed and sobbed. I thought they forgot about me. I thought I would rot in that cell and nobody would ever know. Hours passed as I lay there shivering on the cold, hard, unmerciful bed.

It was so cold. I was so tired.

JELLO

THE RIDE HOME WAS SILENT. Joy hardly said anything. I'd never seen her like that. Bailing her hero out of prison may have been too much for her. She might as well have been driving a hearse. Her hero was *dead*. I felt like a racehorse she'd bet all her money on and lost. I'd let my fan base down. If it wasn't enough that I had killed someone else, now I was dead. Dead to my biggest fan.

I had spent the entire night in a jail cell, with very few blinks of sleep, and now I had to go to court.

The judge, a woman who looked like a blue jay, gawked at me like she wanted to slap my hand.

"Destroying public property...I see...," she said, as she rifled through the case file. "I realize this is Venice Beach, Miz Waters, but these walls are private property. Do you have anything to say, Miz Waters?"

I was about to say something sarcastic about Lascaux, the cave drawings in the South of France (spending a night in jail kind of made me feel like a badass), but she did kind of remind me of my grandmother. I didn't get along great with Grandma, and she did scare me a little.

"No, ma'am," I said, thinking about the nude selfie. Where was it now? Had Axel's mom made copies of it and decorated every bus bench in LA? That would have been a good advertising tactic, actually.

"Nothing?" insisted Grandma Judge.

"I'm sorry?"

I didn't mean it. She knew it. She studied me like a problem child, like she wanted me to feel as much shame as possible, to glow red like a roman candle and explode.

"500 hours of community service," she said, tapping the gavel like she'd smashed a little bug. Her heart wasn't even in it.

It was *really* weak, how she brought down the gavel.

"500 hours," Joy whispered, "that is *excessive*."

No matter how much she hated me, she still wanted the best for me. Joy was my best friend. Having an actual relative as a best friend makes you feel like you were born in the right place at the right time.

Almost everyone can't stand who they're related to, who their parents are, who their siblings are, who their kids are. But even if I wasn't related to Joy, I'd still want to be friends with her.

I'd find out soon enough, her silence wasn't about her shattered image of me at all. As usual, I was just on the freight train of my own narcissism. The prism in which I see the world is, no matter how much I'd like to deny it, *me, me, me*.

Joy had my key and was unlocking the door for me, like I was some kind of invalid. She had problems with the key – inserting it, turning it. She cursed under her breath. Funny thing about keys, even if the key is designed for the actual hole it's supposed to fit perfectly into, there's still a certain way you're meant to insert it, play with it, to get it to open. This was the same lock from 17 years ago. It got feisty, like most 17-year-olds.

"Fuck," Joy kept saying as I stood in the hallway, zombie-like. Yeah, I wanted to help her, but I was so disconnected from reality, my hand-brain coordination was barely functioning; along with my empathy, good mood, and ability to be shocked. *That was about to change.*

There is really no feeling like coming back home after spending a night in the slammer. You realize how much of your life is just about comfort. Your chair. Your sofa. The color coordination of your habitat. Everything is exactly where you want it to be for your own... feelings of safety. I was living a life in which amplifying my comfort was the greatest priority...

...This was the generation we were born into, I'd realized in the cage. Our grandparents worked their asses off, many of them immigrating to the country on boats with spiders and rats and pirates. Their children were born during World War II, when television and toasters were invented, when they no longer had to work in a coal mine to provide for others because they had upgraded to an air-conditioned office. And their children – us, *me* – cashed in, dedicating our lives to as much comfort as we could handle. We complained about whatever we couldn't get. We were junkies for having what we wanted, when we wanted it. I considered myself a low maintenance junkie, but was I really?

As Joy snapped the light on, I saw my cozy couch, my paintings, my flowers, and Suzanne sitting on my favorite chair...

"Suzanne, what are you doing here?"

Now, I was awake. A zombie no more.

"Uncle Paul. Aunt Daisy?"

Joy remained a fucking silhouette beside the door.
"Cynthia?"
WTF?
And last, but not least...
"Darcy? And, Hugh?"

I didn't ask what they were doing here. I knew. Joy emerged from the darkness like a ghost which had materialized into human shape. The conflicted grin on her face said it all. *She set this up.*
"Joy..."
"I'm sorry, Savvy," she pleaded, "I'm so..."
"I told you, I didn't want to celebrate my fortieth birthday. You fucking promised!" I still thought I was funny.
"Savvy, this is not your birthday, this is an intervention."
Duh.
They all got up in unison, like a cult, and poorly attempted to hug me at the same time, kind of like with Indiana Jones when he visited the starving village. People took turns hugging me, some doubling up on me. I swear, it was the closest thing to getting molested, at forty.
Joy was the last one. I did not reciprocate.
I whispered, "You're behind this, aren't you?"
Her guilty look said 'yes' even though her mouth was motionless, like a ventriloquist dummy out of sync with its master. And then, she started to sob. To her credit, quietly. Not the bawling kid in the supermarket variety, thank God. I hugged her back.
"It's alright," I said, "but let's make this fast."
Not sleeping for nearly thirty hours creates a unique blend of fantasy and reality. I mean, they become close. They're lovers. Merged into one. You question tangible

things, like the glass of water in your hand, the couch you sit on, the ground beneath your feet. You would kill for five minutes of sleep. But it doesn't matter if your eyelids aren't closed, your unconscious is bleeding everywhere. You are seeing things along with reality. But when reality itself is strange, when the strangest possible combination of people in your social circle are sitting in your living room, then what?

Most of them had never even met each other, and some hadn't even known the others *existed*. If a real, true intervention was to be effective, it would have to work like a professional basketball team. Players would need to have played together for years. These guys had just met in that hour, and clearly there was no set plan. It was a social landmine that had 'Joy' written all over it.

I would find out later that she had glanced at my iPhone and high-jacked the numbers quickly, before I could catch her. She'd scrolled through it like Russian Roulette. She only got a four. The rest were her parents. And it also felt like they'd been forced into this. It was like Joy had Googled "how to help a friend who drank too much and went to jail" and came up with "intervention." Her heart was in the right place, but I wanted to puncture that heart with a number two pencil, two hours later, when still no one knew how to move this forward.

I kept insisting I did not have a problem.

Aunt Daisy, who was not that different from Joy, said, "Sure you don't, sweetie."

Uncle Paul, who of course disagreed with her, said, "Don't be so hard on her."

Anytime anyone said anything, he kept saying, "Don't be so hard on her."

Cynthia, an art critic who had been reviewing my work for two decades, and with whom I really wanted to maintain a fucking professional relationship, looked like she was standing on quicksand. While the poor lady sank, she tried to resist, giggling nervously, interjecting stories about other artists and their alcohol problems.

"If you were a man, people would applaud you. Look at Van Gogh. He was a horrible..."

"Don't be so hard on her," Uncle Paul said.

"I don't think I would applaud her for drinking, just because she was a man," Aunt Daisy said.

Darcy was the tale of two extremes. Bouts of silence or long monologs. She was a very wealthy woman who had taken some of my classes at the gallery, which I teach for extra money. (*Yes, needing extra money is a recurring theme for me.*) She buys my paintings like groceries, particularly the geriatric lovers' portraits, as I mentioned. She didn't go anywhere without her husband, Hugh. But, Hugh never really said much, so that counteracted his persistent presence around Darcy.

"Maybe it's good for her art. Maybe she's just going through, like, an early mid-life thing. Maybe it's not the dead carousel engineer. Maybe he was just the catalyst. Everyone who was at her last exhibition saw a new Savannah Waters. I know I did. She's not crying for help. She's just evolving. That's what I say," she gleamed.

"Don't be so hard on her," said Uncle Paul.

His wife at last slapped his arm, "Stop saying that, Paul."

"What, I just think we shouldn't be...hard on Savannah."

"You alright, Savannah?" That's all Hugh could say.

It was so awful, I actually had the urge to check my phone to see what new horrible names awaited me.

"Murderer" was getting old. Had I evolved to "Grim Reaper," or perhaps even "Child Killer"? Way more fun than the passive-aggressive freak show, masked as an intervention.

The only person who remained silent was Suzanne, my gallery owner. She said nothing the whole afternoon. She gazed at me with the intensity of Grandma Judge. Her pupils, extra black, extra bug-eyed. Her folded arms, extra folded. Her posture, super uptight. It was for her benefit, I think, that I finally agreed to go to an AA meeting. After pleading for two hours that I did not actually *have* a problem, that I was paying my price to society via 500 hours of community service, I succumbed to Suzanne's chilling silence.

"Don't be so hard on her," I wish Uncle Paul had added to Suzanne's silence. But he was only responding to dialogue, not empty pockets of sound aimed at me like rifles.

"I will go to an AA Meeting, I promise. I will go tomorrow."

Everyone hugged me one last time – the same deal, an awkward gangbang of affection with intertwining arms, pretzeled into one another, gentle hummings of "aww, hang in there," "we love you," and Suzanne's continued blankness (though she also hugged me?).

Joy insisted, "I will drive her."

I was officially an invalid. I'd lost my ability to drive, now...

"Thank you, Joy."

"Great job, Joy."

"You're such a good friend and cousin."

Jesus, I wanted to throw up. ...No, I really did. I wasn't feeling good. My stomach was no longer a silent partner. I wanted to go to the bathroom, but I was afraid someone would follow me inside to make sure I wasn't drinking. As soon as the cult bailed, except for Joy, I hit the john for forty minutes, but I'll spare you the details.

Then, I checked my texts, emails, and so on, and I'll spare you those details, too. You've already heard it, and let's just say, it was *similar* to what I'd imagined. *Maybe worse?* But, I continued to read "blah blah blah…" until I stumbled upon a text from my old friend Jimmy, an artist I worked with a long time ago, that made me suddenly miss my cuddly intervention group, and even Uncle Paul's Tourette's-like "don't be so hard on her."

Remember the painting? The self-nude? It was auctioned by "KissedbyAngels". Mrs. Parsons. Axel told me how his mother used to tell him his eyes were kissed by angels. It had to be her. I'd made an OK income on eBay up until that afternoon. Averaged a few hundred bucks for a sale – once in a while, four figures – but nothing like what was unleashed by Mrs. Parsons.

Jimmy and I had a very cool, platonic working friendship until he moved to the east coast for a project several years ago, and never returned. He didn't like many people, as he was a typical introverted artsy type. But we got along well. Jimmy loved his Google. When he wasn't painting, he was at his computer researching hot topics and reading blog after blog. We reached out to each other occasionally; it was usually him emailing me some gossip he collected from incessant scrolling. This time it was about me.

Someone in France, one Chuck DeGoal, bought my nude selfie...for $75,000. Meanwhile, the image of me in all my glory had been hanging there on the web, on one of the biggest sites on Earth, if only for 48 hours. The good thing about Chuck buying it was that the bids and the painting had been removed. *After millions had seen it.* Mrs. Parsons had collected the 75K, evidently, and shipped it off to France.

I wanted to throw up. Again. And wished I could throw up everything inside me.

But I had nothing left.

I couldn't even barf up my soul, because it was inside the fucking painting.

I was just a skeleton. Bones. Bone marrow. Jello.

"Well, at least someone bought it for that much," Joy offered, on our way to "The Room."

Once there, I started to get angry. The most I'd ever made from a painting had been from a portrait of a couple by the Santa Monica Pier for $12,000. This painting of my naked face, naked neck, naked tits, naked arms, naked thighs, and naked everything-between-my thighs, went for $75,000, and I wouldn't see a cent of it. More importantly, I would likely never see the painting again either. And even more importantly, strangers would see this painting. And herein lies the reason why I had lived by the cardinal rule of always refusing to paint myself. Especially naked. *Don't do it, in case this shit happens!* I'd broken it, and now I was paying the price.

If Axel was right, there was a world where all of my paintings sold for millions, but this one, of me baring my soul, was worthless on eBay. Maybe there was a "buy now for $5" purchase where the person bought it, received it, and fucking burned it in their fireplace. If this thought exists, this scenario exists somewhere in the universe, doesn't it? It was comforting to consider that notion. Well, maybe comforting was not the right word. It was slightly helpful. The carousel engineer had bacon bits of wisdom after all.

FAT CAT

"HI, I'M GINA, and I'm an alcoholic..."

I tuned out pretty quickly. Kept thinking about the probabilities of this multiverse. Of the different combinations with my intergalactic sitcoms, I obsessed over the world in which I was an evil dictator, for some reason.

I still hadn't really slept much, and was potentially losing my mind.

It was a world where everything I did had zero consequences. I'll spare you the thoughts that go through the mind of a hardened criminal.

I'm really having fun with this.

But, to get an idea, just think about your world as a dictator, about having absolutely no consequences for your actions...just how downright evil you would be.

I relished in my evil thoughts.

How I would track down this Chuck DeGoal asshole and take back my painting. Guess that doesn't sound too evil. How I would tell everyone at the intervention, I really want a drink. How I would tell Joy, "I'm not an alcoholic."

I guess these weren't the most evil actions one can concoct. I started to feel guilty anyway. And exhausted. I started thinking about Gaspar, and the hands, and how promising that night had been. Until Axel's mother called. Oh my God, poor Axel. I can't believe he's dead. Joy ripping off my numbers from my iPhone, that backstabbing whore. A rush of emotion plummeted through my weak body like a wipe-out, you know, of the surfing variety. What the hell happened to my life?

"Hi, I'm Carlos, and I'm an alcoholic..."

Finally, my mind started to take in where I actually was. A room inside of a church… flyers, posters, and a huge-ass sign that said 'DO NOT FEED THE CAT'. The black cat was big, the size of a basketball. Wherever it jumped, you heard a *thud*. Its preying eyes gazed at you with judgment, not unlike Grandma Judge.

The second entity she has personified in the last 48 hours...is this part of the penalty?

Goddamn, 500 hours of community service. That is one shitload of hours. There's only 24 in one day. Most insects don't even live 500 hours. Was that the norm? A first offense. A respected local artist down on her luck? Grief stricken? Sorta? Geez.

"...I just cared about drink," Carlos said. "Everything was an obstacle to get to more drink. What I said to people, whatever job I got, my goals for the day, they all had to do with an endgame of getting more drink. I lost my wife, my kids, my friends, and all of my savings. Everything for drink."

Carlos was cute. But they strictly forbid opposite sex sponsors in AA.

In any case, *this* wasn't for me.

"Hi, I'm Savannah and I'm an...alcoholic?"

It just didn't feel right.

Maybe I am an alcoholic. I don't know.

There's some history in my family (like every family on Earth). I have an uncle who was clean until he was 45 and, overnight, poof, the 40 proof genie shot out of the bottle and took his life to the curb. But I just didn't feel dependent.

"...I spray-painted broken hearts all over the neighborhood and hardly remember it..."

It wasn't enough. These people were baring their souls and their pleading eyes begged me to match, or even, top them.

"...I was attacked by a faceless man..."

They gasped. I was giving my audience what they wanted.

"But the cops arrested me instead of him."

They were on the edge of their seats.

"Because I was drunk and had spray-paint cans, they cuffed me like an animal and dragged me to jail. It was the darkest night of my soul. I was forty, going nowhere... locked in a cage... my life vanishing... all for drink."

I really did not believe this was happening. I'm such a fucking liar.

"...And when I came home and saw my friends and relatives and the people who cared about me, I just cried."

I might as well do porn. Because this is emotional pornography. But you should have seen the look on everyone's faces. It was what they wanted to hear and I was too weak, confused – sick? – not to give it to them. The obese cat, though...it knew. It knew I was full of shit.

There was a standing ovation when I was done.

Everyone hugged me, sort of like at the intervention. Some people, like Carlos, cried. I touched them. For a second, I thought maybe I should run for office. The obese cat gawked at me threateningly, as if it was saying, "Don't come back, bitch."

It was difficult just to get out of there. They kept hugging me and stroking my hair, as I passed through clouds of cigarette smoke outside.

"It was awful," I told Joy as we sat at Starbucks on Main and Hill. I actually loathe giving my hard-earned cash to that corporation, but who else could make an iced triple-grande soy latte taste so fucking delicious? Who? Tell me. There is something to be said for two weeks of intensive barista training.

"It was?" She looked defeated.

But, I could see her mind working. She had a Plan B.

I could also see that, if I did not at least entertain this Plan B, she would do more research, one thing would lead to another, and I could wind up being in her custody or something, locked up in an institution, painting the walls with my own feces, braindead. I don't know, maybe not. But, I'd hear her out.

"Well, we can't stop there," she said. You could see it was really, really difficult for her to play "big sister" with me. To her credit, she was *wo-manning* up to the task and being bigger than herself. I'd never had more admiration for Joy than I did at that very moment. Maybe that's why I agreed to the next proposal.

"You have to see a psychiatrist. I have just the person."

DEAD SOCKS

"HOW CAN I HELP YOU?" asked the psychiatrist. His name was Dr. Rivers. He had the poker face. The stonewalling face. The mighty sheen that all doctors have, as if there is a secret telephone in their office that calls God. They discuss life and death; who should live, who should die, and who's beyond fucked up and who will die. They tell jokes because they are actually in control of who will live, who will die, and who will just remain beyond fucked up.

Only six weeks ago, I had a great show. I was the toast of Venice Beach. People were telling me how great I was. Now, I was a murderer-alcoholic-public vandalizer who was seeing a shrink. Me, the artist who memorialized men's hands. Speaking of hands, Dr. Rivers had a nice set. His fingers had an authority to them, a strength, like spiders that could lift objects much bigger than their own size (or was that ants?). His fingers were patient, yet active, rugged, and yet defined. He held his pen with commitment. He was very self-assured, which was why he scared the shit out of me.

Meanwhile, Joy was outside, sitting in the 70's style lounge on a squishy brown leather couch, probably leafing through *Self* Magazines circa 2010. Didn't she have a job? How did she get this much time off? Had she told her boss, "My cousin is so fucked up, if I don't help her, she'll be dead, and I'll have no one to look up to?" She's probably so bored. I bet she's striking up a conversation with other "friends and family", creating her own little Al-Anon.

"Just last month, she was the toast of Venice Beach," she'd sob, "now, she's a full-blown alcoholic and she has a death wish. She doesn't even want to be here. I had to do an intervention. I just care about her so much… do you think I should have her lobotomized?"

"Oh, you poor dear," an old woman says, hugging her as she bawls violently. Then the staff would offer her a box of tissues and a drink of water.

"Ms. Waters?" Dr. Rivers gestured for my attention.

"Yes," I responded, realizing I had gotten lost in yet another bizarre daydream. I looked right at the doctor, whose face was now illuminated by the sun as it beamed through the blinds to his right. He looked like one of those young-looking old guys. His silvery hair was tousled and pulled back, his face had collected a lot of character over his years on this planet, and his eyes, they were kind. Yet big. He didn't blink much. You could see the highlights of his retinas. They looked like the top of parachutes. Whatever, I just wanted to get the fuck out of there. I looked over at the clock. Jesus, only 7 minutes had passed.

"How long is this?" I asked him.

"How long is what?"

"This...uh...appointment."

He shrugged and made a notation on his clipboard. He probably wrote, "this chick is really impatient". Or maybe he's drawing a naked picture of me. Ugh. The nude selfie. I couldn't believe it was still out there. WTF???

He then leaned back in his chair, looking relaxed and intense at the same time. "What happened?"

I felt really hot. My palms were sweaty. The look was jarring. Déjà vu like. But it wasn't déjà. I had seen that look before. When I was eight, my mom took me shopping for the first day of school. She insisted on white kneesocks, but I really wanted the powder pink ones. I screamed and cried and begged, maybe even caused a little scene. To no avail (I'm still working on this). Once home, in the privacy of my bedroom, I took out markers and drew slashes all over the white socks. The next day, my father was standing at my bedroom doorway, holding what looked like dead flowers, but they were the soiled socks, sadly dangling from his hands. "What happened?"

Dr. Rivers had that same exact look.

"What happened?"

"Nothing *happened*," I lied. I felt like *the dead socks*.

He cleared his throat and wrote what seemed like a fair amount of shit on his clipboard. Didn't I just tell him, nothing happened?

"Why are you here, Ms. Waters?"

"Why is anybody here? Why are you here? Isn't that the question we all ask ourselves at one time or another? Ha! Ha, ha, ha!"

He wrote for what felt like five minutes after I said that, and it was abundantly clear that he did not find me amusing. In an attempt to be less rude, I glanced down at my phone rather than the wall clock to check the time. Dead. Shit. I stole a peek at the clock, and he did NOT write for five minutes. Only for *one minute*. I had been in the room for a grand total of eight minutes, but it felt like 40. It was like detention or wormhole heaven or… yes, my wall was starting to crack.

"Can I use your laptop?" I asked him.

"Perhaps, but you must tell me why."

He was still a fucking wall. You could throw bowling balls at it. Wrecking balls. Dinosaurs could not trample on his motherfucking wall. It would still be a wall. I was no match. I gave up. I'm so sad.

"There's a…well, I'm a painter…"

"Um hmmm…"

"Yeah, I do OK. That is, if you're wondering if I make a living at it."

"Sure."

He jotted more notes.

"I mean, it doesn't come automatically. It takes hustling. I have to go on eBay, Etsy… I have shows, too, I just had an exhibition last month on Abbot Kinney."

"I see, so you want to use my computer to check if someone purchased one of your works ?"

"Kind of. I, um…" My voice grew weak. He stared into my eyes and it was like he punctured little balloons in them, and each balloon was full of tears. I sobbed. It was the first time I'd really cried like that over Axel. I guess there is something about psychiatrists. Barbara Walters has it too. Deflated, and a little relieved, I spilled back into the leather chair. And blew my nose gracefully, even though by now I probably looked like Rudolph the Red Nosed Reindeer.

I sort of proceeded to… you know, tell him *everything*. He could have written my fucking biography by the end of that. And he looked like that's what he was doing, too. The scribbling was relentless, like a court stenographer.

Like I was a university professor and he was trying to keep up with me. Like he had a coloring book of my life in the gutter and he had a box of Crayolas, and a very short time to add color to my hell....

"Are you just writing what I'm telling you?" I asked him.

"Some of it. But not all of it."

You always expected him to tell you a little more, but the "little more" never came. He was a human cliffhanger. Please just say one more word. One more. No, no, that's next week's show.

The good news was that I looked at the clock, and lo and *be-fucking-hold*, 51 minutes had passed.

The bad news? I didn't want it to be over. I'd kind of enjoyed pouring my heart out to a total stranger; and that it was his job to make sense out of the mess he'd just heard. What genius came up with this? Oh yeah, Sigmund Freud. He must have made a fortune.

"Ms. Waters. It's not your fault."

Those words were jarring. I recoiled. The blood in my face drained. And he said it again. Why were these words disturbing?

"It's not your fault," he repeated.

What was this, goddamn *Good Will Hunting*?

"What's not my fault? I don't..."

"Your ex-lover."

I couldn't believe he'd used the word, "lover". That's weird. That's crossing the line a little bit, don't you think? I mean, I hate the idea of still using the word "boyfriend" at my age. But "lover" was a little too...intimate, for me.

"How do you know?"

He shrunk back (no pun intended) as if he knew he had stepped over the line. And for the first time, he employed a *back-pedaling* voice.

"Based on the information given to me," he answered.

"That's nice of you to say."

Then, he looked at me really seriously, as if he knew something I didn't. As if his eyes were trying to communicate a different message to me. Was he checking me out? I was a mess. My hair was sad and wilted. My skin was reptilian from lack of sleep. I was out of shape and malnourished. If he was making a pass at me, *he* needed a shrink.

"I wasn't saying it to be nice...did you still need to check my laptop?"

Right, I had explained my motivation during my sob-filled soliloquy. I'd sent Chuck DeGoal a message. He was the French guy on eBay who'd bought my painting for 75k. I'd spent hours the night before writing him a weepy message about why I needed the painting back. Would he sell it to me? I'd checked to see if he replied about 50 times.

The Doc stood up and let me sit in his doctor's chair. It felt powerful, kind of like Kevin Spacey at the end of *House of Cards* Season 2. His computer screen was on Skyscanner and it looked like he was buying tickets to Milan. *Fuck you.* Who needs Italy, anyway? God, I do. I'd kill to go to Italy.

"eBay, yes?" he asked, reaching over me to type "eBay".

We typed in my account. And there was indeed a message from Chuck. We both read it. He murmured the message. Me too. We sounded like a Tibetan chant, but the eBay message was far from *that*.

"Dear Vincent Van Gal (my eBay name),

Your message is very moving, but I must refuse your request. As you can see, I spent 75K on this very unique painting from a great artist. If that is really you, you should understand that once an artist creates the art-form, it belongs to the world. I am part of this world. I purchased this powerful image fairly and she is now mine..."

I broke down in tears again. I couldn't believe there were any left. The doctor was hovering behind me, still reading the message. Very focused on what Chuck had written, like my weeping and sniffling were nonexistent. He was *that* focused. Then, he stood up straight and took a deep sigh. I stood up, too, and that's when I noticed the leather jacket draped on the back of his chair. Was that a pack of cigarettes in the breast pocket? I hadn't really surveyed the room until that moment. I was surrounded by "biker" memorabilia: little bronzed Harley archetypes, and signed photos of the doctor himself, surrounded by gangs of leather-clad men and their machines, suggesting some sort of motorcycle travelogue. My eyes lit up.

"Do you...?"

Those two words were as far as I got. I was going to ask him if he rode motorcycles. And I thought we would be discussing his adventures, I guess, but that never happened. He looked me up and down one more time before vanishing. That was it. Interesting communicator.

"He rides Harleys? And he's a doctor?" Joy asked, driving me back home.

"*You* found him."

"OK, so what did Doctor Hell's Angels have to say?"

"He asked me if I could stop drinking for 30 days."

"What did you say?"

"I don't know. I must have looked so pale, he changed it to 10."

A week later, Dr. Rivers' wall started showing some cracks. I mean, a doctor showing vulnerability is still inhuman, *unless you really look*. It's very nuanced. Grins as opposed to smiles, raised eyebrows as opposed to eye-fucks, enunciations of Christian names as opposed to nicknames. Or was I reading too much into it?

His shirt sleeves were rolled up this afternoon. His naked forearms were sort of mighty looking, as if he could get pissed off and punch a hole right through the wall. These guns gave Dr. Rivers a mortal quality, even though he hadn't displayed an inkling of human emotion since I'd met him.

His doctorly gaze was again simultaneously intense and relaxed, like he knew he was dealing with something really serious, but wasn't panicking about it. Like toilet training a kitten or something. Joy, for instance, would make a federal case out of this, but Dr. Rivers chose the following words:

"So, you've been lucky. But, one day you will get hurt, or get a DUI, or worse… if you continue down this road. When was the last time you had a full physical with blood work? Have you ever had an EKG?"

"Um, I've had a gynecological exam…this year."

Dr. Rivers called in one of his girls and explained to her what he wanted done: full exam, blood work, electrocardiogram….

"Then take her to the back room and have her fill out the questionnaires."

He stood up (with his naked forearms) and walked towards the door, revealing a stylishly worn pair of True Religions, and shiny Ferragamos peeking out from their hems. I wondered how old he was; it was a bit of an enigma, actually.

I thought about him while I was lying naked on a sheet of exam table paper. The nurse had just weighed me (yikes, that wine weighed a lot), taken all my vitals, and sucked a shitload of blood from my arm before sticking magnetic discs all over my body, like she was a deejay and I was a turntable.

After the sci-fi movie physical, I followed the nurse back to his office (my clothes back on), where she asked me to fill out some questionnaires, but told me not to think too much about the answers.

Anxiety Screening Quiz, Bipolar Screening Quiz, Psychopathy Quiz, ADHD Quiz.

Jesus, I haven't filled out bubble tests since I was a virgin.

Question 43. There have been times when I have felt both high (elated) and low (depressed) at the same time.

1. Not at all, 2. Just a little, 3. Somewhat, 4. Moderately, 5. Quite a lot, 6. Very much.

The diabolical test was filled with riddles like this. It made my head spin. Don't put too much thought into it, Savvy. No thought. I kept telling myself this. Don't do it. Don't do it. But I did. I thought very seriously about not taking it seriously.

Before I finished the test, Dr. Rivers dropped by and, I guess, watched me fill in the bubbles. He was taking notes. Or drawing a naked picture of me (I wish).

"I won't be here when you're finished. Can you come back in two days?"

"Sure. I mean, I think so."

"Any luck with the eBay guy?"

"No, and I wrote him several more messages, too. He gave me his address in France, and told me that if I really wanted it, to come and get it."

"Why don't you?"

"I can't just go to France." That was insane advice.

"You want your painting back, don't you?"

"Yes, I do. But, I can't just go alone to a stranger's house on another continent. I mean, besides the cost of actually traveling there, he's not necessarily offering to give me the painting back. He's just being childish. He's saying..."

"How's the abstaining?"

I couldn't believe he'd just cut me off.

"I haven't had a drink."

"Do you want a drink?"

For a moment, I thought he was asking me out. Was he? I decided to act like he was asking me out.

"Sure, what did you have in mind?"

This time, he chuckled, too, showing the first sign of... what, humanity?

Two days later, he told me, "Your liver is perfectly healthy and all of your tests came back fine: good cholesterol levels, nice thyroid, you don't have HIV..."

"Gasp." I wondered if he would have proclaimed a positive test with such nonchalance, but it made me think of sex. I surveyed his shoulders and wondered what he would look like naked.

"You're the least depressed person I have ever met, but you could be a little bit bipolar."

"Thank you."

"What you shared with me about your..."

"Ex-lover."

"Yes, him. I would categorize that as an isolated incident. I'm willing to bet this type of scenario is not common in your life. You have enjoyment in your work. You like to read. You like to create."

"Yeah, I'm pretty boring."

"Your mind is active like a volcano. That's not boring."

Wow. First, ex-lover. Now, my mind was active like a volcano. Was I reading too much into this?

"There are some different medications that aid in abstaining from alcohol, and they have been around for decades. The first one that came out is called anti-buse; it actually makes you violently ill if you drink alcohol – it's really stupid, and I do not recommend the treatment for anyone. We have a medication called *Naltrexone*, which we administer here in the form of a shot, called *Vivitrol*. It is a simpler approach, as you are not responsible for taking a pill every day; you just come to my office once a month to get your shot. But," he leaned in and stared directly in my eyes, "there is no such thing as a miracle drug."

"Oh, so it's like," I chose my words carefully, "*A Clockwork Orange*?"

He looked up abruptly with an intrigued grin. "Yes, very much like that. You shouldn't become ill, but, yes, it is a conditioning technique."

A week later, he asked me if I'd had a drink.

I nodded. "Well, I did ten days… and then I had to test it out."

"I knew you would," he admitted, almost with pride.

"It didn't really make me feel sick, but I really didn't want another drink, either."

"Good, so it worked." He actually smiled.

"Mm, Dr. Rivers, is it appropriate to friend your patients on Facebook?"

"Why not?" The night of our last appointment, he had sent me a friend request. "I was disappointed that you didn't accept."

He had a very attractive profile picture, presumably taken several years ago, and albums of motorcycle adventures all over the globe. You could throw a dart on it and he'd biked there.

Joy, of course, was very unhappy about this news.

"He tried to friend you on Facebook?"

"It's not a big deal."

"I'm so sorry. He came highly recommended."

"Joy, really, he's fun. I like him. It's not a big deal."

"Yes, it is. You have to stop seeing him." She said "seeing him" as if he was a lover, which only made my imagination go wild with images of me hugging the doctor from behind as he soared his Harley through the Italian countryside.

"I accepted his friend request," I announced.

"Savvy, you have to delete him. This is so inappropriate. He's taking advantage of you. He clearly sees you as more than a patient."

That was the most encouraging thing Joy ever said to me.

DINER

- HELLO THERE
- Hi!
- HOW R U
- Im good... How are you?
- IM FINE HARD DAY
- Oh, are you dealing with problem patients like me?
- U R not
- Aw thats sweet of you to say
- not saying 2 b sweet :)

It occurred to me, I never asked Dr. Rivers how he was. It was always about me. But, there was a reason for that. He was being paid to listen to me. He was not getting paid to Facebook chat. Still, that didn't change the fact that he was now my psychiatrist/FB Friend. And, you know, still employed the same doctorly behaviors. The cliffhanger thing – he did that. After "not saying 2 b sweet," I waited about a minute for him to expand.
Well thanks anyway, I replied.

But he was gone. Vanished. So, eventually I resumed what I was doing, formulating another pleading message to the French guy on eBay. When, all of a sudden...

- *Hello there*

He'd popped back in.

Hello there yourself, I replied.

That became a standard greeting in our Facebook correspondence. Throughout the day, he would pop up with a "hello there" that blindsided me. He was like a cat that would dart across the street when you were least prepared. He never actually really said anything. Was he flirting with me? Was this just something he did with all of his clients? He rode Harleys and smoked cigarettes as a practicing MD, so I supposed this behavior fit his profile. The next time I saw him in his office, it was like I was seeing a completely different person, even though he acted the exact same way. He never referred to our Facebook exchanges, and continued with the "treatment" as if we hadn't made contact several times a day, usually in the most banal way. Did he have an evil twin, like in that Jeremy Irons movie about the Siamese gynecologists?

"If he's flirting with you, I'm suing him," Joy insisted.

"Suing him for what?"

"For flirting with his very vulnerable patient."

"I like him, Joy. I don't care if he's crossing the line."

"So you admit, *he is* crossing the line. I'm going to report him."

"I'll deny everything, so don't."

"I can't believe you're encouraging him."

Yes, I was encouraging him. I gave him every reason to keep going further, even though he kept our transactions rather scientific. I began to wonder what he looked like in front of his laptop, shirtless on his couch, surrounded by biker paraphernalia. Or was he sitting on his Harley, replying to me from his iPhone (which would explain the excessive abbreviations and grammatical abuse, not to mention happy face abuse)? Yeah, that looks like a cheap Apple commercial, but I was a little turned on thinking about it. He could text all he wanted with those hands.

- *Hello there.*

His greetings were so robotic, I began to wonder if Jessica, his assistant nurse, was secretly the one on the other end. I thought of replying with something risqué just to get her to reveal herself.

-*Dr. Rivers, I really enjoyed the way you caressed my ass when you gave me my shot the other day.*

-*It's me Jessica, from Dr. Rivers' office. He will never see you romantically, so you can end this notion.*

I was beginning to accept this notion as reality after nine days straight of ad nauseam.

— *Hello there.*

- *Jessica, I know its you.* (I replied.)

I am not Jessica. I am me. Jake.

That was the first time he insisted that I call him by his Christian name. Strange to transition from Dr. Rivers to "Jake." He did not look like a "Jake."

- *You realize she has a thing for you.*

- *She's protective. She has been my nurse for many years. :)*

Why did he type a happy face?

Why did you type a happy face? (This is now me asking.)

- *cause it's a good thing.*

At least the conversation was taking a different turn.

-*Long weekend coming up. Little scary.* (I didn't mean the "scary" part, but this party needs suspense.)

- *Maybe we should have dinner.*

You know when you wait for something for soooo long, when it does happen, your brain doesn't expect it, because you got so used to just wishing it would happen so you don't, like, accept it? It felt comfortable to just wish he would cross the line. Now, it was *real*. I'm pretty sure that's what they mean when they say "be careful what you wish for". This time, it was me that took a while to type back.

Well...(he typed.)

I couldn't believe, for once, it wasn't happening in an alternate reality. He actually liked me, his patient, even after everything I'd told him. Was he willing to lose his license and never practice again because he was bewitched by me? Pretty hot, right?

- *Sure. I'd love to have dinner*
- *Ok. Tomorrow. U pic the place*

Saturday was my first day of "community service". With a group of teenagers, I cleaned up graffiti on Speedway Avenue. I had to wear a jumpsuit with green pinstripes, a baseball hat, and goggles, while operating a sand blaster. I always loved graffiti, so it was painful to wash away such a beautiful art. I sprayed at the images with a hose until they began to vanish. The hoodlums, or whatever they were, had created intricate fonts with incredible precision, bursting with contrast and colors, layered on top of each other like wedding cakes. I was crushing wedding cakes. It was difficult to watch it go.

"It sounds like the judge gave you the worst kind of punishment," said Jake, during our date.

"Yeah, she didn't like me."

"My father was a judge."

"Oh really, that explains it."

We were at my favorite Italian restaurant in LA, Rosti's on Montana Avenue.

"Would you like a glass of wine?" he asked. I was confused – was this a test?

"Do you drink wine?"

"Sure, I like to have a glass or two," he replied.

"Well, I've gone 30 days now, so...."

"So make it 31."

"Um, OK," I replied, and ultimately, anticlimactically, we drank water.

Jake had picked me up in a gleaming black Corvette. I'd approached the car with a big grin, like an excited teenager going on her first date, but he'd just stared into space when I got in the car, sort of like when we were in his office. Once he started driving, he finally said "Hi," and then, in between drags of his cigarette, "How are you?" The car resembled a giant bug. He was dressed in black, too, which gave you the impression he was attached to the body of the car. He was indeed cloaked in leather – yes, the same jacket that had been draped over his chair. We sat outside at Rosti's, so he could smoke. He must have gone through six cigarettes during our "date".

I hadn't held back. I'd come dressed to visually please. His eyes were targeting me like he was a computer amassing targets for later, when he would go on full-scale assault of my country.

"Explains what?" he asked.

"The way you are," I said, "you act like the son of a judge."

"I didn't realize there was such a stereotype."

"It sounds like you don't stereotype people enough."

"The reason I bring up my father is because he used to tell me that he could *sense* the worst punishment for criminals. Some of them wanted to go back to jail, for example. Knowing this, he would not send them back. One criminal he told me about stole a car, and he didn't give him a punishment at all."

"Wow."

"The car thief was really upset and kept calling him names, but my father didn't care."

"Are you influenced by your father in your… field?"

"I try to pay attention to my patients without the walls of psychiatry, yes."

"What did you sense about me when you first saw me?"

"That you just needed someone to talk to. Someone who wouldn't judge you."

"Ha, ha, ha. Well, your dad would be proud of you."

"Yes, he…"

And suddenly his phone went off. And he picked it up. He looked at me quizzically like I had something to do with it. And he left the table. Without saying "excuse me" or anything. He walked about 20 feet away and had what I presumed was a professional phone call. Meanwhile, people at other tables gazed me like I was "the mistress" and Jake was talking to "his wife."

"I know Natasha has a problem… I understand she has a condition, but I'm not in the position to treat her… because we're friends… I know, I know… we're too close, Vince…"

That was the most humanity I've seen him express. In regards to this "Natasha". Ex-wife. Ex-girlfriend. He wouldn't say. And I didn't ask. Once he got that emotion off his chest, he was back to stonewalling. Meaning, his voice rarely changed volumes. His face rarely moved a muscle. His eyes sometimes would not blink for long stretches of time, making you wonder if he was having some kind of weird Vietnam flashback, even though he hadn't served in that war.

His face lit up once more when he talked about his daughters — two, whom he'd adopted at a very young age. Bernice and Meredith. He didn't see them much, except on Holidays, but he was very fond of them. He was once married, I assumed. He couldn't have adopted two girls as a bachelor, could he? I didn't ask.

"I think you would really benefit from having children of your own," he offered. "You don't understand how kids can contribute to your life until they're in your life." It was nice of him to say that about me, even though there was no chance in hell I was ever squeezing out any offspring. Though, I have nothing against them. Ultimately, I know he meant it as a compliment, but it made feel a little uncomfortable, given the, you know, circumstances.

"OK, sure," I said, " you want some of this broccolini?"

Anyway, I had a good time. We were two people who found each other attractive, for better or worse. We were exploring that instinct. I hadn't participated in this type of interaction, particularly sober, since Axel. He was fun, despite his dryness, which even at times reminded me of Mount Rushmore. You know, the carvings of the presidents. Except, he was a doctor. My doctor. Shit, what was I doing? And who was this "Natasha?" I would find out soon enough.

You could tell he had a sense of humor, even though he didn't operate it much. Like a Rolls Royce he had in his garage that he only drove a few times each year.

At 9:43, I shared a cigarette with him. I hadn't smoked since… Axel's funeral. Right. The guy with the hands. I looked at Jake's hands. They looked the same. He took the top down on the Corvette. Like Axel, he drove through the PCH. He insisted it was the only stretch in LA where he could enjoy his ride. There isn't much to say when the top's down, so I tried to relax and enjoy it. *I did.* But there was a sinister sense of déjà vu. I couldn't stop thinking of Axel and that first night we spent together. I saw his face in my mind, and remembered the way he smelled. It was relentless. When I turned to gaze at the

Doc, he gave me a thin smile. As if he could read my mind, and he patted me on the head like you do little dogs. You know how little dogs think they're tough, but they're really not? His petting sort of communicated that. "You think you're tough, but you're just cute." Maybe he meant something else. It was affectionate by his standards, in any case.

The drive back from PCH was a little nerve-wracking, since I now anticipated the "kiss". We weren't talking much, because we were driving into the wind most of the time, so I just kept thinking about the impending kiss, and getting really nervous. As per my techniques of relaxation, I tried to think of the kiss itself as scientifically as possible. This strange display of affection, an ex Gerald (an anthropologist) had explained to me, was born from "kiss feeding", a process used by mothers to feed their infants by passing chewed-up food into their babies' mouths. How did we start with that and get to what we do today, which is to use this feeding process to confirm "attraction"? I don't know about you, but if I kissed a guy and there was food in his mouth, I would literally throw up into his throat. If it was my mom, holy shit, I can't even get my mind around that.

"OK, well have a good night," I announced as he drove me to my apartment gate. We both sort of moved into each other at the same time, and when our lips met, they locked. It felt soft and warm and neither of us felt like unlocking for at least five seconds (which in kiss time feels eternal). It was nice. It was nothing like kissing my mom with food in her mouth – not that I know what that's like (or do I?).

I'd barely had enough time to change my clothes and hop on the computer when Facebook started singing to me again.

- *U R AN AMAZING WOMEN*

(Pretty sure he meant that "singular".)

- *Thank u*
- *I really enjoyed our diner*

(Um, we didn't go to a diner.)

- *Me too.*

Again, he disappeared for a while. Was he consulting a book or a coach? It was bizarre. How he would leave mid-momentum like that.

- *IM Sorry your appointed to remove the graffiti.*

Oh yeah, I had to get up early the next morning for another shift. I had a solid 484 hours left of erasing gorgeous graffiti. It felt like working in a concentration camp for art. Imagine beautiful canvasses in a bonfire. That's what it was like.

U mentioned you like motorcycles. Maybe we can take a drive for 4th of july (Few seconds' pause, then.)

if you dont have plans

I was slightly turned off by his eagerness, but yet I typed:

- *Sure*
- *Is that a yes*
- *I have plans during the day.*
- *Oh.*
- *But, perhaps in the evening.*
- *So evening?*
- *Sure.*
- *Evening :)*

I was also a little turned off by the relentless employment of the happy face.

He didn't smile like this in real life, so what business did he have typing the colon and parenthesis? But... it felt good to be pursued by a doctor. I had never dated one before. Being an artist meant shacking up with either druggies or millionaires who pretended they liked art, and sometimes they were just rich druggies themselves. Being courted by a man of science, who also rode Harleys, was a good feeling. What did I have to complain about? He was responsible, yet burned rubber. I liked that combination.

"You cannot go on another date with him, Savvy," declared Joy.

"I'm not doing anything on the 4th, and I don't want to drink. I just want to hang out with him."

"This is all my fault. I can't believe he's such a creep."

"He's a not a creep. He's been very respectful. And besides, my treatment is practically over. I have one more shot of the fun-blocker next week, and that's it. I'm going."

FIREWORKS

THE GREAT DOCTOR lived in the tallest apartment building in Santa Monica. It was rather majestic, perched up above the shoreline with an efficient guard-gate-valet-doorman system. Once I made it through the guard and valet, the last soldier illuminated the 14th floor button *pour moi*.

When the elevator door opened, I looked down either side of the hallway. Found door number 1415. A tall double door that made you wonder why doors had to be this tall. Nobody is this tall. Behind it, you could hear the ocean, and I knew why. The doctor had already flaunted his front row seats to the Pacific.

My palms were sweaty and I suddenly felt aware of my looming sobriety. When was the last time I was sober on the 4th? Probably when I was 12. I took a deep breath, wiped my hand on my linen skirt, and wrapped it around the door-knocker.

"Bang, bang!" Wow, that was loud. But, silence followed. Amplified by my sobriety. What the hell was he

doing? What the hell was I doing? He knew I was coming. This was like Facebook chatting, but I was standing outside his door, and therefore I couldn't surf the web or beg the French eBay guy for the umpteenth time to free my nude selfie.

The door finally swung open to reveal Mr. Nonchalance himself. He stood there in a white robe unraveled to the navel with unruly, thinning hair grazing his shoulders, and a Cheshire cat grin. I saw him at that moment in a way I had never seen him before. Like I was staring at Jesus meets Hugh Hefner.

"Hi," he said, and looked me up and down, just as he had in his office, and took a drag of his cigarette. He smoked like cancer had never existed.

"Hi?" I replied, hoping he didn't hear the question mark. I breezed past him like it was perfectly normal that he greeted me in a robe, like I'd witnessed a crime that I didn't want to report. I started chatting nervously about my day at the pool. I told him about the $14.00 virgin daiquiri I ordered, and how the waiter spilled some of it on me but still charged me $14.00. Then I went into the pool because I was all sticky. He wasn't listening and I didn't care. I probably wouldn't either because it was so goddamn boring.

When I finally shut up, I realized that his eyes were following me around the room like I was prey. I stopped moving and asked if I could use his shower and get changed. I had spent the day at the SLS hotel, which was pretty close to where the Doc lived and traffic was brutal on the 4th.

"Your hair is all wet," he said.

Did he hear a word I said about the swimming pool?

"Yes," I agreed, "it is."

He led me to this impeccable, Cleopatrian bathroom. The kind you could imagine Joan Collins and Elizabeth Taylor frolicking in. Together. I entered. Shut the door. I stood there with my back to the door, hand still on the knob. When I glanced at myself in the mirror, I just laughed. "Jesus Hefner," I said to myself.

Once showered, I pulled my hair back, not overly concerned at this point, and shimmied into a pair of jeans, coupled with a wife-beater and little black boots I had packed with the motorcycle ride in mind.

"I'm ready!" I exclaimed upon exiting the marble bathroom, and, to my dismay, found the doctor still in his bathrobe. He was on the phone, and appeared like he would remain on the phone for a while.

"Natasha is not my problem… and she will not be my problem," he said to the phone.

Once again, the infamous "Natasha" was at the center of this conversation. Who was she? Now, I had to know. Since Rosti's, Jake had been on several calls about this mystery woman. I wasn't jealous of her, I just heard her name so many times. And this afternoon, I would hear it tons more. Natasha, this, Natasha that. You would think she was married to the Prince of Wales.

"That was fast!" he said, as he hung up the phone, as if he didn't just make me watch him talk on the phone for 10 minutes.

"What was fast?" I asked.

"Your…shower."

"Who is this Natasha?"

I was too tactful about this, I guess. At first, he gave me the chagriny "none of your business" look, but to my surprise, he provided an answer that had the appearance of truth.

"She's the wife of my good friend. She suffers from various fears. I know the type of patient she is. I cannot treat her, but Vincent, he's under the impression that I must tend to her."

"If she wasn't your friend's wife, would she be your patient?"

"Sure," he answered.

"What's wrong with her exactly?"

Now, I was prying.

"She's terrified of... extra-terrestrials."

Wow. I thought he was going to say, she had drinking or drug problem, or she was sexually abused or something. But aliens. That left me dumbstruck. I had more questions, but didn't know how to ask them. Even Jake appeared slightly crestfallen at the problem. As if he could handle it, but was bound to not to get involved, because he was too close to the person. This rule of course was being very broken with me, but it was hard to follow this man's logic.

Jake took this opportunity to assure me he would be ready in five, smashed out a cigarette (a new one) in the largest ashtray I had ever seen (the size of a flying saucer, no pun intended, or slightly intended), and he sashayed into the master bedroom, flowing ringlets in tow.

I had to wait more than five minutes for him to get dressed. Strange; with the men in my life, I usually have been on the receiving end of "waiting around". I generally dress pretty quickly, and at a moment's notice I can glam it up or dress it down at the speed of greased lightning. Somehow, I've been stuck with guys who vanish into the bathroom like they were swallowed by Jonah's whale. I believe in patterns and reasons, so there must be something I'm emitting to create these scenarios, to make the men so insecure about themselves that they have to check their nose hair for thirty minutes before we can get the ball rolling. Why they're not prepared at the agreed-to appointment time is not clear. On the other hand, it's always an opportunity to check out their library. Everyone has one. The Doc had your typical collection of Henry Miller, Bukowski, and Hemmingway, but he also had a lot of books written by women. Erica Jong, Anne Rand, Danielle Steele (?), and even Jackie Collins (I found out later he knew both of them, or claimed he did). What caught my eye was the Charles Baudelaire poetry book, face down on the glass table. Clearly, he had been reading it.

Of course I picked it up and checked out where he was.

This winged traveler, how he is awkward and weak!
He, lately so handsome, how comic he is and uncomely!
Someone bothers his beak with a short pipe,
Another imitates, limping, the ill thing that flew!

Sounded familiar, right? Speak of the devil, he emerged from the bathroom with a cigarette dangling from his mouth. And recited the exact passage of the poem I was reading. Amazing.

"The winged traveler, how he is awkward and weak. He, lately so handsome, how comic he is and uncomely."

"You smoke a lot for a doctor," I said, trying to not appear impressed, even though I really was. Who can resist men who recite poetry and blow smoke rings?

"Do you want an espresso?" he asked, very aware I was impressed.

"No thanks, I'd like to get going."

His hair was under control, and he was wearing a pair of sexy jeans with nothing else but a few ropey bracelets that accentuated his brawny hands, and a chain that caressed his lean, but still muscular chest. The butterflies came back, and we were almost ready to take our ride.

The bike ride was exhilarating. Very quickly, I forgave him for making me wait. The Harley was music to my ears, a gurgling mess of laryngitic aggression that deafened every sound in the vicinity. Holding my doctor closely was strange, and not what I fantasized about, but it was satisfying and, ironically, just the therapy I needed.

We watched the fireworks in Malibu and it dawned on me that fireworks were Crayola-colored semen. Just look at the way the display explodes and swivels. It's striking how much it looks like a 6th grade sex education video. The Doc and I were sitting on the sand. I was holding his arm, gazing up at the powerful life-giving metaphor, in a way I had never seen it before. I grabbed a fist-full of sand and let it seep through my fingers. He held his hand beneath mine and caught every grain. *Maybe not every grain, but you get the picture.*

There was a traffic jam on PCH, but not for us. We zigzagged between cars like the powerful sperm that would arrive at the egg and leave the other 199,000 behind. It was intoxicating. I began to feel OK again, for the first time since the night of my show. I was wearing my doctor's denim jacket, clutching his waist as he sped through a maze of pissed off LA drivers.

Suddenly, we were making out like high-schoolers in the elevator. I took a break from French kissing him to ask, "How old are you?"

"Fifty-eight."

The enthusiastic reply was a big turn-on. He was proud of his age and glad to be alive. I was also relieved that he wasn't like 80 or something, which in LA was not impossible.

By the time we burst into his apartment, we were both out of breath. He didn't turn any lights on, so we were left at the mercy of whatever the moonlight gave us. It wasn't much that night, and in the darkness, it was like we were both blind. We touched each other's faces, lips, earlobes. Volcanic blood was bursting through me. Literally. My vaginal walls were flooding. I felt disinhibited, impervious to pain. I don't ever remember being so turned on.

I was breathing heavily. We both were. When his hands grabbed various parts of my body, it felt like my flesh belonged to him. He slid his hand into my jeans, and without effort, landed a finger on my favorite spot, like a magnet drew him to it. I shuddered. I let out a little yelp. And suddenly, I was a fireworks display. Erupting. He took my hand and led me to the bedroom, where he gently undressed me, lay me on the bed, and put his soft lips and tongue right between my thighs. It was intense, immediate, all-encompassing. When he entered me, I had a mini-seizure, I felt transported, I felt like I was no longer controlling my body, he was. We kissed like we were devouring each other. Soon, reality blurred and I descended into the unconscious. I don't recall what I dreamt, but Axel was there. So was my self-nude painting, floating in the ocean (you could hear the ocean from Jake's bedroom); Jessica was also there (and she was really nice?), there were fireworks, and there was graffiti, but the doctor was not there.

I woke up in the middle of the night, startled that I had actually slept with my psychiatrist.

ALPS?

I DON'T KNOW WHY I LEFT. I *snuck* out in the wee hours of July 5th, tiptoeing to the door like someone escaping prison. I bolted to the elevator, past the doorman, *who looked like a mannequin*, and descended into the light blue glow of empty 5 a.m. streets. I liked Jake. I liked what we did. So, why did I feel this way?

As you mature, the inherent wisdom of the elderly begins to take shape, and it dawns on you that they weren't full of shit about *everything*. Everyone, including parents, grandparents, and even teachers, lied to you at some point because they had power over you. They could tell the inquisitive, miniature person anything they wanted. I always asked a lot of questions. I'm sure that got exhausting. One of the things I learned that wasn't bullshit was that you can repress pain. Once, when I fell down (I don't recall for what reason; I fell a lot), my dad picked me up, and through my tear-ridden wailing, he calmly told me something that I never forgot.

"Savvy, I know you can hear me...I have to tell you something important. When you become an adult one day, you're going to fall again and again, but often times you won't feel the pain until much later. So, you should be happy that you feel this pain right now. It will be over soon. This is something you're going to miss when you're an adult."

So, this is what Dad meant. I was feeling the sting of my past relationship. Not Axel's death, nor the persecution and all that other shit, but the relationship. The potential. The potential that died because I got tired of him. Did I kill our potential and Axel? What if he never did drugs before...what if they were right...what if...

I was barely outside his building when my phone dinged.

- *Thinkin bout u* - was the first text, followed by,
- *can't wait to have more "us" time* -
- *Thank you*, I replied, caught off guard by the emotion in Jake's texts, and I couldn't really think of anything else to say.
- *Your special. Was sad you left : (*

He never said anything emotional to me in person, and these text messages were doing nothing to help me shake the creepy residue I was feeling. In real life, flesh to flesh, eyeball to eyeball, he was still stonewalling. You could actually squeeze more of a reaction from a statue. "I was sad you left"? Those words would never sprinkle out of his actual mouth. But in text, he was geysering it.

I was still traumatized from those months with Axel. They were magical. They were real. They were reminiscent of young love. And in some ways, *best friend love.* You know, when you're six and you meet a same-sex kid that likes everything you like. You overlap everything you say to each other. You can't stop laughing for hours, even though neither of you is high. You feel empty without your friend. You can't wait to hang out again. It was like that with Axel. It was intense. I missed it badly. But I didn't miss the bear trap that had been the reality.

Something in me did not trust Dr. Rivers. After all, he was a psychiatrist who had sworn an oath to treat his patients with a certain professional conduct; he broke that oath to pursue me. Was I really that irresistible, or was this how he operated? I'd like to go with irresistible, of course. Even though Freud warned all psychologists about sleeping with their patients. The old man was not into sex, which is why he wrote about it so much. So he found all the high-class babes throwing themselves at him repellent.

As I walked home through the quiet early morning streets of LA, trying to clear my head and make sense of it all, I received another text. This one made me freeze in my tracks. I looked at it several times, like a bill you receive at the end of dinner, and you want to make sure it adds up.

- *I WANT U TO COME WITH 2 ALPS*

The Alps. The Italian Alps?

He's inviting me to Italy?

- *Hotels are paid 4. I will get ur tix.*

Then, before I had a chance to digest any of it, or even chew and swallow for that matter, he added…

- *please say yes*

I paused. Then responded…

- *Are you sure you like me that much? -*

I wanted to change the tone, and maybe buy a little time. The thought of traveling through the Alps, likely on the back of his Harley, was highly tempting, but this man was a stranger, and becoming increasingly stranger by the second.

- *Why don't we have diner next sat to discuss? -* the doctor suggested, and I obliged. That would give me time to think it over, and possibly warm Joy up to the idea.

During the week, I kept thinking, no, obsessing over it. I had visions of Spaghetti alle Vongole washed down with Chianti at lunchtime, the luscious language spoken by hot Italian men on Vespas, a perfectly frothy cappuccino sipped while sight-seeing through...

...Of course, Joy demolished this fantasy.

"You are not going. I can't believe I have to say this. Oh my God, I am so upset. I'm so...you're my best friend and my cousin, and I love you. I just don't want to see you get hurt or chopped up..."

Huh?

"...or get raped..."

Does she have a drinking problem?

"...or get your organs taken out..."

I'm officially leaning on going now.

"...or any number of weird things that could happen to you."

"Joy, he's just asking me to go on a trip to Italy."

"You just had your first date. You just...philandered with him."

"Philandered?"

"And whatever, that's your choice. I'm not judging you, but..."

"Joy, calm down. I'm not going, alright? I was just..."

"Good. Because if you went... I can't even imagine. I would be so worried... Thank God you said no."

Well, I hadn't actually said *no*. This was something I really wanted, had actually coveted, from the moment I met him. But, being texted such an overture was off-putting. Dr. Rivers, I understood, was a coquette, an eponym generally attributed to women, but in this case it seemed perfectly fitting, and perfectly in line with these narcissistic types. They play hot and cold like it's a tennis ball. You don't need to volley with them, as they will hit as many balls in your direction as they want, like one of those tennis ball machines they use in practice. They fire all of them at you. Stop. Fire. Stop. Fire. Stop. Fire. You never know when the next one is coming or when it won't come at all.

Nothing until Saturday, and then he fired again.

- *R OUI STILL ON 4 TONITE*

Oui? That could not have been auto-complete. It wasn't cute, and didn't even make sense. I was paying for a double ristretto at Venice Grind, and before I even got situated enough to reply, my iPhone ignited again.

- *GUESS U CHANGED UR MIND 2 BAD*

OK, his coquetry was now reaching new heights. My attraction bulb was flickering. His compulsive assaults had become a huge turn-off. I suddenly felt like I was dating Lolita, and that's not how I want to envision my man, a knee-socked nymphette that changes her mind on a whim, gets hurt too easily, and is way too text-happy (I'm sure if Lolita were written today, she would be text-crazy).

Meanwhile, I had just sucked down an industrial strength espresso of the bitter, grimacing variety, and I could feel my heart pumping in my forearm. I was not in the mood for this bullshit.

- *I'm sorry. I am not available for dinner tonight* -

Enough was enough. But somehow, I don't know how, he managed to text back at lightning speed. He was good at it. His fingers were quick. I could attest to that.

- *I'm sorry if I scared u, but I know the way I feel about you and yes, I'm sure i like you that much. spending 24 hours a day with you for 3 weeks - yes I can handle that. if the feeling is not mutual please tell me.*

- *Not Mutual* - I texted back, dropping another axe, and then very quickly feeling like a dick. Even if he was coming on too strong, I wanted to be human about it. I knew

"Not Mutual" was painful, even though he probably felt no pain. I started texting back an equally long message.

- *I barely know you and do not feel right* -

I changed "right" to "comfortable" then back to "right" and then to "appropriate," and then just decided to fucking call him. I don't understand why people spend eight times the amount of time to text a message they could conclude in a much shorter time. Wasn't that the original goal of texting?

"Hello," he answered after several rings, his physical voice refusing to participate in the passionate text plea to join him to Italy.

"Listen, uh, Doctor...I mean, Jake. I barely know you, and I just don't feel comfortable going away to another continent, staying at a hotel with a total stranger. I just...don't. But really, thank you for the offer. It's very..."

I couldn't find the proper noun. It's very kind? It's very sudden? It's a beautiful offer? Wow, I actually thought that. Gracious? That would have been good, but my inner thesaurus wasn't working that efficiently this afternoon.

"OK, I understand," he said. Then he hung up. Before I got over the fact he'd just hung up on me, he sent an epic text:

- *It stings a little bit, but I will leave you alone. I just thought it would be fun and spontaneous and I really enjoy ur company. I just don't understand why you would choose nothing over something, but it's ok.*

He had to be a clone of somebody else. Something was missing.

Over the next week, Joy and I hung out a lot. I did as much community service as they would allow me to do. Financially, I was on fumes. I hadn't been hustling or even posting my paintings on eBay because the sight of the fucking eBay logo sent me into a tailspin. Being sober through all this didn't suck as much as I might have thought; it became a sort of medal of honor.

I was still on the "Clockwork Orange" drug Dr. Rivers had given me (it honestly feels like I'm talking about another person and not the guy who invited me to the Alps), and the thought of pouring a drink down my throat felt foreign and a little gross. I finally remembered what alcohol tasted like back when I was about seven and snuck a taste of Jack Daniels for the first time. I gagged because it tasted toxic. Because alcohol IS toxic.

"I'm so proud of you," Joy said, as we had dinner with her parents, Uncle Paul and Aunt Daisy.

"Don't be so hard on her," Uncle Paul said and turned his head to his wife.

"I didn't say anything," said Aunt Daisy.

But eventually, she did make a passive-aggressive comment or two, and even if Joy swore she did not talk to her mom about my situation, I could tell she had. But I didn't give a shit, honestly.

"Mom," she kept saying, giving her the look that reminded her, "You're not supposed to know."

"I told you to not be so hard on her," Uncle Paul said once more.

After dinner, a very bland chicken cacciatore that Aunt Daisy had made, clearly using mostly canned goods, Joy declared, "I'm so glad you decided not to go to Italy."

Overcome by a processed food-induced melancholy, I replied, "Yeah, I think I made the right decision."

Meanwhile, I could not escape the awareness of the silence reverberating from my cell phone. Was he really so bad? Did he do anything wrong, but just like me a lot and act on it passionately? Why *would* I choose nothing over something?

Days passed without a word from Dr. Rivers, and not without a thought of him either. Despite everyone's insistence that I had made the right decision (especially the intervention gang-bangers), I saw my Italian fantasy vaporize. It was like an acid bomb had been dropped on it, slowly annihilating everything. Views of Mount Blanc and Italian cows grazing in the pasture. Gone. Delicately-shaven prosciutto served with indigenous mountain cheese. Gone. And, the hot Vespa-riding Italian men. Gone.

Suzanne was still cold and not returning any of my calls, though once in a while she would send an obligatory "How are you?" text. She was so passive aggressive, it made me sick.

When things went well, she was awesome, so full of life, great sense of humor. She'd gone after me pretty aggressively when she first saw my work.

"You have to show your work at my gallery. Have to, have to, have to," she said during her pitch to me at the Rose Café.

"Thanks," I remember saying. "I love your enthusiasm. It is very genuine."

"You can't buy passion," Suzanne said, "and I'm passionate about what you do. It's hard to explain why a certain artist moves a person in a certain way, but you just have that effect on me..."

I suspect that Suzanne was more blown away that I was big fan of the painter, Suzanne Valadon. An accident that Suzanne's hero was also named Suzanne? You be the judge. Valadon was a teenage model in turn of the century

Paris, who posed for Toulouse-Lautrec, Degas and Renoir. She had a kid by maybe one of those guys, while becoming a painter in her own right. Her paintings stay in your mind long after you've stared at them. The majority of her stuff was female nudes. Her entire life, Suzanne did basically whatever the fuck she wanted. For example, if someone invited her to Italy, she would have gone. Even if Italy was across the continent from France.

I still had this pit in my stomach, like a stubborn child holding fast to her word, but going against something she really wanted to do. Was I an idiot? I had just passed on the trip of a lifetime, and at this point, I couldn't even remember why. There was no way I could back-pedal now...could I? Besides, he had probably filled my seat on the back of his bike. God, why hadn't he tried just a little harder to convince me?

Please, God, make him ask me one more time.

Please, Santa Claus, Easter Bunny, Tooth Fairy…

Where are any of you when members of the human race really need you?

iCOFFIN

ONE WEEK before the doctor left for Europe, I was stricken with a sense of anxiety; I reached for my phone. The price of pride had fallen in the stock market. I was ready to ask if the offer to go to Italy was still available. *Just ask*. Of course, I couldn't *ask* him. He would never bat an eye. But his texting persona had vulnerabilities. It could pour out Shakespearean replies. That's where I decided to focus my campaign.

- *Hi, how are you? Ready for your trip?* (I tested the waters.)
- *hi! was wondering about you. Yep, leaving one week from tomorrow.*
- *Great. Did you find a replacement for the back of your bike? LOL*
- *no, i did not look for a replacement nor were you a fill-in.*

Relieved, but still nervous, I knew this was my opportunity.

- *If possible, I'd like to change my mind.*

My heart was racing. I stared at my phone. Nothing. Shit. At least five minutes went by, but it felt like five fucking hours.

I'd blown it.

I'd spend the next month in LA looking for a new gallery to show my non-existent work in and wiping off graffiti from the neighborhood. I had been let go by Suzanne, who claimed that my "actions of late were not in line with the image of her gallery".

"I just can't have a public vandalizer representing my gallery," she had finally told me. Yet, last month, she exhibited the works of Ramone Clifton, who has been in jail several times. The truth was, my work wasn't selling as much as it used to. She needed young blood. This was her opportunity to axe me, but she was giving up on me too early. She would regret this, and regret was an emotion I had grown very intimate with. In an alternate universe, my paintings were selling like hotcakes. Cynthia wrote an entire book on my palatial success. Suzanne and I were drinking Chardonnay as she bid me farewell on my trip to Italy. But wait, in order for this to occur, I would have had to meet Dr. Rivers, which means Axel would still have died, leading me to debauchery and public defacing. But, I would still have a gallery.

It sucked not to have a gallery anymore. For years, I loved telling people, "yes, it will be in my gallery"..."please call my gallery"..."meet you at my gallery"...of course, it was never mine. I didn't own it.

It's one of those LA or New York or San Francisco things, where even if you work in an office, you say it's "yours". But nothing is yours. Not even the goddamn skin and blood that make up your flesh and bones. Your skin is replaced every couple of years. Your body is only, like, 3%

original. Everything else is bacteria, other's people's skin, and all the crap that's in the air. But that's probably why that 3% is so important. My gallery made my 3% of originality feel like it was 4%. It gave me confidence. I made me feel important. It gave me balls, which you need to have in a coldblooded town like Los Angeles.

I could also call the gallery staff for things. They had a stamp machine. They picked up the tab of artist crap sometimes. They made the flyers. They supplied everything, like a parent does. Stuff that in my mind I thought would last forever. I guess she was like the mother I was suckling. I really liked Suzanne too. I suspected she was gay for a while. I didn't think she was attracted to me or anything, I just thought she might be gay.
You get into thinking shit like that in big cities. The Faux gaydar. You spend afternoons, even full days wondering who's gay and who isn't. This was probably what it was like during the McCarthy era when everyone wondered who was a communist.

"I'm sorry," she said, when she let me go. This was on the phone. And I recall not feeling surprised. But there was the eerie feeling that it would hurt more later, like if I happened to be up at 4am, when every mistake you ever made floodgates every thought (maybe there's a reason you're supposed to be deep in REM at that time).

"You shouldn't be sorry, it's OK," I told Suzanne calmly. There was really long silence on both ends of the phone at that point.
"So, how are you otherwise?" she asked.
"I'm OK. You?"

She didn't even answer how she was. But I guess, that happens a lot. She just jumped to the next question.

"What are you working on?"

"Staying out of prison," I answered. I forgot what else was exchanged after. But hours went by before I realized I no longer had a gallery. Did this have anything to do with my sudden need to accept Jake's Italian invitation? Probably.

I couldn't make the connection. I'm not a psychologist. But I knew the feeling of loss too well. "Hand Maid" was a good show, written up in all the papers, but that's all bullshit, unless you're Lucien Freud or somebody like that. I sold two paintings that night. Suzanne picked up the bill for the opening.

Crickets showed up to the exhibition thereafter. After my fall, all the paintings were taken down and sat inside a box in my apartment. The apartment of death.

"OK, well, I hope we can still be friends," Suzanne actually said.

For the first time in my life, I hated coming back home. Normally a neat person, I let things go. Dirty clothes on the floor. Unwashed cups. TV on 24/7, even though I usually just stared at the images with the sound off. I turned up the volume a couple times when I came upon a Rick Steves program, whom I loathe.

The guy looks like he's going to work in a corporate office, but in actuality he's visiting a small town in Germany or France or Italy. Watching his show was the only time I felt like not going to Italy. But it didn't mean I wasn't going to Italy. I hoped. I actually prayed, then took a deep breath, tossed my iPhone on the couch like I hadn't a care in the world, and began to undress. Then, I glanced over my shoulder to that little black iCoffin, almost pleadingly, before entering the bathroom. Nothing. I shampooed, conditioned, buffed, and took an extraordinarily long time to shave everything that needed to be shaved. When the water stopped running, I acted cool, psychologically tricking myself into believing I didn't give a shit about anything. I moisturized and combed my hair, until finally there was nothing left to do but exit the bathroom and lunge at the iCoffin.

Nothing.

"It's not the end of the world," I told myself, which was an odd thing to say. How did I know it wasn't the end of the world? It could be. But they say it doesn't happen overnight, that the process takes time, like anything.

Ten minutes later, I had resigned myself to the fact that I had lost the opportunity for the trip of a lifetime, and I couldn't even remember why I had turned it down. Sure, he's eccentric; yes, he is an emotional textophile, yet acts like a robot to my face. But, was that really a reason to turn him down, Savannah? The love-making was sweet. Love-making? What was this, a fucking Woody Allen movie? Jesus Christ, I needed a drink. I could just walk over to the bar on Admirality and sip a glass of wine. Or guzzle one, two, or three. Calm down, Savvy. Remember the last time this happened. You wound up in a cage.

Fuck it. I threw on a sun dress and strappy sandals, and bolted to the elevator.

I was click-clacking through the parking lot when my iPhone beckoned me.

A message. My knees almost lost equilibrium.

I'm sure I looked like one of those guys with gold fever. I stopped in my tracks, heart pumping, and unlocked my phone to read the following text: *sorry it took so long for me to get back to you. was with vip patient all day. the offer is always open for you.*

A sense of serenity took over my body, and I realized that all of my anxiety was in vain. So, instead of drinking, I went back to my apartment and texted with the Doc for the rest of the night, making arrangements for our upcoming adventure.

RAMEN

LOTS AND LOTS OF WORK had to go into the planning of my journey, especially given the delayed acceptance.

Jake's friend Vince, who had pioneered the whole trip, had his assistant on top of it. She was arranging flights, hotels, and transfers for me. She came to the conclusion that the flight would be $6,000 more if I was going first-class. *I'm sorry, it's just too much*, Jake pleaded. *Will you be OK in coach? Please say yes.*

I'd be OK in a fucking cargo plane with chickens.
Sure, I'll be fine.
Good. I'll get you a script for Xanax so you can sleep.

Sure, I no longer had a gallery, but I was going to Italy. The feeling that others were working on my behalf, making calls, reservations, and decisions felt good. I don't generally make a habit of getting highs out of these situations, but this one time, I really needed it. Maybe it was Axel, the hands, the prison, the painting, Suzanne...I needed a vacation from all of it, from myself really. It was like the movie "The Exorcist", except that there wasn't a demon inside me, it was just me...and I needed to get out.

It was all good except for one thing. Joy.

I could not pass that buck to the assistant, or could I? Couldn't the assistant call Joy to relay the message: "Miss Savannah will be departing for Italy in a few days with the doctor. She will call you upon her return. Bub-bye, Joy."

Shit, this was the one thing I had to do myself.

We had plans to meet. I actually hadn't seen her in a couple of days, which was a long time, considering she had been practically my probation officer.

We met at Kanpai, after 10 p.m., because that's when they serve their mind-blowing Chasu Ramen. I needed comfort. I needed magic. I needed Chasu. It was like going on a blind date. I couldn't sleep the night before, imagining her freaking out and throwing delicious bowls of Ramen against the wall. She'd call the cops, the mental institution. They'd hold me down in a straitjacket and fry my brain, and somehow she would have like *custody over me?* Was that even possible?

"Hi," she said very calmly, her eyes gleaming diabolically.

I was already slurping my bowl of condolences when she arrived. I skipped the pleasantries.

"I'm going to Italy," I said before suckling down more delicious porkfat broth from the gigantic wooden spoon.

"I knew you would," she insisted sinisterly, then – "I was prepared."

Oh shit, I did not like the sound of that.

"You can go," she said parentally, "but you're not going alone."

I wasn't going alone, I thought. I was going with Dr. Rivers.

"Darcy and Hugh are going with you."

Suddenly, I felt like throwing up Chasu. In her fucking face!

We argued. Nervous Japanese waitstaff glared. Caucasian patrons didn't give a shit. Joy won the argument. I would be chaperoned like a 40-year-old Paris Hilton, or what's-her-name from the Disney movies.

I had to meet with Dr. Rivers the next day to tell him the news. I was too exhausted to text anymore. I thought my goddamn thumb would fall off.

We met at a Starbucks across from his office. A lot of people seemed to know him there. They kept coming up to our table with their huge $8 drinks, graciously shaking his hand like he was a bishop. "Hello Doctor," they would say, or "Hey Jake." He even flirted with a couple of women, who, to be fair, began the flirting: "Hey Doc, what are you up to, no good?" Both times, he replied, "Depends when you get off work." He looked at me like he hadn't actually just said that. Like he had spoken suggestively to these women in private. It was weird. But he was weird. If I didn't have sort of bad news to lay on him, I would have done more than scowl.

"You decided not to go to Italy?" he asked.

"No, I'm going."

He looked surprised. "Then, what's with the long face?"

"I'm not going alone," I said.

"Of course, I will be there."

"Jake, I am not going alone," I elaborated. This was a boring conversation, trust me. Jake mostly asked me to repeat myself until he accepted that Darcy and Hugh were coming too. The whole thing was getting surreal. I *almost* didn't want to go anymore. There was too much baggage, too many people to deal with. And wasn't the whole point of traveling to feel free?

"Who are Darcy and Hugh?" he asked, not appearing like he cared much.

"Darcy is a rich...former student of mine. Well, more like a fan of my work. She was somehow sucked into the intervention group. Remember, I told you about it when we met?"

When we met, that's funny. I said that as if we met accidentally, not clinically, the way it happened.

"Sure," he said, "I understand."

He looked like he could give a damn. But how would I know? I was dealing with the passive-aggressive master. We were face to face, as opposed to text to text, so therefore I was clueless. He was staring out the window and didn't move a muscle when he announced, "There's something I have to tell you, too. It's important for you to know before we embark on this journey together."

"OK." Not much could faze me now. Was he an angel, a demon, an alien, the second coming? None of those would have shocked me.

"I am a heroin addict. I have been clean for twenty years, but I still go to NA meetings. I remember every single day what it was like to be a victim of addiction, and I remember every single day how excruciating it was to come clean."

"I had no idea," I said, stunned, as the thought of young Jake lying in the fetal position in some shit hole with a needle hanging out of his arm began to circulate in my mind. I imagined a young man that didn't even look like Jake, but some guy in a General Hospital episode. Some stud who was unshaven, desperate, but great looking, wandering on the streets of San Francisco, forced to do anything to make a buck, and I mean anything. His weakness and vulnerability made my stomach hurt. He was so frail and cute, with death literally at his doorstep. I don't know if it was because of Axel, but I had tears in my eyes.

"Was this before you became a psychiatrist?"

"It is the reason I shifted my practice to psychiatry, with a focus on addiction," he concluded.

"It wasn't a ruse to pick up hot, vulnerable women?" I joked.

"This is the first time I've ever done this," he said, very seriously. "I would be out of business if this was a regular thing. You're different. In any case, if you no longer want to go..."

I'm definitely going now.

THE GANG

    I WAS THE IMAGE OF REPOSE in a plush Marie Antoinette-like sitting area, meaning I would have my cake and eat it too. My eyes were barely open as they surveyed the surroundings: a canopy bed, curtained French doors, fictitious countryside hills, saturated with multicolored flowers. I felt the sun's hand nudge me awake, as I awoke from my Xanax-induced slumber. I rubbed my eyes and tried to digest the fact that I was in Lugano, f-ing Switzerland! The land of chocolate, rogue bank accounts, and what…Heidi?

    It was hard to believe I had made it across the continent. Away from the grind of LA. Away from the rat race. Away from Joy, Suzanne, Maria, Axel's memories, my corpse-like apartment. I felt like a fugitive. Like I got away with something, which is pretty much what I feel like when I travel. Like I'm cheating somehow. If you consider that we've only been flying commercially for about 100 years, that's pretty much how you're supposed to feel, right?

I had a limp copy of Charles Baudelaire's poems in my left hand. I'd bent the spine of the book so frequently, you could hear it creak like an old door. I enjoyed the sensation, like I wanted to snap the book in half. Tear it with my bare hands.

"Baudelaire," said the man who had been sitting next to me on the flight. He looked impressed, like I should be illiterate. He was cute though. Plus, I was high and flying 600 mph across the Atlantic. I could have been sitting on either side of Pol Pot and Joseph Goebbels and I wouldn't have known it. Of course, that would have made interesting conversation.

My neighbor had big eyes, made bigger through his glasses. His head was shaved, but it looked like his hair was once blonde. He had an adorable, escaped from a mental asylum look. These days, any look can be retro and cute, no matter how sinister.

"Yes, the Albatross," I answered, my voice probably more flirtatious than it should have sounded. I was half conscious, and thus, sounded like I was still in bed. But my neighbor, he was wide awake. He reminded me of an exotic bird who was always looking for scraps, hopping near you. Until you moved. The bird would recoil quickly. But once you stopped paying attention, said bird would wander close again, seeking breadcrumbs.

I'll spare you the boredom of how two strangers introduce themselves on an airplane. BTW, I had a window seat, so I was boxed in. Just me and Jack, in the back, with only the bathroom behind us. I was cornered. And he, Jack Hallenbeck, looked at me like I was cornered. Funny thing is, when we first sat on the plane, I categorized him as someone who would keep his mouth shut for 6 hours (after the layover in Boston). Jack had a serious look. Like he knew something was up. He was on his phone until the moment the plane took off. His expression looked dire, almost apocalyptic. Now, he was smiling, like he somehow shed that serious adult skin and became a child again.

"You're an artist," he said.

"I don't like the word," I replied, "but yeah, I guess. And you? An artist?"

Normally, I would have been impressed that he knew I dabbled in the arts, but right now, I didn't care. Nothing could impress me. I felt tranquilized.

"I was a broker," he admitted.

"Stockbroker," I clarified.

"Yep."

"Why did you...stop doing that?"

He chuckled, then said, "Because it's all going down."

On an airplane, that statement should freak me out. But since the Xanax had kicked in, I was honestly ready for the plane to plunge to the depths of hell. It did cross my mind that you couldn't say something like "it's all going down" on a 747.

"Can you elaborate on...that?" I asked.

"Sure, if you want to hear it," he said, like a boy who gestures you into a private corner to whisper you a secret.

"Why not," I said.

"Remember the '08 crash?"

"Who doesn't?"

I don't imagine you're supposed to say "crash" either. Too late, there were four people waiting to use the bathroom, standing right above us. Their faces, ashen. They did not want to hear Jack Hallenbeck's story.

"Next one will be ten times worse," he said.

"Wow," I said, in a Keanu Reeves-like fashion, chuckling.

"Yep, maybe twenty times worse," he added, "and it could happen at any time. In a matter of days, or even hours. You know people with money? They could lose it all in a matter of hours."

One person who was waiting to use the john went back to their seat.

"Like...what do you mean?" I said, smiling brokenly.

"Do you know how much money the Fed is printing?"

"How much?"

"Three trillion a year," he said.

"That's a lot," I admitted.

"That's a lot of zeros. That's unprecedented. No government in history has ever done this. That's all the government can do now, is print money. You know how much money the Fed printed before 2008?"

"I don't know, how much?"

"A trillion...in 100 years. Now, we're doing 3 trillion per year."

I was almost ashamed to ask, "And why is that...uh, bad?"

"You know Bernie Madoff?"

"Not personally," I answered.

"You understand the Ponzi scheme...Madoff was taking investors' money and putting it in junk stocks that had no actual value? Well, that's what the Fed is doing. We're printing oceans of money with nothing to back it up."

Now, I understand why Jack Hallenbeck's expression was so dire when he walked in. He had come to peace with this information and converted it into humor, which is how homo sapiens come to terms with any horrible news. I went out with a cop once, a long time ago. Henry McReady. Loved his name. McReady told me that cops are always getting in trouble for making jokes at crime scenes.

Like, the relative of a victim will overhear cops joking around and accuse them of being insensitive. But McReady would tell me, cops saw such horrible stuff, stuff normal people never saw, could never see...and making jokes was their only way of dealing with it. That's when I realized why humor is such a necessary instrument in human life. It's how we deal with horrible shit, right?

"So America is just one huge Ponzi scheme," I concluded.

"You think I'm BSing. I am not," he laughed.

"I don't know," I said, "I'm just...sitting next to you. Listening to you before I pass out."

"Where are you going?"

"Switzerland. Meeting my boyfriend there."

Was Jake my boyfriend? He was very old to be called a "boyfriend". This word had a nice ring to it when I was 16, but now that I was 40… I was thinking, a new word needs to be invented. Man friend? Homo sapien friend? Homo erectus friend?

"Enjoy it. Enjoy as much as you can."

"Why?" I asked. "Why should I enjoy?" I asked again, with a curious look on my face. The Xanax was really taking over my body now.

"Because it could be the last great time you have before it all goes down."

"Like an albatross," I added.

He was very private about why he was going to Switzerland. No doubt to visit his Swiss bank accounts. Whether or not Hallenbeck was right, he was right that you had to enjoy it while you had it. Because when it's gone, it's gone, baby.

My dad used to tell me, "Everything we have, we will probably lose one day. You know, all this stuff, TVs, cars, remote controls, we haven't had it very long." At the time,

I thought he meant that we, our family, did not have it for very long. Since we only bought that TV a couple of weeks ago. Now, I get it.

Yeah, Jake is temporary. I'm temporary. You're temporary.

All pleasurable things are
temporary. Food. Sex. Good conversation.

I think I was reading "The Albatross" over and over again to harness a clue of what was in store for me. I read it over and over again like a song you get obsessed over and play in a loop. Was Jake the albatross? Awkward but strong, handsome yet uncomely, his wings dragging him to the ground. You admire him, yet find him puzzling. A man who makes a living helping others, yet is almost retarded in his ability to communicate his emotions. Only through the advent of the iPhone can he channel his feelings. Oh my God, he's a junkie of electronic messaging. His emotions are hostage.

The texting vanished when I arrived here first. Jake was still in-flight, first-class, knocked out on a prescription of his own making. He was coming in from London, where he'd stopped to visit his daughters who study abroad. He talked about them with great affection. It was strange to date a father, someone who has co-created two children, and essentially lived another life. He was now on borrowed time. Had his marriage not ended (I'd discovered that he was indeed married), he would have been at home, not divorced. He didn't discuss this too much. I just knew he had returned to the purgatory of bachelordom and didn't seem too upset about it. The routine of marriage was too much for him. You can tell, he's a man who likes to be left alone. I was never so happy waiting around for someone before.

I was in a daydream of being in Lugano, Switzerland, and also in… the reality of being in Lugano, Switzerland. I have never daydreamt about a place and been there simultaneously before. Close my eyes. Lugano. Open my eyes. Lugano. One eye closed, one eye open. Same shit. Lugano, Lugano, Lugano.

Ping.

His first-class flight must have landed in Geneva. Before I had a chance to reply, he sent:

What r u wearing

As I giggled, he sent another one,

What r u not wearing

As I scowled, he sent another,

I want to smell your hair

As I swooned, he sent another,

I want to kiss your toes

As I laughed like a crazy person, he sent another,

I long 2 b between u

As I felt warm, he sent another,

I want to kiss your neck

As I loosened my shoulders, he sent another,

I want to kiss all 10 of your fingers

As I said "What?" he sent another,

I want to caress your shoulders

As turned my head and wondered how many more were coming, he sent another

I want u warm n ready

O-kay. I was getting super horny. I forgot to eat or drink water. I couldn't wait for the next sweet, sexy, raunchy message. I was somehow flattered that he bothered to spell "your" as opposed to "ur." He was becoming an addiction to me, too. I could not wait for the ping. I was on pings and needles.

However, I'm the kind of girl that needs the illusion of control. Who isn't, right? I mean, unless you're a woman living in the Middle East, and even then... have you ever seen Persian films? Those chicks are really bossy. My way of controlling this situation was to make sure, when the Doc walked in, he was going to begin the process of taking me in 30 seconds or less. When that door opened, I didn't want to hear about his stupid first-class flight, the airport, the limo, his daughters, how beautiful this place was...I was dressed to be undressed.

So, I waited. And waited. And waited.

In a variety of Playboy centerfold positions on the bed.

But I started to feel like the sound of one hand clapping.

I could do better things with that hand. I started thinking about my flight over. There is something very provocative to me about airplanes, particularly at night. They are almost like floating hotels, but there are no separate rooms and everyone is touching. I always wondered what it would be like to have a sexual encounter on an airplane. I mean, not with a lover or companion you are traveling with, but with a stranger. The thought gets me so hot. It is one of my many fantasies... So, there I was, boxed in by the window, when a Paul Newman looking man (circa salad dressing days) asked the man next to me (Jack Hallenbeck) if he could have his seat.

Jack obliged, and the handsome man sat down next to me.

"I was hoping I would get to sit next to a beautiful girl," he said with a deep, captain voice. He had friendly blue eyes and a bright, experienced grin. We began to chat. He was a Spanish and German mix, which was a wonderful combo. He told me stories about adventures he'd had all over the world and I listened. With my head rested on the seat, I was staring into his eyes when he said, "If you don't stop looking at me like that, I'm going to kiss you."

And then he did. He cupped my face, then violently pulled it towards him. Stuck his lips into mine. His tongue forced its way into my mouth. Exploring my mouth as I yelped. His hand massaged my right breast. Soaking wet at this point, I mentally begged for him to go further. Soon, the sensation I felt on my bare thigh, I realized was his hand. I was conveniently wearing a flimsy little skirt. He squeezed my thigh and tickled it, teasing me before he touched my panty line. I gasped.

"Shhh. No one can see." Something about that turned me on, too. Forbidden. Lip-locked, helpless, I looked around and caught one or two peeping toms, including a male flight attendant who met my gaze, and gave me a knowing grin. It was all too hot. The stranger slid his fingers inside my panties and I exploded. Albeit quietly. "Otre Ves," he whispered in my ear. And I did. "Otre Ves," one more time. "Otre Ves…"

When I was just about to come for the fourth time, I was snapped back to reality with a steady, confident knock on the door.

Knock, knock, knock…"

"Just a minute!" I moved faster than a kid on Christmas morning, straightened my dress, glanced at myself in the mirror, and flung the door open.

"Good evening, my dear," said the 50 to 80-year-old man who I think spoke with a British accent, pink sweater tied around his neck.

"Yes, good evening…uh, sir," I replied, swiveling my head as if I was gently rejecting whatever he was offering.

"You must be Savanner," said the 50 to 80-year-old effeminate Brit. Clearly, he knew who I was. Did he work for the hotel?

"Please don't call me 'sir'. I'm Vincent," he announced, "Vincent DeVillier."

I shook his hand. He had a firm, wealthy man handshake, which I had learned to detect in my line of work.

"But you can call me Vince," he winked.

He had a devilish glint in his eyes, and a flamboyant way about him. So, this was Vince. The famous, or rather, infamous Vince.

"Yes, right," I recalled, "you're, uh...Doc...I mean, Jake's friend."

"That's right." He grinned, seemingly slightly drunk. "Jake texted me from the airport. He'll be here shortly. He said it would be good for you to get out of the room. Perhaps, you will kindly join us for supper?"

"Us?" I said, suddenly recalling that it was not just the Doc and I on this journey. Right, yes, there were others. And they were meeting us on the Piazza della Riforma for a late supper? I haven't heard that word, supper, since "Little House on the Prairie".

For some reason, I'd had this idea that maybe, since it hadn't been mentioned for a while, others were not coming. I was desperately trying to preserve the desert island sensation of this getaway. I would fail in this endeavor. Miserably.

"Our...gang, so to speak," said Vince.

"Gang?" Hell's Angels? Crips? Bloods?

"You're in the Swiss countryside, my dear. It's beautiful. The views are dazzling, the food divine. The only thing missing is your presence. Please, join us. You look stunning, by the way. Simply a marvel." What he said made sense. I could accept that I was stunning, sure.

"OK, Vince, let's go."

He held out his hand, and we embarked down the hallway, out to the veranda, and down a cobblestone path, illuminated with paper candle lanterns. Greeted by well-dressed Italians, we scuzi-ed and prego-ed our way there. I kept wondering if they could sense I just came almost four times. But I didn't make a big thing of it. You're pretty chill when you came that much.

Yes, it was Switzerland, but it was pretty much Italy. Even the sun was Italian, setting in large brushstrokes of orange, red, and blue, all over the distant mountains and the sky. I took a deep breath.

"Come along, Savanner," said Vince, and we continued on our way. We arrived at a large canopy set up right on the edge of a cliff, with a white tablecloth setting, an abundance of flowers, and flickering white candles. They were all there. All but Jake.

The gang was sitting at a candle-lit table, like a super friendly cult. You could see the dark blue water sparkling from the moonlight in the background. This could not be real, could it? Only the day before I was hanging out at Rite-Aid in Marina Del Rey, California. Now, I was breathing in a fucking fairy tale. I was Snow White and these were the seven rich assholes. People's voices were overlapping. Slingshots of accents. Females sounded more female. Males sounded more male. Sipping and eating made my ears perk. Delicious smells were come-hithering my olfactory glands. I was so relaxed, I could have been talked into participating in a Manson Murder.

The only person I recognized was Darcy, and her husband Hugh, but the other faces and hands that came at me were disorienting, like a merry-go-round of eyes and mouths, teeth, gums, and eerie sounds.

Meet Antoine. (I'm seven feet tall. I have giant hands.) Meet his wife, Maribel. (I'm five foot, two. I look pint-sized compared to him. My voice is chirpy. We have children, many of them, and we're always texting them.)

Meet Colin. (I'm in a wheelchair and I'm Irish. I never smile. But I love to drink. I have a driver named Parker. I look like I'm 17. I have a galaxy of freckles. I'm actually 27. I laugh at jokes but never say a word. This is a job for me. Period. I'm half everyone's age, except for...)

... Vince's wife, Natasha. (I'm about 1,000 years younger than Vince. He calls me, "my little Natasha". I'm quiet and reserved, yet cutely sexy. I look like I'm scared of everything, but I'm very fascinating, because I'm a mystery you want to solve.)

"Natasha," I emphasized," I've been dying to meet you."

Vince scowled. Speechless for the first time. But Natasha, her expression did not change. She looked at me like she expected me to say exactly that.

"I've been wanting to meet you too," she replied, stone-faced, as if this was a poker tournament. The remainder of the table were all engaged in their own conversations. They weren't privy to Natasha and I's tête-à-tête, kind of. The only available seat was beside her. So that's where I sat. The young woman's eyes locked in on me, as I took the chair.

"Great, we both wanted to meet each other and now we're sitting together," I said cheerfully. And meant it. The scent of the food was spine-tingling.

"It is then, mutual," Natasha added. But I let her have the last word here. I nodded, tore myself from the eye contact and dove into the food.

There was lot brought to the table already. The mountain air made all of my senses come alive. I was ravenous, though the food looked almost too good to eat. A crystal cheese platter displayed generous hunks of Gruyere, Stilton, Gouda, and Brie… and delicately sliced Italian meats: Salami, Soppressata, Prosciutto, and Pepperoni. I ripped off a hunk of perfectly crusty baguette and started with the Brie and a little bit of orange marmalade. My taste buds were alive. I shut my eyes and let all of the textures and flavors dance around in my mouth. There were bottles of wine on the table and no doctor to tell me "no". And I was off the Clockwork Orange stuff too.

Once more, I was daydreaming about what I was seeing…how I would marinate a bite of Stilton, while I was actually doing it! I chased each bite with a generous sip of Amarone della Valpolicella 2007. As I lost myself in a food and wine-induced bliss, I don't think I said a word to anybody. I was winning the battle of feeling like I was on a desert island. I was just me, the cheese, the 2007…when the waiter gently tapped my shoulder.

"Be careful, Miss. This plate is hot." There was more to fantasize about. The heaping platter displayed whole grilled branzino, perfectly charred and decorated with rosemary sprigs and lemon slices. The aroma was divine, spring in your nostrils, Heidi grazing the fields with her muttons inside your nasal cavity. The accompaniments marched on… heirloom tomatoes with feta and basil, truffle risotto, Italian green beans with thinly-sliced almonds, and new potatoes roasted with whole garlic cloves.

I could see Darcy employing her shit-eating grin from across the table, beaming in my direction like we were getting away with something.

"Isn't the sea bass outrageous?" Darcy asked. She loved to pose everything in questions, as if she expected you to agree with her, no matter what.

"Isn't the cheese to die for? Isn't the hotel just splendid? Isn't the wine simply soul-quenching?"

"Yes Darcy," I agreed, "it's certainly soul quenching."

Still, seeing a familiar face was calming, albeit that of Darcy, my de facto probation officer. There was no way she was going to forbid me from any vices. What the hell was she going to say, "isn't it great that you're not drinking wine in Europe?" Her husband, Hugh, was another story. Well, a quiet story. He said almost nothing, except once in a while, he would ask me, "You OK, Savannah? Everything alright?"

I sipped my Amarone and nodded. It was the first drink I'd had in a long time, and I needed instant gratification, something to soothe my nerves, even as I could see Natasha glaring at me from the corner of my eye. Sometimes, I smiled at her, sometimes I looked like I was having a fourth orgasm. But her expression, I swear, never changed.

"Why did you want to meet me?" she finally asked.

"I've heard so much about you," I said.

"Oh, like what?"

Vince eyed us uncomfortably, like something bad was about to happen. I knew then I was in a trap. I couldn't answer. I couldn't not answer.

I was rescued by my iPhone. It vibrated. I jerked and said, "Excuse me, Natasha," trying to sound as nonchalant as possible.

The text master was back. He had actually sent me 13 more texts, but I hadn't even felt it. The cheese, 2007, and all the other goodies owned me.

- *WILL B THERE SOON :)*

Not a particularly sexy message, but it was thrilling to hear from him, nonetheless. I texted back, if only to ward off Natasha, who I could see was waiting for me to respond. And would probably wait for hours for me to respond. She had that posture. And she wasn't eating much. She possessed the only pair of arms that were not moving.

- *How far are you?*
- *1/2 HOUR B4 WERE ALONE*

Whatever. The roof of my mouth was the most relaxed it had ever been. My tongue was trembling from the profundity of flavors. I think my soul came.

Meanwhile, Natasha was, I'm pretty sure, peeking at my phone, but pretending like she wasn't. She hardly moved her neck and face, but her eyes were constantly active, like one of those cat clocks. I would normally be very on edge to be socially micromanaged like this. I was just so damned relaxed. Nothing could bother me. If an H-bomb went off outside, I would have said, "Just look at that beautiful mushroom." Although I should have been, I was not threatened by her.

"Are you excited about the trip?" I asked.

Her facial muscles hardly moved. She was made for plastic surgery. She hadn't had any work done yet (she looked like she was barely pushing thirty), but her every action was prepared for it. She was like a statue with a heartbeat. A flesh and blood Venus de Milo. John Barrymore once said, if they found the arms of Venus de Milo, they would have found boxing gloves.

"I'm not big on motorcycles, but Vincent enjoys them," she said softly.

That would become one of her two most common remarks. "I'm not big on [whatever]", and the other was...

"I don't disagree with it," which she said in response to the hotel. I'd asked her if she liked her room, and she said she did not disagree with her room.

It was easier than saying she agreed with it, which sounds even stranger, because how do you agree with a room? Anyway, she said those two sentences 80% of the time, whenever her mouth opened. Her flamboyant husband explained this behavior.

"Oh, don't be so British," he launched at her.

"I'm not big on being called...that," she replied.

"So ironic. I'm British, but you're such an English woman."

"Why do you insist on calling me an English woman?"

"Because, darling, you're so proper. Savanner, isn't she proper? You're also very uptight."

The entire table seemed to nod, confirming this. I don't think everyone realized that their body language (me included) confirmed her rigidity. Natasha noticed it, and straightened out her posture even more. She must have been from somewhere in Eastern Europe, though her attitude was very American. She'd probably moved to the States during her childhood. Her accent was neither foreign nor American. The tug of war of her origins created a lisp whenever she spoke, though barely detectable. Mostly, she seemed bored and uninterested in just about everything. This dinner would live on in the memory of everyone at this table, except for Natasha's. Well, maybe she'll remember it. Just not in the same way.

- *I WANT U*, texted Doc.

The libidinal nature of his texts stormed back. He must have been bored in his cab. Speaking of cab, I hadn't been drunk since that debauched evening on Abbot Kinney. The rebellious teenager inside me was batting her eyes, a sleeping giant, awakening. She urged me to keep Jake waiting before texting him again. She did resent the "it'll be good for her" thing. What a dick, I swear, she said. And I agreed with the teenage girl inside me. I stopped answering the texts. "Fuck him, he's not your dad," she said. I agreed. Yes, thank God for that.

- *Inside you is the most thrilling place to visit*

But each one got more aggressive, more pornographic.

- *Images of u on all 4s in brain*

I turned off the sounds, but the light kept blinking, like my will-power.

"Your kids?" Antoine asked. This was the giant black man sitting across from me. I'm serious, he must have been nearly seven feet tall. His hands were really big, too. Like paddles. He could play ping pong with his bare hands. His wife, Maribel, was a petite white woman, just like all the women at the table. But, when you saw Maribel in contrast to her husband, she looked miniature. Like Smurfette dating Gargamel. She frequently completed his sentences.

"Antoine was asking if that's your child… texting you?"

That made me laugh…hysterically. The idea of Jake being my child. A second ago, he was my father, now he was my son. Funny how quickly things change.

"What's so funny?" asked Antoine, who was very soft-spoken, almost as if he'd adopted that style of speaking to balance out how gigantic he was.

"Oh, oh," I said, realizing the entire table was waiting for my answer, "it's just…not my kid. I don't have one, that's all."

"We have five children," Maribel said.

"Oh, great," I said, as if she had just purchased five kids at the store last week. "That's awesome." I cringe when I use the word "awesome". I'm not even sure why I was so enthusiastic about her having five offspring. I guess, she just looked really small, and bearing five children out of there must have been challenging, even if it hadn't happened all at the same time. I'd forgotten how fun it was to get a little buzzed. Even though Natasha was really looking at me now. Like she was reading all of my thoughts, even my unconscious. Stuff I couldn't read. She was reading it.

"They text us all the time," Antoine added, explaining that he and his wife were just projecting when they'd seen the numerous amount of texts firing at me. Little did they know, these texts were the last thing you ever wanted to associate with children, unless you're French, maybe?

"Antoine is a famous basketball player," Darcy announced, as if it were intimate information. Meanwhile, she had just met the guy, but was clearly proud of her new semi-celebrity acquaintance. I later learned that he was one of Jake's patients. He played for the Miami Heat and Golden State Warriors. He was a small forward. He'd made a ton of money, but was very modest.

"I was a basketball player, but never really known. Except for hardcore fans," Antoine said. "It was a fun career, though. I really miss it."

"But now you get to be around your kids more," Maribel insisted. Antoine squeezed her hand. Cute.

"Why did you want to meet me?" asked Natasha again. I smiled at her, and knew there was no way I was going to sleep without coming up with something.

"I heard you were very beautiful," I smiled. I don't know if she believed me. I was lying through my teeth. She wasn't bad looking, but she wasn't someone who you'd hear is beautiful through a third person. Didn't matter. She blushed. She went scarlet. My bullshit worked. Wow. If I hear about another guy who can't get laid, I'm going to seriously slap him. Women are easy. You can lie to their face with how hot they are and they will believe every word. For now, this would do. But for how long?

When Jake finally arrived, I played it cool. It was my turn to straighten out my posture. Amp up the classiness. Smile thinly. Dare I say, emit grace and beauty? I was buying my own bullshit now.

Of course, Jake greeted Antoine first. Such a star-fucker. He actually hugged him like they were relatives.

"Great to see you! How are the kids?" And on and on…what a fake piece of shit. Then he stuck his hand in his pocket and pulled out, I think, a bottle of pills (I heard it rattle), and he slipped it into Antoine's hand with the dexterity of someone who has done it a million times.

"Thanks, Doc."

He patted the ball player's shoulder.

"You are the best," thanked Antoine again, radiating with joy, like the Fountain of Youth was in that bottle. Maybe that's how he got so big.

"There he is!" announced Vince, who was next in line. They hugged like father and son. Jake also slipped him an F.O.Y. bottle. He was like a pharmaceutical Santa Claus. But instead of reindeer bells, you heard pill bottles rattling. I couldn't believe I was going to let this guy fuck me later. I was seeing people in threes by now, so I guess I could have done worse.

He actually said "hi" to everybody else and didn't even bother to give me the surreptitious wink or glance. My rebellious teenage girl was on high octane by now. She hated him. She wanted him dead. She wanted to throw him off this mountain.

"Has Colin shared with you his World War II Theory of Love?" Vincent asked me. I looked up at Jake, who was still standing there smiling like he was on the red carpet of a Hollywood awards ceremony.

"Oh you must hear it… but, not tonight," he said, massaging my shoulders from behind, and he kissed my head. It was very clinical, but feeling his face and arm, even though it was business-like, created a calm sensation inside me. The teenage girl said, "I can't believe you're going to let this dick touch you. Ew!"

He then announced, "I'm completely exhausted, my friends. I'm afraid I won't be joining you for this meal. But every meal hereafter, I will be there."

"Liar," the teenage girl said.

Everyone said "aw" and "too bad" and "good night".

Jake then looked at me in anticipation, as he was waiting for me to escort him to our bedroom. He had spoken for both of us. His exhaustion was my exhaustion.

"I'm going to have dessert and get to know our friends more," I told him. "And, I'd actually like to hear Colin's Theory of Love very much."

The Text Master froze for a moment, then cocked his head sideways like a peacock. He attempted a smile, but grimaced instead, unable to hide his shock.

"OK, see you later," he said, and walked away like he had three legs. He did.

"I'd love to hear about your World War II Theory of Love," I declared again, from across the table. Colin wasn't shy. I'd heard his voice throughout the evening frequently, just not directed at me. Everyone seemed uneasy, though, as if they had heard it before, except for Vincent, who acted like a kid who wanted to hear his favorite bedtime story for the 50th time.

"Colin has devised the perfect theory of love, using World War II as the basis. Go on, share your profound insight with our mademoiselle," Vincent prefaced.

Colin stared at me, even though the whole table was all ears. I could tell not everyone had heard this sermon.

"I believe that, in the game of love, one can always be categorized as one of the nations in World War II. For instance, in the inception of your relationship, say, you're passive at the beginning, but become deeply entangled, you're Great Britain. If you get emotionally attached, but act like you're not, you're France. If you refuse to get involved until you get fucked, you're the United States. And so on, and so forth."

"What would Russia be?" asked Hugh, of all people. But Colin was still looking at me when he announced this, "Russia would be someone who builds a solid relationship, is betrayed, and then wins the heart of her lover, only to tear his heart out. However, she then lives the rest of her life mistrustful of people."

I looked at all of these strangers surrounding me with love on the other side of the world from California. Each had a relationship all their own, just like the countries and their wars, as Colin lectured. Meanwhile, Jake was still sending me texts. Raunchy ones. The last one was –

- I need you rite fucking now...:)

"Make the motherfucker wait," said the teenage girl. And I obeyed her. And then, Darcy got going. She had a Rick Steves travel book opened; she had earmarked the crap out of it. She was reading out of it, out loud. You can tell, when she traveled, she was the one who did all the planning.

"...Oh, that's why the streets are called Piazza here, and not Strasse..."

No one was really interested, but that didn't stop her. Because everyone was very aware this was an Italian region of Switzerland. Because you heard only Italian here. Still, Darcy liked travel facts. She really, really liked them. Like Rain Man.

"...Oh, I'd love to do a boat cruise tomorrow and...and a mountain lift...oh, and I'd love to get a gelato tonight at the," she read, "Piazza Cioccaro."

By this time, the entire table wanted to join Jake in the bedroom. The teenage girl was snoring. I took the opportunity to excuse myself from the table.

By the time I returned to the room, Jake tackled me at the doorway and started kissing me everywhere. He pinned me to the wall. Took his time unbuttoning my shirt. When he finally tore open the last two buttons, I moaned.

Soon, he had me on the floor. He held me with one hand by the back of the neck. The other hand explored my body until he found what he was looking for. He started out gently with his finger right on target, and put his lips on mine. He held my neck firmly. I couldn't move, unless he let me.

He breathed into my mouth. His fingers seemed to play the piano on my highly sensitized instrument. He had my head locked. He wouldn't let it go. I whimpered. I gasped, inches from his mouth. Faster, harder, and then he hit my note... Ahhhh! Just as I was about to howl, he engulfed my mouth with his and swallowed my scream like he was taking some of my soul (the same one that came earlier). I lay there in a daze as he got up and lit a cigarette.

"What about you?" I questioned.

"That was for me," he replied.

CHURROS

THE MOTORCYCLE is the last bridge to riding a horse, the main mode of transport in the last century. Closest thing to a horse, or what Jake liked to call, "the beast".

The beast awakens: *Blumblumblumblum!*

The beast marches: *Potatapotatapotatapotatapotatapotata!*

The beast hauls ass: *Rummmmmmmmmmmm-bla-ruuuummmmmmmmmmmmmmmmmmmmmmmm-bla-rummmmmmmmm!*

It's the reason why people ride, despite how dangerous it is. And the possibility of violence is attractive. When you're humming at 70-80 mph, all you see is what's around you… the asphalt, liquefied like a gray aqueduct, the trees, which blur like an endless Cezanne landscape, and the blue sky, which seems to stay still, no matter what you do.

After a while, it's like flying. If you're in the back, not controlling anything, it feels like you're hanging on to an albatross. He's taking you wherever he wants to go. You trust in his thrust.

I couldn't have imagined Darcy on the back of a bike, let alone wearing a helmet, but she looked very natural in one. And so did the other wives, whom I also couldn't have imagined wearing leather and strapping themselves to their albatrosses. It dawned on me how primal it was to tear down these highways at blistering speed, with little margin of error. I remember, in Driver's Ed, a policeman came by to give us a talk. He said there's only two kinds of motorcycle accidents: bad ones and really bad ones.

But I'd never felt safer. The sound of the wind, ripping into the shield of plastic protecting my face, was somehow soothing. It almost lulled me to sleep. Holding onto Jake's belly, his flank (as Colin would say later, "the second most vulnerable part of a man"), this conjoined me to him. The way his stomach would expand, which I felt through his shirt, was very spiritual. It was as if he was pregnant and I was feeling something growing inside him that belonged to both of us.

Rummmmmmmmmmmm-bla-ruuuummmmmmmmmmmmmmmmmmm!

Our beast.

Our beast of peace.

The winding roads only added to the feeling of weightlessness.

I could see the faces of Darcy, Natasha, and Maribel; the expression of profound tranquility, even through their designer sunglasses; I mean, inside their mothers' wombs tranquil. The irony of man and machine, the laryngitic cacophony of the Harleys. Rich, carefree women normally subject to imagined fears because they have no real ones, millionaire husbands who have already peaked, desperately hanging onto any pulse they can find, and me, the 40-year-old artiste still looking for love in all the wrong places, likely doomed to repeat the same shit over and over again. There was poetry in this moment.

I let my mind go, but Darcy basically didn't shut up all morning about our next destination, thus she was at the forefront of my thoughts. She'd been reading up on Rick Steves about Chur, Switzerland, which I mistakenly pronounced like "churro", the delicious cinnamon sticks frequently found at Disneyland. I found out the hard way it's pronounced "Coira." And it's the oldest settlement in Switzerland, dating back, like, 4000 years. Coy-ra, she said. Then said it again. Basically, I was bullied into saying it correctly. Guess it's better than her actually doing her job as my probation officer.

Natasha studied me while I repeated what Darcy said. Coy-ra.

"How did you sleep?" I asked Natasha.

"I wouldn't disagree with the mattress," she said, "and you?"

"Oh, I agreed with mine. I agreed with it on every topic."

She grimaced and maybe smiled. I don't know. I kind of preferred when she had no expression. In bed, Jake asked me if I said anything to Natasha.

"What do you mean, anything?"

"Anything as in...anything."

"I spoke with her, so I must have said something. Was I not supposed to?"

"It's fine," he said gently. Still high from the orgasm and the being in Europe thing, I didn't broach. But in the back of my mind, I saw dark clouds on the horizon. I just brushed these dark clouds under the rug. Because I was in motherfucking Churros, Switzerland. That's what you do when you're in Churros. You brush dark clouds under the goddamn rug. Seriously, I just got here. I could brush an apocalypse under the rug. Speaking of Churros, that's what Europe is, Disneyland for adults. The buildings all look like It's a Small World. The old town centers all look like the Disneyland entrance. And Space Mountain, Matterhorn, that's being on the road, that's riding with the Albatross...

...potatapotatapotatapotatapotatapotata...
We were coming to a stop. Like a rollercoaster, the end is always a letdown. Even though these rides didn't go for just five minutes, but four or five hours. I could ride on the back of the bike forever. If I get dementia and I'm stuck in one memory, I hope it's this ride. Before my feet touched the ground.

That's when the magic vanishes. We stopped about every hour for a break and I would be reminded there is such a thing as ground. But it's always funny how the men back up their bikes bull-leggedly. They're so awkward-looking. Albatrosses.

But Disneyland for adults has magic to burn. Let-downs have short lives.

This view was achingly beautiful. The mountains were capped with snow. They stood so high, they penetrated the clouds. The grass. The cloud formations. Ugh! You could just propose to it. Seriously. This is probably what a virgin looks like to men who lust after virgins. Like this view, right here. Jesus. Fucking. Christ. It hurts to look at it.

"Isn't it gorgeous?"
"The weather is perfect, right?"
"I can hardly wait to get to the City West Chur Hotel."
"Me too."
"I heard great things about it."

Nothing was being exchanged that meant anything...and I didn't care to differentiate who said what. The wind massaged my face. Sedated me into zen-like permanence. So, there's a naked painting of me somewhere in France. Who cares? So, I have no gallery. Who cares? So Jake has his arm around Natasha, who...

...What?

They were having a discussion. The girl was on the verge of tears. They looked like they were...breaking up.

Vince seemed unaware, or he just didn't care. He had one glove off, laughing and flirting with Maribel, Antoine's wife.

"It's like gliding, isn't it?" he asked her.

"I love it," she answered.

Antoine was stretching his legs, alone, about fifty yards away. I was stuck with Darcy, her deaf-mute husband, and Colin, who had wheeled himself away from Parker and the van.

"What's wrong with Natasha?" I asked.

"Oh, she's going to deal with what she has to deal with," Darcy said forgivingly.

"Extraterrestrials," Colin added.

Darcy scowled at him, as if this was a secret.

"Aliens," she clarified.

"She fears them," Colin summarized.

I might have been acting like I didn't know, but I'm not sure why. Maybe it had something to do with Jake asking if I "said anything" to her. I told her, I heard she was beautiful. Did that cause this breakdown? Who falls apart because of that? Unless they find out it was...a lie.

"It's very serious, Savvy, a debilitating fear," Darcy said, as if she were now an authority on alien fears.

"The fear can manifest itself in the open plains, where aliens frolic," Colin continued. I was never sure if he was being sarcastic, but I lean towards that.

"A perfect landing ground, just look at all the space," Darcy added, "this is perfect for an alien airport or something."

About 20 yards away, I noticed Colin's driver urinating against a tree, the golden jet reflecting sunlight, like he was pissing gold. It was an oddly beautiful image I never admitted to anyone.

Before I had time to preserve the perverted memory, Darcy grabbed my hand and took me aside. Step into my office kind of thing. Of course, her "office" was only five feet away from anyone. They could all hear.

"I heard that you're homeless," she began.

"Homeless?" I grimaced. Colin looked puzzled, as he had scooted two feet closer to us. Hugh acted like he didn't hear.

"Your art, that is," she clarified.

"Oh...right. Yeah, you know, it's...whatever," I said, not really desiring to discuss it with her.

"What if we opened a gallery?" she offered.

"We?" I asked.

"You and I," she clarified, again. I needed a lot of clarification this afternoon, apparently.

"Yeah, why not?" I said, looking at Colin as if he were my advisor. He shrugged, or maybe he didn't. He was smoking a cigarette.

"You can begin with my portrait. I mean, Hugh and I. We haven't had one done in ages, and, well, I think it's time… "

Meanwhile, Jake was really consoling Natasha. He was hugging her. It looked like he was boarding a train to go to the trenches or something, and handing her a pill bottle as a farewell present.

"There's the old Doc, working his magic," said Antoine, now in our circle. He spoke as if he were reminiscing about how Jake saved his life once upon a time.

"You know what that's like?" I asked.

"Oh yeah, I had many nights like that. But my fear wasn't about aliens. It was about the pressure of the NBA."

"Of the opposing team?" I asked.

"No. Usually, it was within. My teammates. The GM. The media. The opponent was always the easiest part. At least you knew what they wanted. That was simple. The Doc taught me that."

"Ironic," I replied.

"Where's Maribel? Oh, there she is," Antoine said, finding his wife talking to Vince, who seemed to be acting effeminate on purpose. Probably his technique, a carte blanche to flirt with wives. She wasn't reciprocating. And the whole sweeping under the rug thing was mutual. Everybody was doing it. For now.

The sound of the Harleys was a graceful, flatulent symphony that couldn't have come sooner. We were all strapped to our respective albatrosses. Vince took off first. Then Antoine. Then us.

"There's something wrong," Jake said.

Blumblumblumblumblum...

...The engine cut out.

"What's wrong?" I asked, concerned. I really wanted to take off.

"I...don't know," he admitted. A little early, I thought. Guys usually fake there's nothing wrong for a while before they admit that. But Jake, for whatever reason, didn't bother with the facade. It wasn't his. He was insured. And thus, he called it a day.

"You're not going to check...the whatever. To see if maybe you can get it going?"

"Savannah, I don't know anything about fixing a bike," he said as he called the rental place. I couldn't believe it. He didn't even try to restart the thing. He just threw in the towel. Just like that. A caveman didn't just fail to start a fire and call for help right away. What the hell was wrong with him?

It was like being on the verge of an orgasm...and not releasing it. I felt very unforgiving. I was suddenly in the mood to feel worse than the situation...you know, to prove how bad it was. This is how the saying "hell hath no fury like a woman scorned" was invented. I walked away from Jake and Colin, watching the sun bathe the alien landing ground. It was still gorgeous. I calmed down against my will. This stupid beautiful backdrop. No matter what happens, it swallows you.

"I ordered another Harley. They'll deliver it to us in two hours at the hotel," Jake announced. The rental people would come and tow this bike. Wonderful omen.

Colin would drive us back to the hotel...in the car. Yuck. But yes, we were still in Europe. So, I buried it under the rug. I put on my happy face and rode along. As opposed to, you know, walking to the hotel.

It was a quiet ride. No one felt like talking. We were all mourning the death of the bike. I could tell Jake was crushed. The Albatross lost his wings. He was flying across vast oceans and fell flat on his ass. What could he do but start texting people about it?

I looked outside. Kept it on mute. Jake was texting someone. Colin was surfing the web with his iPhone. BBC News. I could see it from here. I noticed Parker, the driver, was also checking his phone. I felt like everyone was smoking weed except me.

It was a loooong ride. Someone would eventually open his mouth. It would be, surprisingly, Jake, who started talking about unicorns of all things.

"Unicorns are real," he said. I had no idea what he was talking about. But neither did anyone else in the car.

"Are they?"

"Sure they are," he said, "most of these myths are real. They are what we call today...rhinoceros."

"Ah, they were mistaken as horses with horns, whereas they were another creature, I see where you're getting at."

Thankfully, this is all I recall from this conversation. Eventually, the World War II thing came up. Alright, I'm the one who brought it up. Guilty as charged.

"What country is Natasha?" I asked.

"Natasha is well-maintained. She stands up for herself, but her weaknesses are too great for the enemy. I believe she's Yugoslavia."

"Hitler razed Yugoslavia, I believe," Jake added. "Operation Punishment."

"So the enemy in this game is Germany?" I asked.

"The theory does not presuppose any enemies, such as Germany, Japan, or Italy. The metaphors have more to do with the countries, and their states of mind in relation to the person in question."

"It's a very valid analysis," Jake interjected. "You should write a book, breaking down each country with case studies. It would sell."

Jake's voice was sort of irritating. Holding onto his belly on the back of the bike was a contrasting experience. On a bike, he calmed me. Eliminated all the ugly things about the world, like the commercialization of stuff. The riding experience reattached you to the trees, the horizon, and all the pretty amazing shit that we're surrounded by that we never see.

I supposed I hadn't really heard his voice in a while, and when I finally did, he was talking about the details of getting a new bike delivered, then unicorns, and finally how this unwritten book could be converted into a commercial sensation.

"I'm not interested in that," Colin concluded.

"Would you mind if I wrote the study?" Jake asked.

"Be my guest," Colin offered.

What a materialistic jerk, I thought. Here is a humble, intelligent, insightful man sharing his philosophy, and all Jake wants to do is get into Barnes and Noble's and sign a bunch of autographs. He'll probably mention Colin in the special thanks section, along with 500 other friends who "inspired" him.

I felt the need to create further discomfort on the subject.

"So, what personality would be Germany?" I dared to ask.

"Germany would be a person who is very aggressive; someone who is hot and cold. When he attacks, he attacks with intensity. This person's ego is tremendous. He believes he is always correct and can have who he wants."

As you can imagine, I was glaring at Jake this whole time. He was playing with his iPhone, probably Facebooking about how amazing everything was or sending someone a text just to show off. What a poser.

"But this person, he bites off more than he can chew. Eventually, if he does not get what he wants, he becomes childlike...and eventually, he implodes."

That's not good.

The City West Chur Hotel was a brand new hotel. Like it just came out of the packaging. The building was placed in a very odd position, by the train tracks, and butted right up to a giant mall. An adjoining structure had "SEXY SHOP" plastered on the side of it. I laughed and asked Jake if he'd like to go check it out. He just brushed me off. He was probably too busy thinking about his book. I thought it would be fun. I didn't realize this would be the beginning of many shrugs.

Jake and I managed to mostly avoid each other as we got ready for dinner. Was this our first official fight? There was no screaming, no shouting, no cursing. Just nothing. Which was how he was usually. But you could feel the aggression and animosity. You could feel rage underneath him. We took turns in the bathroom, grunting and mumbling to each other. There was a moment when we nearly spoke, but the phone rang and he had to go downstairs to check out the new bike. He vanished for a long time. Actually, he didn't even come back. He texted me to tell me to come down for dinner. When I got to the lobby, I saw him talking to Natasha. Far away from the group. Everybody had somehow found their favorite person to cling to. Except me. Darcy claimed me, of course, which meant Hugh also claimed me. They were a two-for-one, but you never knew Hugh was even there.

"They speak a very specific style of German here, you know," Darcy said. I had no idea what that meant. Even with Jake stonewalling me, I was still in a cheerful mood. We wandered through Chur, or Coira, together. Admired the buildings. The fountain. An old couple. Darcy did, anyway. They looked like they could barely walk. It was cute. They were wearing their best outfits. They needed to hold each other just for support. Their faces were profoundly wrinkled. I would have loved to paint them.

"Isn't that ancient couple just adorable? You know they've been around since, like, World War I. They were little kids, playing hide n' seek. They witnessed the industrial revolution."

"And they probably never left this neighborhood," I added.

"They're in Europe, Savvy, of course they've left. You can't not leave. All the countries are so close together. That's why everyone speaks so many languages. They have to. In the US, our closest neighbors are Canada and Mexico, and only one of them does not speak English. Rick Steves says, Americans are desperate...desperate for culture. You know, he's right."

"When you're old, you want to be like those two?" I asked.

"I would be delighted to be them. Look how cute they are. I can't wait for Hugh and I to grow old together, can I? What do you think, Hugh? You want to grow old with me?"

He didn't answer. I was surprised she even posed him a question. He didn't react, one way or another. I don't think she expected him to answer. She would have been shocked if he ever said anything. I wonder how he asked her out?

We, the gang, had dinner again. But now, it was like we all knew each other. We found the only place open in this strange little non-town in the mountains. We had completely left the Italians. No more piazzas, Darcy reminded us. We were now in Strasse-land. And she added, as the de facto history teacher of the group, it was pronounced Coira. Everyone was getting pretty tired of that.

We didn't actually know each other very well at all, but, in the same way women living together eventually synchronize their periods, we were harmonizing. It felt like I was there for months, and like I had known everyone for years, even though it had been about 72 hours. Natasha sat across from me this time. She looked directly at me. A lot. Even while chewing her food. Of course, whatever plate was displayed before her would only be 10% eaten. I felt like saying, "Are you going to finish that?" after every course. Discussions overall were less first-impressionistic. Vince brought up the unicorn thing. Jake emphasized that all mythical creatures were real. He said the Loch Ness Monster was a crocodile. People argued. I ate. People laughed. The food continued to be moan-worthy. Natasha stared daggers at me. I smiled back. Pan-cooked chamois with juniper and game sauce, butter spätzli and red cabbage with apple. Oh my. I didn't know food could be that good. After the final course, all the couples split up. Jake and I walked back to the hotel. Alone. And I emphasize this. Maribel and Antoine went souvenir shopping. Darcy dragged Hugh God knows where. Parker drove Vince God knows where. I believe Jake and I were the only duet going home.

The pavement was extra loud. The lobby was extra empty. The elevator felt like it was taking a thousand years.

"I always get the biggest room, for some reason," he stated proudly, as he unlocked the door.

It could have something to do with the bag of treats you handed Vince upon arrival, I thought to myself. But suddenly I felt alone. I was with him, but there was a sudden rush of emptiness. And strangeness, as in, he felt like a stranger. And then it dawned on me, maybe I'd been

right to leave his apartment on the July 5th
morning. Maybe my first instincts were right. Yes, they
usually are. I hardly knew the guy.

"I'm going to take a shower," I announced as soon as
we entered the room. And what a lovely shower it was.
Sleeping Beauty would have masturbated herself to sleep in
here. The shower pressure was perfect, caressing,
baptizing. The mirror reflected me to perfection as I exited
the shower with wet hair and feminine grace. The fog from
the dampness amplified the fairy tale image. I hardly even
realized I was jet lagged.

When I exited one of the loveliest bathrooms you
could ever shower in, the whole room smelled like
smoke. That's correct. There was a fog in here, too. Jake
smoked wherever the fuck he wanted to. I approached
him. He flicked the cigarette out the window.

"Well, I guess I'm gonna go to bed," I sighed.
"Turn around," he said, exhaling a cloud of smoke.
"Why?"
"Just do as I say."

So, I turned my back to Jake and stared down at the
bed with anticipation. I gasped when I felt a soft silk fabric
touch my eyelids and snap them shut. Darkness. I couldn't
believe what was happening. Did he go to the Sexy Shop
without me? Getting laid tonight had been the furthest
thing from my mind. Now, I grinned as my heart pounded
with excitement. I heard something jingling as he took me
by the shoulders and placed me on the bed.

"What are you doing?" I asked.
"Shhh."

He grabbed my left arm and stretched it to the upper
corner of the bed. *Crack!* I was cuffed. *Clonk!* Then, the
right.

"I've never done this before."

"We can stop whenever you want," said Jake.

I didn't say anything, but I realized I was smiling.

Then it was silent for a while. Like he'd vanished. Like the door was wide open and I was handcuffed and blindfolded.

"Jake? Jake?!" I almost screamed, before realizing that I didn't want anyone to come to the rescue. Minutes passed. It seemed like eternity. I calmed myself down. Controlled my breathing. Searched for any sound he might make. I was determined to show him how cool I was.

Then, without warning, he ripped my robe open to expose my body, as I was now strapped down at the ankles, as well. My breathing was labored, my bare nipples erect as he kissed them and gently pulled on them with his teeth. Then he kissed me. Softly at first, then forcefully with his tongue and wet lips. His kisses made my adrenaline pump, and I squirmed and struggled, feeling the heat exploding between my thighs. The metal clanging echoed throughout the room like it was a dungeon. He kissed me everywhere, and brushed his lips over my panties, whispering, "Not yet." When I couldn't take it anymore, he ripped off my soaked panties and began stroking me with his tongue.

One. Two. Three. And I was done.

I screamed at the top of my lungs, fighting the cuffs like I had the strength to tear them off. I didn't. All my muscles tensed. He suctioned his mouth on me while reaching down to release my legs. Then, he climbed on top of me and gently unfastened my wrists just as he entered me. I hugged him with my whole body. He thrust into me.

One. Two. Three. And, just like that, he was done, too.

SPIDERS

"I'M HAPPY THAT IT'S A NICE RETREAT," said Joy.

"It is," I assured her.

"You are wearing a helmet, I hope," she reminded, sort of motherly.

"Sure, I have all the safety features, Joy."

Then, we ran out of stuff to say. Joy, the person I'd spent the most time with in my adult life. The person I could always count on, and from whom I never felt estranged.

"What else? What else?" she repeated.

"Look, it's pretty late. Let's talk later in the week," I mercifully announced.

"Sure, yeah, you're like nine hours ahead, right?"

It was late, but I wasn't tired. I was a little lonely. Jake was staring at his eyelids, lightly snoring, cigarette half-lit in his hands. I had my eye on his fire hazard while sitting Indian-style in front of my laptop, Skyping with Joy. The moment she answered, I knew I shouldn't have called her. But I actually did miss her. I missed her proximity. I missed the comfort of knowing we could meet somewhere. If my life was threatened in LA, she would be the first person I'd call. And if I hadn't put out Jake's cigarette, many lives would have been threatened.

    I gently lifted the Marlboro light from his fingers, took a drag, and flushed it down the toilet. This was when a light beamed across the room. It was totally dark in here, so the tiniest flash would stick out like a sore thumb. Especially the flash of an iPhone. I shouldn't have, but I followed it like a boat follows a lighthouse. I told myself that if it goes off before I get there, I wouldn't push any buttons to see who it is. But it's an Apple product, they're hell-bent on eliminating all privacy. So, I had an eternity to peek. Surprise, surprise...

    Natasha: *I really need to see you. I'm in the lobby. Come down please.*

    I realize the message wasn't for me, but the jet lag was like having five shots of espresso. My mind thought it was the middle of the day. I knew I was nowhere near sleep. And Jake was not going to entertain me, so I took the initiative. I went to the lobby. It was almost two in the morning. But you could hear the fetid sound of voices from bedrooms, or from the one café bar that was still open at this time.

    When I walked down the stairs, it was like a Hitchcock movie. I could see the shape of Natasha sitting alone. I couldn't see her face, since it was obscured by the balustrade. Forever, I couldn't see her face. Just her body. She was wearing a jacket over her sleeping clothes. Sipping a glass of water. I could see her disembodied arm lift the glass. She took tiny sips. The amount of water looked the same when she put the glass back on the hotel coaster. I don't know if I wanted to see her in tears, vulnerable, needing someone to talk to, or if part of me wanted to confront her about texting Jake at this time. I know they weren't "together", so why did I care?

The moment I had a good look at her face, she was locked in on me. She was not in tears. She didn't look weak. She didn't look surprised. At all. As if the text had been for me. I thought I was silhouetted from her vantage point, but her eyes seemed to pierce through that. She was looking directly at me. At my eyes. Like we were face to face already. What could I do? I feigned surprised from halfway up the stairs.

"Natasha? What are you doing up? I couldn't sleep either."

"I'm not big on jet lag," she said, never taking her eyes off me.

I didn't ask to sit across from her, of course. I just did. Her unblinking eyes gave me the chills. But I poker-faced my way through it, I think. Truth was, it was exciting to do anything at this time. All those years of being forced to sleep at a certain time puts staying up late at the top of the list in the game of youth.

"Is Vince asleep?" I asked.

"I don't know. He could be. Or he could be watching porn," she said cavalierly.

"Huh," I said, noticing she was gazing at something on the ceiling. I couldn't see what it was.

"There's three spiders there. A female and two males. When we arrived, there were four males. They're lining up. To meet her."

"She's...killing them?"

I kept craning my neck to see the erotic spider in question.

"Afterwards. She kills them...afterwards," Natasha whispered, as if the arachnids could hear us talking about their sex life.

"The males are waiting willingly?"

"The experience is worth it to them," she concluded as she took another small sip of water. Still, I couldn't see the spiders in question. I trusted that she could see that far. I just couldn't.

"It's worth it to the guys, but what about to her?" I asked.

"She will give birth to a pile of baby spiders afterwards."

"But with no fathers."

"She's pregnant...until she's not...and then she is again."

I wasn't sure what she was getting at. But I steered the conversation elsewhere.

"That's how we used to do it," I said.

"What do you mean?"

"Our grandmothers, great-grandmothers, they had eight, nine, ten children, it was normal. Can you imagine having that many children? Spending your entire twenties just being a baby machine?"

"My parents only had one child."

"And your grandparents?"

"I never knew them."

"But," I repeated, "can you imagine just being pregnant for an entire decade?"

I could tell the conversation was making her uncomfortable. That's probably why I wouldn't let it go. I have a tendency to do that. To be socially confrontational, in case you haven't noticed.

"That would be fine with me," she said, "I'd like that. But Vince disagrees."

"If you do manage to be pregnant for that long, you would only need one box of tampons for, like, 10 years."

I thought this would make her blush, but instead her eyes seemed to blacken. Her expression became more concrete. She played along. I was in over my head.

"The first time I bled, my mother told me there was a ghost in my stomach."

"Wow, I've never heard it described like that before."

"She said, every month there will be another ghost."

"Sure, it's like a haunted house for forty years, right?"

"Are you going to pursue your painting?" she asked suddenly.

This one came out of left field. Was she talking about what I think she was talking about? I think she was. But I didn't want to admit it. I acted stupid.

"What painting? Huh?"

"The painting," she said, "that you want back."

I couldn't fake it anymore. She won. My smile was a shit-eating grin. And I was probably blushing. And she was studying every facet of my transformation. She was like the spider on the ceiling. The one she was probably making up. Crazy bitch. But smart, too. She checkmated me.

"I don't know," I said, "I might."

"You should, she said. "I would not be big on a painting of me in that way...out there." She dropped the final blow. I needed some air.

I walked through the desolate streets. Alone. Pissed off at Jake for telling Natasha about my private life. It had to be Jake. He knows her. They talk. Obviously, she texts him in the middle of the night.

Thinking about the self-nude only made me obsess over it more. The painting was, after all, in France. I could go there to get it. Chuck said to come and get it. So, I should, right? Maybe that's my purpose here. I couldn't believe Jake told her about my private life. What else did he tell her? And to think, we had just had such a nice night together.

Jake was opening up. Acting human. I was thinking for the first time, maybe I could love this man. It was a very brief, microscopic thought. I didn't love him. It was a synthesis of a thought. I'm just saying, the post-coital conversation moved the relationship forward.

"The Albatross was my father's favorite poem," Jake said.

"Really," I said.

"He spoke fluent French, my father."

"He did?"

"He rode a motorcycle."

"Did you… get along with him?"

"I wouldn't say that. We didn't have much of a relationship."

"He was a judge, right?"

He didn't reply, but I could hear him nod. The lights were off.

"And your mother?"

"She cheated on him," he said.

"I meant, what did she do for a living?"

"Little odd jobs. She worked in a movie theater. She worked in playhouses."

"Was she an actress?"

"She worked at the ticket counters, usually. Later, after they divorced, she became a stewardess. She loved movies where characters died. She was always upset when a character did not die. Death was fascinating to her."

"Ah," I said, as if I'd discovered something about him. But I couldn't intellectualize it. Albatross, mommy, airplanes, death...there was something there, but I didn't know what. I wasn't a shrink, was I?

"Why do you... think you became a drug addict?" I dared to ask.

"There's a lot of logical answers. You can blame me, you could blame our culture, you could blame my parents. You can say, I'm an addictive type."

"You do love to text."

"You know, two-thirds of your brain controls your hands? That's why amputees suffer from phantom hands syndrome."

He was not apologizing for texting. He would never do that. If you took away his iPhone, he would shrivel up like the Wicked Witch.

"I became a doctor because I needed the control. When I was on drugs, I didn't like how my memory vanished. How real life moments became like dreams. When you're having a dream of... you kill someone, you're chased by the police, you divorce that from your consciousness. Being on drugs like I was, it was like being cut in half. Being a psychiatrist, it keeps me very conscious. It keeps me in the present."

It sounded great at the time, but was Jake really in the present now? He was borderline, shall we say, "challenged" when it came to emotions. Maybe all the drugs he did really fucked him up. Maybe he was Axel, if Axel made it this far? I learned in my one meeting in AA that once you're an addict, you're always one. It's a disease. You can only learn to live with it. My heart went out to him. Maybe this is the best he could do. I just wished he hadn't opened his mouth to Natasha about me, or did he?

I was the only one walking around in the middle of the night except for two women, talking and laughing about a mile away. I couldn't really see them, but I could hear their mousy murmuring bouncing from the narrow cobblestone streets. They were having a warm conversation. It was comforting to me, reminded me of Joy.

This city really is a Disneyland for adults. The houses are colorful, like giant Legos, if they melted a little bit. It's always fun to check out closed shop windows.

Everywhere you looked, you saw Bündnerfleisch, Bündner Gertensuppe and capuns...meaning tissue-thin slices of air-dried beef, barley soup with vegetables and Swiss chard leaves stuffed with meat and cheese, respectively.

There were enough gelateria stands to line up to the moon, seriously, which by the way looked glorious tonight. The moon did. Crescent-shaped. Or croissant-shaped, if you're thinking about a nude painting of yourself being gazed at by total strangers.

Every goddamn bakery was hocking the world famous Bündner Nusstorte, this rich shortbread thing with walnut caramel filling. The Alpenstadt-Torte was also in your face. Yeah, that's a sponge cake with cherries and sweet caramelized nuts. There's a reason why you want to walk down these cobblestone streets when all the shops are fucking locked down. You feel like a bank robber circling Fort Knox.

There's also this thing called Bündner Steinböcke, gianduja-filled chocolates in the shape of the ibex. Whatever. It's good stuff. I tried it earlier. Maribel bought some and bullied everyone into adding a bazillion calories, not that I care. Antoine ate a ton. Said when he was a pro, keeping the weight in check was the toughest part. He's a giant, so he eats a lot. He killed his Bündner Steinböckes.

One of my invention ideas is a procedure where you can borrow someone's stomach. So you can just eat without morals. You know how some royalty had a room they went into just so they could throw up? So they could eat all day. Like a wine tasting. I never spit wine back in. It's gross. And it's just the worst tease. Once it goes in, it does not come out. Well, not the same end, anyway. Imagine if you could just borrow several stomachs. Eat fucking Nusstortes and Bündnerfleisches for days. Literally.

There were a lot of kitchen shops too. They were big on cutting boards. In the shape of animals. Goats and other mountain beasts. It was cute. But I was getting hungry, so I didn't really care about souvenirs. I began to wish one of these places was open. Didn't bakers show up at 3 a.m. and start churning butter and milk and all that crap? My stomach was having fantasies now. I don't think I had snacks at the hotel. No chips. No cookies. Just cigarettes. Always a mistake to not have snacks when you're traveling. I shouldn't have been hungry. We ate like conquerors for days now, like we were raping and pillaging towns; taking all their virgins with one hand, holding a drumstick with the other.

"The Apple symbol, that's from Adam and Eve, right?"

And then, I heard a familiar voice. It was the two women.

"I'm not big on Genesis," responded one of them. Natasha? Didn't I just leave her in the lobby?

"But I mean, that's the Apple symbol. It's the bitten Apple from the Garden of Eden, right? Everyone is hooked on their iWhat-nots. It represents, like, the Tree of Knowledge and we are in the Information Age, right?"

The other one was Darcy. I couldn't see them. But I heard them like they were right behind me. At this time, with no one around, voices echo. They go everywhere like butterflies. They're in the sky, on the ground and in your ear. Naturally, I did whatever I could to follow them.

"What do you know about Landeck?" Natasha asked.

"It's an old medieval town. It was once a border town like Tijuana. You had to go through it if you wanted to get anywhere."

I wanted to hear them talk about me, but after listening to them bullshit for what seemed like an hour, I almost gave up. I don't know if I was disappointed or relieved. But I did know, Darcy was likely the one who ratted me out. I was in harmony with Jake again. I was relishing this feeling when…

"What do you think about what Jake said, about the unicorn?"

"I think it makes sense. I never thought about it."

"He said that every thought we have really does exist. Just in another dimension. He calls it the multiverse."

WTF? Like Axel's multiverse? Was I hearing this right? Maybe it was a junkie thing. But that would mean Axel was doing drugs before I dumped him. So, maybe I didn't kill him. Or maybe I did.

"So, when do we begin the portrait?" Darcy asked.

I was in the lobby, drinking a cup of coffee, sort of watching a Futbol game, still dazed from the night before even though it was already noon.

I noticed Parker eating by himself in the corner of the room. He moved his mouth like a bird, as if he were eating secretly. Was Colin such an asshole boss, he didn't even allow his driver a lunch break?

"Shall we begin tomorrow…the portrait?"

I'd forgotten I had agreed to this. Darcy could tell. So she did what any wealthy person does. I was still not verbal, at this point.

"I'm happy to pay you for it," she said.

This was when it dawned on me that she had always planned for this. She had discussed it with Hugh, in LA, and said something along the lines of, "Wouldn't it be great if Savvy painted our portrait?"

Hugh probably nodded or shrugged "yes" in the same way I was nodding or shrugging "yes".

"How did you sleep?" I asked.

"Like a baby. Like I was still in the womb," she offered. Creepy thing to say. Something Rosemary's Baby would say, if it could speak.

"You slept the whole night? Because I'm super jet lagged," I explained.

"Yes. I was deep, deep, deep in my unconscious," she lied.

"Well, we're going to the land of Freud," I offered.

"I don't understand." She suddenly looked baffled.

"You know, 'unconscious', Freud...he, like, invented the concept."

"Oh yes," she shrieked. I can't believe she just lied about sleeping all night. Or maybe she's just crazy. I'm on a bike trip with crazy women and old guys desperately in search of their youth. Very dangerous.

I could see down into the lobby. Of course, there were Jake and Natasha, having a coffee together. Away from the others. Vince was sitting with Maribel. Antoine was sitting with Colin. It was bizarre. Like a game of Tetris where all the pieces stopped fitting.

BEAST MASTER

WE WERE SOMEWHERE IN THE HEART of the old Austrian Empire at the Sporthotel Weisseepitze. The place was very wooden, very Grimm-brothers-ish, as in "Cautionary Tale". As in, you felt like you were inside a forest, even though you were in a building. As in, the girls were dressed in Dutch outfits, like the Swiss Miss hot cocoa packages. I used to drink cups and cups of that stuff. Little did I know, it wasn't really chocolate. What the hell was it? But now, I saw the real chocolates. I tasted the real chocolates.

Yes, I was in Austria, "The Sound of Music" Land, where Ethan Hawke and Julie Delpy met in Before Sunrise, and of course, where Sigmund Freud invented "penis envy". Well, it didn't occur here, where I was sending a message to my eBay nemesis, but indeed, it all happened in this country.

Jake called our replacement bike "the new beast". I called him "The Beast Master". He called me "The Beast Mistress". To me, it sounded like the beast was married and I was having an affair with him, like I was homewrecking the family of Mrs. Beast. I don't know, Mistress just doesn't have the same ring as "Master". It didn't sound like I had command or dominance over anything.

The ride here was once again magical, dream-like. The grass was yellow, the color of the sun. We floated through rolling hills, slowing down through windy streets imbedded in mountains and little villages that must have been around since forever. Because no one would build a house in that position now. It's amazing that residences were built from scratch in these locations. This is where the fear of heights was invented. We were definitely in the adult version of Space Mountain, where crashing your bike wasn't the only concern. Leaping thousands of feet (um, from your bed) off the side of a mountain was a close second. Close, close second.

The shadows of the clouds changed shapes constantly. The sun appeared and disappeared, like it was playing hide and seek – not like in California, where it just played Monopoly. Jake's stomach, now slightly larger from all the rich, yummy food, felt warm and comforting. The bike did not break down this time. Thank the Lord.

The gang synchronized like bumblebees. Sometimes Jake took the lead, sometimes Vince, sometimes Antoine. The roads snaked around mountains, with turns so sharp you thought for sure someone was going to be sucked into the hands of gravity. But, nobody was. It was graceful, and magical, and the air had a sweet perfume, growing cooler as we climbed the mountains and warmer as we descended. In the rear-view mirror, far away like a bug, was Colin's ride, which would vanish completely at some points... I would think he was gone... then, poof! The van would peek out over another hill or bend.

We stopped at a restaurant. We always did. This one was more like a rest stop. They served strudels and schnitzel and sausages. Delicious. Homemade. You heard cows and pigs in the vicinity. Schnitzels had amazing snap. Other bikers gathered at this viewpoint, which was complete with souvenir shops and a dazzling, yet vertigo-inducing, mountaintop view. Antoine must have eaten half a dozen sausages. Natasha, half of one.

"I'm not big on this much meat," Natasha said with a forced smile that unnerved everyone.

Jake and I were standing aloof from the group, observing them. I mentioned to Jake that I saw her the night before. Told him about the spider conversation. He paused, as if computing what she said.

"Spiders," he said, "there were no spiders there. It was so clean."

"I know, right?" I asked.

"What time was this?"

"About two in the morning," I answered, yawning. Now, I was very tired. Heavy bags under my eyes. I was the eye bag lady. "Eye bag" sounds like "Ibeck," doesn't it?

"You were up at three?" he asked, lighting up a cigarette. I just got done telling him all about my late night adventure. Guess he only heard part of it. Guess he wasn't on the clock. I must have said "2 a.m." about twenty times.

"You said you didn't want to be her doctor before? Are you her doctor now?" I asked.

"I'm not doctoring her," he said.

"You're talking to her."

"She's my friend's wife."

"True."

"She's suffering."

"So, you're medicating her. I don't care. I'm just asking, because..."

"I am not medicating her. I prefer not to discuss this anymore," he said with finality. And walked away from me, fastening his helmet. What is up with that? I seriously did not care. He could remedy her all he wanted to. But why couldn't he admit it? I followed him to the bike where the gang was already revving their engines. That was the end of that conversation.

I was in my room alone. Unless you count my Apple product as my companion. I'm sending messages to my eBay nemesis. Jake was out there, probably sitting with Natasha..."not treating" her. He did actually mention this again when we arrived.

He asked me not to mention anything alien-related to Natasha; no alien movies, books, etc. Funny thing is, I wouldn't have. But now that it's in my head, whenever I see her, I see extraterrestrials everywhere. I think back to all the alien media I've ever seen: ET, Close Encounters, Fire in the Sky (apparently based on a true story), The X-Files, and a TV show called V that I used to watch as a teenager on Friday nights. It stood for "Visitors". When I look at a person's face, I see their alien features. Colin has the most V-shaped face. Natasha actually has reptilian eyes. Maybe she's a self-hater.

For the first time, I noticed that she was usually the person who checked us in. She spoke a ton of languages, I guess. German was one of them. This was never mentioned, but I do recall her ordering for us in German. I'm sure she speaks Romanian or Hungarian, or one of those Vampiric languages. My mind was getting sort of infatuated with her. The mystery of Natasha. I guess Jake was, too. He was spending more time with her than with me. The night of the handcuffs seemed like ages ago. I was actually afraid, that night, about how far out of control things would get. But I sadly had nothing to fear. He didn't make any more moves. I asked him several times if he wanted to visit a monument, a museum, or take a walk. He just shrugged. It never feels great when you get nostalgic feelings from 48 hours ago. Was Jake pissed that I confronted him about treating Natasha?

"This is my time to rest," he said.

"But, it's just to explore a little, stretch our legs, take some photos, maybe…"

"I'm not a tourist, Savannah."

Fifteen minutes later, he left the room. What was I supposed to do, but get into it with my eBay nemesis. It was looking dire. This guy was going to hold onto my painting with his cold, dead fingers.

I wrote: *"I will do anything to get that painting back."*

He wrote back: *"I've decided to keep it permanently. I've grown very attached to her."* In the past, he might have sounded apologetic about this, but now his tone was different. He was a man in possession of a prize he wasn't letting go. That was his new message to me.

"What can I do. I am here. In Europe."

"In vain," he wrote back, *"you can visit her if you'd like, but she is mine."*

"I will pay you what you paid for her," I suggested.

"You don't have the money. And besides, this is not about money."

"I WANT HER BACK. GIVE HER BACK TO ME."

"NOOOOOOOOOOOOOOOO," he wrote. Holding on to the "o" button for that long is never good. When you're on the wrong side of the "no". Which I was.

"I'm coming to get her with an army," I threatened.

"You will need one," he wrote.

"Have you seen Braveheart? Have you seen Taken? I am American. I am coming to get what's mine. That painting is mine."

"We will see about that," he wrote calmly.

Ugh. Jesus. I hated this guy. This stubborn French asshole.

For the first time, the gang did not have dinner together. Which pissed me off even more because Jake didn't want to do anything. Everyone's stomach needed a vacation. I'm sure the ladies were alarmed when they could barely get their arms around their men. Remember that innovative stomach idea I had? Could have come in useful right about now, right? Maribel suggested we take the night off from a big dinner. No one fought her. We all gave each other knowing looks. We showed our bellies some mercy.

Darcy suggested that we begin the "painting project". I had forgotten about that. Almost completely. This is when I hate that I'm someone who likes to keep my word. I'm not 100% foolproof, but I try. When I'm called on it, I usually do it. When someone says, "You said you would do that," I feel compelled to do that which I promised. So, even though I was disliking Darcy a lot, I managed to eke out, "We'll do it, Darcy, just not right now."

To which she replied,"Okey-dokey." And then, she saw another very old couple that she deeply admired and expressed herself. Talked about how cute they were, like how someone talks about chihuahuas. How ca-yute!

I wanted to slap her. I swear. It had to be her, right? Who told Natasha about my self-nude? What a big mouth. It's not her fault. What else is she going to do? If she ever had to be interrogated, it would be the easiest shift ever. They would just bring her some tea, ask her one question, and listen to her talk for about 80 hours until the Gestapo or whoever got what they needed. No forced extraction necessary.

At least I didn't have to hang out with her tonight. I was alone. Good. It felt great to be by myself. I was going to head out to a restaurant, eat alone, not exchange anything socially with anyone. Feel my own skin. Get in touch with my own flesh and blood. It was thrilling to anticipate this treat.

Except in the lobby, Vince was standing there, his elbow propped on the counter, bursting two empty glasses with melted ice cubes. I was hoping to just nod to him and bolt out the door. Easier said than done.

"Hi Savanner, how are you doing?"

"Good, Vince. What are you up to?"

"Having a drink with you," he said, as I fell into the trap.

OK, I had a drink with Vince. He was very touchy-feely. He was caressing one of my hands, which I would remove, but he would find out a way to caress the other hand. Like he was an octopus, and I was his prey.

"Tell me about the genesis of your latest masterpiece."

"The painting...Darcy and Hugh?"

"The temporary title of your piece, I hope?"

"I haven't started it...yet. I don't know."

"Tell me about your process, darling."

I was sipping a very delicious glass of red wine, which he ordered. I don't remember what. But damn, it was delicious.

"Well, it's pretty dull. I sketch the subjects. I peruse through a file I have of potential outfits, colors they could be wearing."

Did I actually say "peruse"? His way of speaking was infectious.

"When I begin the actual painting, I'll be looking for the light to hit them just the right way."

I had never been so disinterested in talking about my process. What I didn't tell Vince was that I really did not feel up to doing this project, but I'm sure it came out. It was a habit cemented deeply into my way of life, like a criminal who knows only how to rob banks or liquor stores. He gets out of prison, promises never to do it again, but then gets an offer and does it again, out of habit. It's hardwired. I trained myself like how you train a dog to roll over and play dead, and not sleep on the bed. I've been painting since I was about five. I'm a forty-year-old dog. I'm the Vampire Lestat of dogs.

I used to draw on the walls. My parents weren't into that. But I did it, anyway. My mom would spend a lot of time wiping it off. I guess I know what she must have felt like now with my criminal sentence. My stomach still hurts when I think of the graffiti I've been scraping off the walls. The community doesn't know what it's missing. Many of the murals that were once there, instead of blank suburban, drab, dead colors, have vanished. There was a beautiful one on Motor and Centinella of a Latina woman that they just painted black over. I should have taken a picture of it. Now, it's not there anymore. I'm not saying the Crayola I scrawled on the wall was as good, but it was honest. It was what I was feeling at the time.

When I joked to Vince that Natasha and Jake were spending so much quality time together, he didn't appear the least bit concerned.

"That's my English girl. She's so used to the city. She needs the hustle and bustle. Without the old ant farm of metropolis, she reverts to blind panic. Ha, ha." He sucked his cigar and gazed off into the distance.

Blind panic? That did not sound good.

"Is she going to be OK?" I asked, smiling thinly.

Vince shrugged. Or maybe he didn't even do that.

"But aren't you a little...bothered that Natasha is...spending so much time with Jake?" I asked again.

"I'm not a shrink. Jake's a shrink. He's good at it. He helped you, didn't he?"

"I don't know the answer to that."

Did he help me?

Is it one of those things we must judge based on hindsight?

"I knew Jake when he was the at the doorstep of his career. I recall thinking how perfect he was for the work. Like you, he's an artist. He would never admit it."

"An artist?" I asked, condescendingly. I was disappointed that Vince was going to be zero help in this matter. That's the only reason why I let him deter me from my alone time.

"He has an eerie fascination with maladies. He sees a sick person; he wants to correct it. Whereas, you see a blank canvas, and you want to fill it."

Actually, that's not the way I approach painting, but I nodded anyway, in defeat. I sucked down what was left of my delicious wine and patted Vince on the back as I stepped off my stool and out of the bar.

I ended up having dinner at Pizzeria Heinz, which had nothing to do with the ketchup. I read about in Trip Advisor. I didn't dig too long; it was like the very first thing. I'm sure Darcy was reading all the Rick Steves literature about the region. She even mentioned in our last painting session how she thought she saw the legend himself, wandering in his "Members Only" jacket, taking notes, licking a gelato cone. She's read so much Rick Steves, she's beginning to hallucinate him, I thought.

As I waited for my delectable pizza, I sketched Darcy and Hugh's faces on a napkin with a pen. I like to really get to know a face when I paint it. Every micro-feature. One of the differences about living in LA is that you don't see many faces. You see cars, with disembodied body parts. If you walk on the streets, you will find desolation.

In Europe, you see faces, faces, faces...everywhere. There's so much communication that happens in a human face, losing it is like losing a language. You think where you live is always normal, but LA is not normal. To go days, weeks without seeing faces will kill you. My business used to be faces. I did couples' portraits for years. I never say this to my clients, but I find my favorite creases or wrinkles to focus on as my center of gravity. It's like the body of water in a city. Once I find these aging features, I work around them. I was still searching for them in Darcy. Hugh was older. He had many wrinkles to choose from. There was work to be done with Darcy.

I knew the pizza would be amazing, because my olfactory receptors were literally dying as I waited to eat my entire pizza from a wood oven. Besides, I was in perfectionist country. I ordered the Hugo, which was a tomato sauce, mozzarella, sliced parmesan, and artichoke hearts. I watched as the chef made the pizza, glancing over his shoulder at me with a flirtatious smirk every few minutes. Exactly ninety seconds later, he rescued it from the oven and brought it over to me with a huge smile on his face. The pizza was heart-shaped. I blushed. Was I really that charming? The dough was crunchy, but pliable too. The sauce was sweet and balanced. It washed down deliciously with a glass of red wine that was brought to me, compliments of the chef. Maybe I am better off on my own.

When I returned to the room, I was hoping Jake would display a pulse. I wanted him to ask me where I'd been, who I'd been having social intercourse with. I would have settled for him asking me to fetch him a glass of water. I would have told him to fuck off, but it would have been nice to be asked. He was passed out. No water. Although, I felt like tossing cold water on his stupid face. Even though he was unconscious, he looked like he didn't care.

I washed my face and lay down next to him. For some reason, I leaned over and kissed him goodnight.

"You're drunk," he mumbled, "I can smell it."

And then, he turned over and started snoring.

"What?" I asked. Did he even know he said that? I slept as far away from him as possible, on the edge of the mattress.

The next morning when I awoke, only the indentations of his body remained, but he was gone. It was like a murder scene, except that the bed was still warm where the body of this man had once been. I was hoping he had vanished, because I had planned on texting him.

- *Good morning* - I texted.

- *Hello, my little sleepy-head :)* - he replied.

Ridiculous. Was this really the only way I was going to drink from the well of romance? Via fucking morse code?

I felt like throwing my iPhone through the window. I felt like I was being intimate with HAL 9000, an artificial intelligence. Maybe that's why he could relate to Natasha. Because he was an alien.

- When are u trotting down? he asked. "Trotting"? Jesus. He must have been hanging out with Vince.

Now, it was time to kick some ass.

- U can go ahead, I'm going to ride with Colin today - I texted.

There was no reply.

He was really good at that.

His textacular poker face.

He always had reasons, later, why he hadn't replied right away, but I was convinced that he saw the message, that he was concocting the next move carefully, and that making me wait was part of his arsenal. Colin was right that relationships are like war. I mean, I'd heard this before, but never considered it this profoundly. Of course, Jake was a warrior at it. He was a shrink. Why wouldn't he know how to get in my head?

- Fine, see you in Merano - he finally texted back, about ten minutes later.

It was not the best day to accompany Colin. He was very moody with his driver, Parker.

"I specifically asked you to fill up the petrol. Now, we'll be even further behind," he cursed. Parker mumbled back incoherently. Colin glanced at me, as if I understood his pain (that of being unable to find good help these days).

"This is the best I could do. I'm not wealthy."

"I didn't think you were," I said.

"My wife insisted this would be good for me," he explained, and gazed out the window. The clouds looked dark and tortured. Maybe it was a good day to ride in the car. The horizon had the look of impending rain.

"You're married?" I asked, accidentally sounding surprised.

"I see, you fancied me the bitter, wheelchaired bachelor, who spouts World War II historical lessons because he has so much time on his hands. Well, you're not far off. My wife is tired of me. Of course, I'm tired of her, too."

I didn't say anything after that. The pitter-patter of the raindrops against the ceiling of the car sounded relaxing. Almost healing. I looked up at the sunroof as the droplets smashed into it, landing in little bubbles. The tiny bubbles would travel with the wind and cling to the larger bubbles, becoming indistinguishable, as they formed really large bubbles. It was like a reverse Pac-Man. Sort of. I don't know, but it was mesmerizing.

The rain was so hard, it almost blinded the windshield.

I was concerned about our biker gang, but they seemed thrilled to venture through the rain. They had apparently all stopped, as they were now dressed like astronauts in over-sized rain gear. When we stopped, the first one I saw was Natasha. She ripped off her helmet with glee, and the look on her face was calm and a little flushed, almost childlike. Her cheeks were red like apples. The smile on her face was adorable.

It made me a little jealous that I was missing this experience.

Jake did not console her this time, since she was in the moment.

He did not say anything to me, aside from, "Where will you be having dinner tonight? With the gang or with me?"

"I don't know," I replied, hoping he would ask me to ride with him.

But he didn't.

And I didn't ask.

Thus, I just watched as the gang zig-zagged through the glistening roads like birds flying south for the winter. The sun eventually made a cameo appearance, ending the rain, and bouncing purple and gold on the wet asphalt. The gang looked like they were floating through the sky.

"Slow down, for God's sake," Colin would chastise his driver, who accidentally slammed on the brakes. "I said, slow down. I didn't say slam the brakes. We could hydroplane and topple down the mountain. Jay-zeus," Colin attacked further.

Parker gripped the steering wheel like he was choking it, like he was ringing its neck, and suddenly, I felt less safe in there. That's not saying much, though, because I never felt unsafe with Jake.

I admit, I was just fighting a battle I couldn't win.

He was the passive-aggressive warrior. Not me.

I was always sort of pathetic with passive-aggression. For decades, I was insistent that what people said had to correspond with what people meant. But the world isn't like that. Anywhere.

PIERCE

DARCY AND HUGH WERE VERY COOPERATIVE. They even found a place to buy me all the supplies I needed in town. They have always been very generous with me, I'll give them that. Hugh was actually the perfect model. He didn't say anything. He was gifted at keeping his position stationary. The man could hold a smile for a long time. If you put a beehive on his head, he wouldn't move an inch. It was surprisingly fun to paint them.

Darcy was, of course, much more fidgety. She asked lots of questions.

"How is my dress?"

"Is the light flattering?"

"Do you think I should sit like this...or like this?"

Normally, this would have pissed me off, but it didn't. Of course, something else started to bother me. When I was in my twenties, I loved the scent of the paint fumes. The toxicity was a medal of honor, but now, it was making me nauseous. It made me sad that I no longer had that immunity.

I thought about Jake, about how estranged from me he was becoming. Somehow, I'd managed to un-know him. Our intimacy was getting stripped like string cheese. I actually apologized for making the comment about "medicating Natasha".

"Oh, don't worry about that," he said.

"No, I shouldn't have said that; it's none of my business," I added.

"Really, it's no big deal." But his face was stone cold. His eyes were empty. His soul was, you know, giving me the "cold soul-der".

But he was still tending to Natasha. Wherever we went, he was by her side. I wasn't jealous. I was more curious. Really curious. Why was it such a mystery? It wasn't. We all knew she suffered from irrational fears. OK, we all knew she believed in (and feared) aliens. We all knew she could snap at any moment. But snap how? I thought for sure the shit would go down when Vince's son dropped by for a visit. That's right, there was another one of him, but younger.

Jake had mentioned this probability, but when I hear the word "son" I think of a 5-year-old boy who only cares about candy. Pierce wanted candy alright, but not the kind 5-year-old boys usually want. He had an Italian girlfriend named Sofia, and a second girl, Brooke. It was unclear why Brooke was there. Was she a second girlfriend or Sofia's BFF? No one knew. Pierce was Vince 2.0, an upgraded version with a horrible virus that would hurt anyone he made contact with. I guess that's why Jake said, "Vince's son may join us...hopefully not."

One Vince was enough.

"Vince is one of those friends," Jake said – more like sighed. He meant, one of those super energy friends that bully you into doing things, like healing their sick wives. Even if you've said "no" a dozen times.

"Pierce is a terror. He has no moral compass."

Pierce sounded oddly fascinating.

"He's a great-looking kid," Jake added, only adding more to the mystique.

"Who's the mother?"

"Vanessa, I think she's in an institution or on an island, I'm not sure."

"Holy shit!"

"I'm beginning to think this entire trip was planned around getting me to treat Natasha."

"What can we expect from Pierce?"

"The unexpected," answered Jake.

We were all finishing breakfast on the patio, when we heard a rumbling that sounded like a bull, but in actuality was a car. But not any car: a Lamborgini Countach. Black. Shiny. Like a giant spider. Like Natasha's spider. We all stared at the quarter million dollar car. Some of us had to turn around and hold our gaze. This was the car that had been on millions of posters in the 80s. Not mine. But I knew guys who had posters.

You could see the driveway from the patio where were sitting. The Countach's door opened like a reverse guillotine. Out came Pierce on one end, and Sofia and Brooke on the other. Pierce was good-looking, in a St. Elmo's Fire kind of way. He was "never worked a day in his life" good-looking. His sense of entitlement was vicious. It swallowed everybody whole; including the two girls he was dragging along.

Sofia was in a bikini and jean shorts. Brooke was buttoning her shirt. Both girls were very young and very sexy. Their minds were owned by Pierce, who hugged his father like they were frat brothers.

"I haven't seen you since the Riviera," said Vince.

"Wasn't it the Maldives?" offered Pierce.

Jake sat back quietly and when Pierce turned to him, the young man's energy dissipated. Jake and Pierce locked in on each other, like two gunslingers paying respect.

"Hello Pierce," Jake offered.

"Hello Dr. Rivers," Pierce said, as a chair was pulled for him by one of his nymphettes. He ordered a café au lait, even though we were not in France. No one corrected him. The waiter in fact said, "Bien sur, Monsieur." Pierce didn't order anything for his girls at this time.

"Where's Natasha, my beautiful stepmother?" asked Pierce. This is when Vince got a little quiet. Jake was looking away, at the parked motorcycles. Alas, this was a day of rest. We were not going anywhere. Jake could not escape.

Natasha was in the restroom when Pierce arrived. She calmly sashayed from the bathroom and didn't bat an eye when she saw Pierce. She just smiled. It was hot out that day, so I suggested we all go to the pool, which we did. We actually monopolized it. An old couple was there when we arrived, but they quickly vanished when the Tasmanian devil took over, meaning Pierce.

"Aren't they cute?" asked Darcy, as the really old couple trudged away. The wife helped her husband out of the pool, and they took their time like they were moving underwater.

"Those relics? Cute? I don't know about cute. Old people are high maintenance these days. But they give nothing back. My Countach is high maintenance, but she gives a lot back, right Sofia?"

He slapped Sofia's ass really hard. *TWACK!* You could hear it echo into the lobby.

"Ow! " she shouted, playfully, as she began to disrobe. In front of everyone. I mean, everything. She didn't care. Her body was very difficult not to look at. Darcy and I even glared at each other in confusion. She was beautiful, she was fictitious. The skin, the breasts, the perfectly trimmed...you know...hairs...I was this close to asking if she wanted a portrait done.

"Darcy is just saying, those old people are nice. They have life experiences," said Brooke.

"What do you know about life experiences?" asked Pierce. "You're not even eighteen yet." Brooke was in the water, wearing sunglasses and a giant hat. Never occurred to me she was under-aged. She looked old for an under-aged teenager. She must have been mature.

It occurred to me that only girls were gazing at Sofia's naked body. Me, Darcy and Brooke. The others were doing their own thing. Hugh was asleep, even though he had just woken up two hours earlier.

Maribel and Antoine were reviewing their iPhones. I'm not even sure if they knew Pierce was Vince's kid. Colin was sipping a glass of wine quietly and it wasn't even noon yet. But, I figured I should probably start drinking too. There was a large metal bucket icing two magnums of Garrus from Chateau D'Esclans Rosé. I quietly helped myself to a glass. Actually, it was plastic. I helped myself to a plastic. I despise drinking out of plastic, particularly wine. I don't know where Parker was. Jake and Vince were having their own private discussion. You could hear them muttering to each other.

"Relax Jake," Vince said.

"Vince, this is the last trip I'm taking with you," Jake said.

"Don't be so dramatic, Doc."

"You assured me I wouldn't have to tend to your wife and now your son is here, too."

"I can't control Pierce. You know I can't, you healed him."

Holy shit, who wasn't a patient of Jake's? I guzzled my wine.

Pierce couldn't hear this because he dove into the swimming pool, causing a mini-tsunami that drenched all of us. It was pretty hot, so I didn't care. And I didn't have my iPhone out. It was usually turned off; I was on an iPhone diet. But Darcy was a little upset. Her hair got messed up and she left in defeat. She even woke up Hugh, who was startled.

"What? Who?" When he saw his wife, he knew the look, didn't say more, and accompanied her upstairs.

Sofia and Brooke fought for Pierce's company, but he bee-lined toward Natasha, who was sunbathing, sort of, as far away from anyone as possible. She was reading a magazine. More like flipping through it.

"Hello Mother," said Pierce.

"I'm not big on being called your mother," stated Natasha.

"But you are. It's legal. Hence, I may refer to you as Mother without getting locked up. You could even breastfeed me and the police couldn't stop you."

Natasha actually giggled. Sofia and Brooke hated her. They would probably collaborate to destroy Natasha if necessary. They'd lose, but it would be fun to watch this duel take place.

"Am I being too provocative?" Pierce asked his stepmother. He was at the foot of her lounge, leaning out of the pool, near her naked feet. His arms were on her sandals. Vince was watching the whole situation, while talking to Jake. I was positioned where I could hear everything. Not intentionally.

"Your son is going to aggravate Natasha's condition, I told you that. But you don't seem to care, Vince."

"I don't care. You shouldn't care either," Vince said.

"Well, it's my profession to care. But that's beside the point," Jake clarified, "I agreed to do this trip to relax. I brought my new girlfriend..."

I can't believe I was being referred to as "girlfriend." It's not shocking, but hearing him use the term really brought out our age difference.

"She's very lovely, Savanner," Vince stated.

Did I mention I was also drinking? It was just supposed to be one glass of rosé. But, there were suddenly four or five buckets of the stuff. At this point, I was talking to Brooke and Sofia, both frolicking in the pool. We were discussing the self-nude in France. Everyone else seems to know, so who cares?

Sofia didn't seem to care. She didn't even understand the problem.

"You're born naked. You die naked," she offered.

"Are you going to get it?" asked Brooke.

"I don't know," I said.

"I would want to meet the man who pays $75,000 for my body," they both said in sync and giggled.

"So you're the Doc's flavor of the month?" asked Pierce. Yes, the question was directed at me. He swam in my direction, and put his arms around his two girls to establish ownership. Everyone was getting pretty hammered, especially considering it still wasn't noon.

"You'll have to ask him," I replied. I couldn't think of a better comeback. But I could see Jake stiffening. I could see Natasha relaxing. She's had more drinks than I could remember. Her rosé glass was empty. Her arms dangled. Her big sunglasses reminded me of two black holes. It felt like she sicced her stepson on me.

"He doesn't answer questions," Pierce said...about Jake. He was right.

"My father has spent hundreds of thousands trying to get an answer from him."

"Like the price of your car?"

"That's not a car, baby, that's a Lamborgini Countach. You know what Countach means in Italian?"

He stuck his tongue in Sofia's throat. Then stuck it in Brooke's throat. Then he asked them to kiss each other. Before he answered his own question.

"Countach means, what a piece of ass!"

I felt like I was trapped in a Girls Gone Wild video. I was feeling dizzy, so I climbed the ladder out of the pool and collapsed on my chaise, covering my eyes with sunglasses in hopes that he would stop talking.

"You know how many quarts of oil that vehicle takes?" he asked me, as he leapt out of the pool, following me.

"One quart?" I asked, unenthusiastically.

"Eighteen. Eighteen quarts."

"Why are you sharing this information with me?"

He leaned over me. His body wet. His face silhouetted, from the sun blistering behind him. He was like a naked Grim Reaper. I could hear Natasha giggling in the background. She wasn't asleep. Or was she laughing in her sleep? Who the hell knew?

"The Countach can only be handled by a man. Takes fifty pounds of pressure just to switch gears."

By now, Jake and Vince were paying attention to our...duel? If I hadn't slammed four glasses of rosé, I might care.

"Pierce, relax, stop raising your voice," requested Vince.

"Don't provoke him," said Jake.

"You see these girls?" Pierce asked me. As water from his body sprinkled on my body. I didn't like the sensation.

"Sure," I said, "I see them." My eyes were shut.

Sofia and Brooke were waiting by Pierce's feet, two mermaids in the swimming pool, enslaved.

"I branded them. They're mine. Show her," Pierce commanded. And both girls turned over and showed us, sure enough, a strange upside down v symbol, that was actually a P for Pierce. One of them was still bleeding from Pierce shoving a hot skewer into her sciatic nerve. It was as awful as you could imagine it. Or did I just imagine it? I blinked my eyes several times but my vision was blurry.

Jake looked at Vince like he wanted to punch him.

"You call this relaxing, Vince?"

But Vince was hammered by now. He didn't have a care in the world.

"This is the last time," Jake said.

Pierce was out to antagonize him.

"The Countach has been a million times more therapeutic to me than that guy."

He was pointing at Jake.

"I've learned many lessons from that vehicle. I've learned what it takes to maintain something. I've learned that nothing comes easy. I've learned, if it's not hard as fuck, then what's the point?"

At this point, Jake stood up. Vince made a weak attempt to stop him and gave up, continued sipping on his rosé.

Antoine was approaching. "Hey man, don't talk to the Doc like that."

"It's OK, Antoine."

"This guy doesn't know shit. He has a degree or whatever, but he's just a legal drug dealer. So my question is, why are you fucking a guy who's supposed to be your doctor?" Pierce spun around and gave me a sadistic smile.

Jake charged Pierce. Antoine got caught. And then all three burst into the swimming pool. The girls laughed. Vince didn't flinch. And Natasha, while everyone was struggling in the water, just walked away. Like she was bored.

NICE JETS

WHEN I WOKE UP ON THE CHAISE, everyone was gone. My head was pounding. I sat up and looked around. There wasn't even a trace of them. No wine bottles, no plastic wine glasses. I wondered if I had dreamt the whole thing, kind of like that movie La Piscine, where fantasy blends with…

"Good morning, Savannah." Suddenly Natasha was standing above me.

"Natasha! Hi. Wow, you scared me."

Sometimes you saw Natasha and feared her, since she had those kind of eyes. Sometimes you felt sorry for her, since she was sobbing and trembling. Sometimes, you wanted to shake Vince and scream, "That's your wife, man! What are you going to do?" Vince never reacted to her whims, not like Jake did.

"Where is Jake?" I asked, but suddenly Natasha was gone. I grabbed my towel and realized that my suit was dry. I must have been sleeping for a while. When I went into the lobby, everyone was waiting around like nothing happened. No sign of Pierce. No Sofia. No Brooke. Parker and Colin were outside smoking and arguing. Jake and Vince were huddled off drinking espressos, and Darcy and Hugh were staring at the TV which displayed some kind of financial information, I think. I found Natasha at a table sipping tea with Maribel and Antoine. They were talking about their kids, like they always did. Somehow, this was making Natasha worse.

"We went to Cambodia last year," Maribel told us. "Beautiful country. Everyone has great smiles. The tuk-tuks are so adorable. The old women, carrying baskets on their heads, even though it's about 110 degrees. All they ask you is, how many kids do you have? The idea of not having children is totally foreign to them. They have as many as they can. They assume you're planning to have one."

"Why is that?" I asked.

"Because their kids will later support them. That's how it works over there," Antoine clarified, "the more kids you have, the more likely they'll help you out when you're old and decrepit."

"It's like a team thing," I said.

"Yeah, yeah, it's a team of earners."

"It's a poor country, but so cute. They don't make much, so the kids are like the 401ks. The kids are the retirement plan."

Natasha's face went ashen, like she wished she was Cambodian. She didn't hear the "poor country" part, she just heard the "as many kids as possible" part.

I thought back to her comment, that she'd be OK being constantly pregnant. Her face looked like it was transforming into concrete. She was also giving Vince those famous eye daggers of hers. It dawned on me, whenever Maribel and Antoine mention their kids, this happened. Of course, Maribel and Antoine talked about their kids 102 % of the time.

The stranger Natasha acted, the more Jake shut down on me. Was he feeling insecure that he could not meet the challenges of dealing with Natasha? Or maybe he was upset about that weird afternoon with Pierce. After our bike ride, he would find solace in whatever hotel room we had. Was he exhausted from treating her? I was exhausted from just the few times I had a casual conversation with her. Did Jake feel trapped and under pressure? I don't know. These questions would remain unanswered for eternity.

I was seriously considering leaving the group. To go to France and get my self-nude back. By force? By charisma? Certainly not with money. I had none. That's why I was only "considering" leaving the group. Once I looked up the tickets, and so how not-cheap it was, I was resigned to my "kept woman" or "concubine" status, but you know, without the sex. Concubine without benefits. I had no choice but to do the painting. At least I had a job. Or, something to do.

From hotel to hotel, the painting would ride with Colin and Parker, and at each hotel I would engage myself deeper into it. We had been traveling for about a week when the jet lag vanished and I began to feel domesticated again. Funny how the mind "normalizes" everything. Before you know it, you know what to expect. Cobblestone streets. A church. Souvenir shops. Gelaterias. Cutting boards in animal shapes. The deepest element of traveling is understanding that it's all the same everywhere. People survive. There's a spiritual center. There's an oppressive government. There's a tradition. Foods. Trinkets. Clothes. We are just taught that we're different, like we're taught milk, college and bread are good for you. In the end, bread is sugar, college cripples you with debt and milk kills you.

When we arrived at the Hotel Therme in Merano, Italy, it was dusk. The sun had been on the edge of the horizon for over an hour. It simply would not give up the ghost. This was a bucolic little town that people visited from all over Europe for its magical "healing baths".

"Legend goes that this town had healing powers," Darcy narrated for the third time, her eyes beaming. She existed for thermal spas and pools.

Of course, Jake did not.

"I'll be in my room," he announced, and as usual, there was a choir of sighs, and "Oh, come on Jake."

He looked disinterested.

Why was he here? Why did he want me here?

Was this excursion somehow part of our therapy?

His predictability was suffocating.

In an hour, he would be in bed, surfing the internet, or watching foreign TV, smoking up our pretty room like it was a gambling den, putting our fire alarms on the edge of their seats. Very likely, he would be having his dinner in bed. By 10 o'clock, he would be deep in rapid eye movement. I was out of moves. There was nothing I could say without sounding desperate.

"You don't want to go to one of these thermal baths?" I pleaded.

"I took a shower already. Very nice jets," he said.

"That's not the same thing."

"Hot water is hot water, in my book," he argued.

"But why come here to this little town and not see what it's all about?"

"I'm here. I'm in the town. I can always say, I've been here."

"Can you? You can say, you've been to the hotel in Merano, but have you actually been in Merano?"

"Why don't you visit one of these thermal adventures, Savannah?"

"I thought it would be fun if we both went."

He didn't say anything.

"Hello?" I interjected, as he switched channels.

"Hello," he echoed.

"I realize I'm not Natasha, but...I am here, and I am asking you a question."

"You are not Natasha. You are not a sick woman. What was the question?"

"Will you go to one of these thermal baths with me?"

"I'm on vacation, Savannah. When I'm on vacation, the rule is to relax. Thermal baths, I'm not sure what they mean."

That's weird because "relaxing" was the last thing he was doing.

"So, that's a no?"

He didn't like to say no, it dawned on me.

"Hello, so, that's a no?"

He kept ignoring me, switching channels and sucking on his cigarette.

"Jake, answer me; that's a no?"

Finally, I snatched the remote from his hand and eye-daggered him.

He looked back.

"So, that's a no?"

"Yes," he answered.

EKHARD

I WOUND UP GOING to the thermal spas with Darcy. I was so lonely that I was willing to hang out with my arch nemesis. She wanted nothing more than to chatter about our new gallery.

"We could call it Darcy and Savvy." You know, that kind of shit. There were lots of old men in towels. It felt very Greek, Aristotelian. We found an empty room that we could enjoy privately. Jets sprayed your ass with such force, you felt like you were levitating. And Jake was wrong – hot water in here was not the same as the shower head. I was very relaxed for the first time since, well...I guess I was pretty relaxed last night. I had never seen Darcy half naked before. She had a pretty nice body for her age, actually. Cute butt. Perky.

"We could open it on the other side of Abbot Kinney. There's an auto shop there that just closed; we could rebuild..."

When I'd had enough of Darcy, I just cut her off...

"Don't you have the impulse to never return to LA, begin a new life in Europe, make new friends, find a new job, learn a new language...don't you want to do that?"

"You really want a new job? You're such a great painter," she said, scowling.

"There's just so much emphasis on career, on how much time you should devote to your trade. You know, in January, Suzanne had a ruptured appendix. They took her to the emergency room and had her sign a waiver. She could have easily not made it out. She was like, what the fuck?"

"Oh," Darcy reacted. She was very uncomfortable around curse words.

"She had this pain and went to the hospital, and just like that, they told her she might be gone. The first thing she thought about was all the people she would never see again. Not paintings. Not work. Not meetings. Not deadlines. Just her friends and family. It's hokey, but it's what matters. I could paint or not paint. Just sitting here with you is..."

Then, of course, she cut me off.

"Wait a minute! I look bad in the portrait. I do, don't I?"

"Darcy, I'm not talking about the portrait."

"I'm not photogenic, I know that. But I thought, with your magic, you could make me photogenic just once. And I could hang it up in my house and people would say to me, just once, Darcy, you're photogenic."

"From a painting? It's not the same thing."

"There would be one image where I looked better in it than in real life. And when people came over, they would say "Darcy, you are so photogenic, look at you, you're so ca-yute."

The woman was sick.

When I first met Darcy, she wanted to be a painter.

She painted things from her purse: nail polish, credit cards. Digits. Expiration date. Her name. She would open her purse and do collages of the mess. They were pretty good, actually, but she just stopped. Without an explanation. Rich people do that. They do not need to explain why they suddenly stop something.

But, I felt like she really understood me, my technique, my way of working. Once she got it, that was it, she was not interested in going beyond.

Her relationship with Hugh was the most important thing to her, even though she rarely spoke about it. So, I took advantage of our half-nakedness and struck. It dawned on me, I never asked her how she met Hugh, how she started dating him.

"We didn't actually date. We knew the same people, and we would have these small parties where we all spent time together on weekends. We hiked together. Ate cake. Went to the beach. That's how many of us met our partners."

Wow, "that's how many of us met our partners"? This was beginning to sound like a cult.

"When one of us liked someone..."

"In the group?"

"...it was usually sort of mutual. Parties would be arranged for us to be together."

"So, it would be like having a date, but with a bunch of people chaperoning you, like in 1890 or something?"

"No, it wasn't like that. It was really nice because there was never any pressure to kiss or say anything. We would spend time together, but without pressure. I can't stand the idea of a date – going out to meet a stranger in the middle of the night, without knowing who he is or what he does or what he makes. Not that I'm just going for that. But, how much a man makes is a good barometer, you know."

"So, Hugh was one of these members."

"You make it sound like a cult," she said, accusingly.

"Darcy, I didn't mean it like that."

Of course, I did.

"Hugh was so cute. When I first met him, we were having a costume party."

"It was Halloween?"

"No, it was May, it was just a costume party... in May."

A costume party in May? I would have loved to be a fly on the wall.

"Hugh was wearing his fencing outfit."

"He fences? Hugh?" I asked, perplexed.

"Yeah, he's really good at it."

"En guard?"

"He's won a bunch of trophies and stuff."

Wow, you really don't know somebody until...well...you ask about them.

"So, he was in his fencing outfit... and what were you wearing?"

"I was a princess."

BIG WOW.

"Aaaahhhh..."

"I couldn't see his face, you know, through his mask."

"It's like talking to a basket, right?"

"I couldn't hear what he was saying either."

"So, what did you...mmh...respond to?"

"Something about him made me feel very comfortable."

Crazy. She couldn't see his face or hear his mumbling through the fencing mask, and yet, she felt something...dare I say, kinetic. Hugh must have crazy pheromones.

"The next time we were supposed to meet, the group had set it up for us...but I got sick. And I had to stay home. The following day, Hugh sent me this package full of fruits, oranges, vitamin C...it was so sweet."

It was a nice story. It humanized these rich assholes. I thought about Jack Hallenbeck's prophecy. What would happen if Darcy and Hugh lost their fortune? If the money system just went kaput. I have a feeling they would still be together. Their bond was titanium. They could have been bugs or frogs, they would somehow find each other. There was a chemical thing.

Did I feel those sensations with Jake? The day I entered his office, saw his hands, used his computer? Yeah, there was something chemical about that. But not recently. Now, it felt corporate.

When I got back to the hotel, I asked Jake if he wanted me to massage his feet, which I knew had to be hurting him after all that pedaling.

"You would do that for me?"

"Of course."

There weren't any oils. But in his unfinished salad, I noticed an unused portion of olive oil. That's what I used. While he surfed the internet, or whatever he was doing, I gave his feet a nice rub-down. He didn't say anything for the first half of this, but eventually, he was so relaxed that he began to share his thoughts.

"You realize, a third of your brain is used to control your hands?"

"Well, you mentioned that, but..."

I didn't know it was his way of sharing something intimate about himself. I love hands, as you know. We do lots of things with our hands. We shake hands. We salute. We hail dictators. We pick our noses. We stick our hands in the worst possible places. We eat. We play music. We text. We flip each other off.

There's some amazing stuff people can do with their hands. Like the guys in the Three Stooges who can poke each other's eyeballs. Like Spock, how he can separate his fingers in his salute. Like the piano. Like the keyboard. I remember typing class. Mr. Meacham. Talk about a dictator. "A, S, D, F, J, K, L, semi-colon… semi-colon, L, K, J, F, D, S, A…" he would bark as he wandered around the classroom. It was the most mechanical I ever felt. But years later, I found myself typing 80 words a minute. I could type as fast as I could think.

Communicating from your brain cascades into your hands. So, it makes sense. Sure, OK. But Jake was snoring by the time I figured this out. The truth was, massaging his feet was as relaxing for me as it was for him. I was there to once more convince him to explore the sites with me. I left his dungeon in defeat.

I thought about Mr. Meacham a lot as I walked through the cute little city. If Jake wanted to be a boring piece of shit, that was his right.

As I walked, I noticed how old this little town was. There were little streams of water flowing beneath little pedestrian bridges creating romantic bosoms along the path. I walked halfway up one of the little bridges. I gazed down at the rambling stream beneath me, and wondered if this body of water had healing powers. I saw a fun house reflection of myself. Did I need to be healed? My hand grasped the rail, and I squatted down to rest my legs. I was faced with a flood of lovers' locks. The gate was adorned with them. Tons of them, old and new, in every color of the rainbow.

I felt a pang in my heart, and couldn't get the fun house version of myself out of my head. I was lonely.

So, I walked down windy cobblestone streets alone, and everything was still open and people were walking and

I would peek into shops and instead of focusing on what they sold, I focused on the people that ran it and this one place had the same guy that probably worked for a hundred years, which Darcy would certainly appreciate, the wrinkles in the ancient human being; and as the night descended, I saw many couples, not necessarily tourists, just people in love, enjoying each other's company, licking each other's ice cream cone, and I couldn't understand why it couldn't be like this with Jake, because the town looked like a goddamn postcard, and one person was more beautiful than the next, and I wished I had my camera, since little bridges arched over flowing bodies of water, and each one led to another unique nook of the neighborhood; and the sun and moon were coming and going at the same time as I walked along the river's edge as the sun began to set, and I realized that I was hungry, as I had been walking for some time but I didn't care because I spotted a café in the distance, with outdoor tables at the river's edge and said to myself, "This is where I will eat," at which point I forgot how much I liked spending time alone, and a sense of serenity took over as I sat down at a table for one, ordered a glass of wine and sipped it slowly, without a care in the world.

Then I had another glass, noticing the table nearby with a boisterous bunch of men, who were all very smart-looking and spoke several languages, each of them glancing at me a few times apiece, since they clearly had very good taste, especially the best looking, the leader, who turned to me and asked why such a beautiful girl was dining alone; and before I had time to think of a clever response, he begged me to join the smiling men, all four of them, each approaching midlife crisis, but only one pulled out a chair for me – the leader, Ekhard – and I said "OK" and Ekhard saw that I was drinking red and poured me a fresh glass of

Brunello, and he was from South Africa and another man was from Spain, another from Geneva, and the other had homes all over the world, but every year they get together and play golf together in a different country, as they all had gone to school together in Switzerland, but still, they were fun and inviting, and there was something so civilized about the way they interacted, so I had fun too, even though I could have sworn I saw Natasha glaring at me from outside the restaurant, but I didn't care and ate with these four men, featuring courses of antipasti and pasta, a roasted duck, and a filet mignon, which we all shared, then two desserts, a flaming coconut cake and tiramisu thing, added to the wonderful, casual vibe of wine, food, and bliss...and I lost time.

"Oh shit!" I exclaimed as I looked at my iPhone clock.

"What is it, darling? You understand you're in the Alps?"

I wanted to relax, but I felt like Cinderella. Except that it was hitting two in the morning. For some reason, even though Jake had zero interest in doing anything, I felt guilty that I was getting back so late, like he was my dad or something. And I realized, it's because he paid for the trip. He paid for my company. I think that's why the Chinese call a gift "giving before taking".

"Let me walk you," Ekhard offered. He was a soothing, unassuming man. He knew nothing about me. He was a stranger. A kind one. It was nice that these men, all married, were just there to have a good time and I was at the center of it. A sort of communal G-rated gang bang.

We walked outside the restaurant. And he kissed me. Without hesitation. It felt like a teenage kiss. Like something you do because your hormones demand it. This wet embrace lasted a good minute. When he let go, there was a suction. I chuckled. And probably looked really stupid. But I felt attractive. The way he was looking at me.

"I really should get going. The hotel is just up there over the hill."

"I'll take you," he offered.

"No, stay here with your friends. I am good on my own."

And I never saw him again.

BULLY

IT WASN'T LONG BEFORE I figured out the puzzle of painting Darcy's face. Once that shoe dropped, the image created itself. It wouldn't be long now before I would have a way out of this crazy trip. I don't want to sound ungrateful. I was under the impression that Jake and I had a relationship we could build on; at the very least, I thought we would fuck like wild rabbits. Neither was happening. Was the romantic in me still holding the schoolgirl wish that, at any moment now, Jake would snap out of his coma and we would create beautiful memories together? Schoolgirls don't know shit. That's why they're in school. And yes, I still had that fantasy in the back of my mind.

But I also believe in contracts. As an artist in 2016, you have to. Or you won't survive. And part of me wishes I had a contract with Jake. The construction of this document repeated in my mind over and over again. Frequently, dancing in my head in a variety of drafts, particularly when I was in the act of painting. Its conclusion read something like this:

RELATIONSHIP CONTRACT FOR TWO PARTIES.

Witnesseth. I, Dr. Jake Rivers, agree to finance a two-week sojourn, in which the majority of transportation will occur via motorcycle (to be supplied by me) through portions of Italy, Austria and Switzerland. The locations will be determined via a colleague, who is arranging further details. We will name this sojourn THE TRIP henceforth.

I agree that said getaway is the result of "intimate relations" with one, Savannah Waters. My interest in THE TRIP is thus to determine one of two possibilities.

a) If a relationship with Ms. Waters is of my interest.

b) If a relationship with Ms. Waters is not of my interest.

In the event either is no longer determined, my aim is to enjoy "the moment" of THE TRIP and fornicate with Ms. Waters within, and perhaps beyond, the boundaries of the law.

I agree that if EITHER the INTEREST or AIM is abandoned, Ms. Waters is free to pursue further relations and/ or acquaintances without my objection.

I also agree to treat my friend's wife's condition if it becomes an emergency. However, this will not interfere with THE TRIP or THE AIM.

Signed and dated, Dr. Jake Rivers
(Jake Rivers)

But wouldn't it be so much easier if we could have these contracts? My plan was to still to bail, but my mind could be changed. It was like a ticking time bomb. If I'm done with the painting and he's still Lord Cold Shoulder Wallace, this concubine is outta here, as the contract stipulates.

"Hi Savannah, where's Jake?" asked Antoine, perhaps the only black man for miles. It was the free time we all had, between checking into the next hotel and dinnertime. The time that Jake spent staring at the ceiling in the hotel room.

He was waiting outside one of the gift shops waiting for his wife. She was browsing for postcards, and she looked like she was taking her sweet time. He looked pretty pussy-whipped, a feeling I knew quite well. He was holding her purse, checking his iPhone, and addressing me. An impressive juggling act.

"He's visiting the greatest relic in town. The hotel room," I replied.

"I heard about that one," he played along, "that's where gladiators used to train to fight lions."

"Yeah, Jake is fighting the deadliest beast."

"He'll get smoked if he's not careful."

We both chuckled. I wasn't sure how much I could discuss. I knew they were friends and Jake had helped him through serious ordeals, but I could tell he knew I was being stonewalled. It was slightly awkward, actually, but we found common ground. I asked about their trip to Southeast Asia.

"Oh yeah, that was crazy. We started in Hanoi. Wow. You don't know what you take for granted until you get there. Like sidewalks. There weren't any."

"So, where do you walk?"

"On the streets along with the mopeds and cars and buses. And there's hardly any street lights. You just go. And they adjust. It's amazing to see the movement, how people just make those adjustments. It's crazy. And if there were any sidewalks, they were being used to sell street food."

"Pho?"

"Oh yeah. That was nice, but Maribel was freaked out half the time. They're making it right there on the streets. I mean, you see hacked-up beef on the sidewalk. On the asphalt. No gloves or nothing. Just bloaw, death on the ground. Yeah."

"But you had it?"

"Oh yeah. The pho was delicious. The spices, whatever they use to accentuate flavors, they're doing it right. They cost like $1.50, maybe cheaper. They have these kindergarten seats, so it was tough for me. I looked like Will Ferrell in that movie Elf. People kept laughing at me."

"Sounds fun."

"Yeah, the bánh mì was like a dollar. Really good. But tiny sandwiches. You had to buy two or three. But here's what you miss the most; the air."

"The oxygen?"

"Oh yeah, we had to buy masks. And I'm, you know, twice the size of everybody, so I must have looked super scary. But you can't breathe. Two blocks, you start coughing, your face is turning green. Maribel thought the sky was just overcast, but it wasn't overcast. That gray shit was just smog. People just live in that. It was sad. People have to do it. But you don't know what you got till it's gone. My mom used to tell me that. I understand what she meant right there."

"How long were you in Hanoi?"

"Too long. Then, we went to Haloong Bay. That was cool. Still has smog, but it was more chill. I walked by one dog restaurant. That was so crazy. There were signs with an image of a friendly dog with Vietnamese writing on it. I followed up a couple steps and there it was...it looked like any restaurant. But you could see the silhouette of people inside, drinking beer, eating Dalmatian burgers or whatever. It was...crazy. But everyone was just living their lives, doing what they always do. I'm not judging. And I love dogs."

In another dimension, I wonder if there was a restaurant that served the meat of your ex-boyfriends. A sick thought, I know, but my mind kept turning these dark images. Of course, like Axel said, if I thought it, it exists somewhere. I had to change the topic to something else. I asked him how he'd met Maribel.

"At college. We went to Duke."

"You were in classes together?"

"No, I...she offered to share a Subway sandwich with me."

"And that was it?"

"Yep."

Wow, that Subway sandwich must have been one of the great investments in American history. Maribel wound up marrying an NBA athlete. Smart girl.

"That's a nice story," I offered. It made me sad, too, finding comfort vicariously through them.

"Yeah," he said.

"More romantic than the bánh mì, " Maribel said gleefully as she emerged from the store, shopping bags in tow.

I walked around with them for a couple hours. They took pictures they could send back to their kids, whom they spoke about a lot. They had a daughter and a son, Michelle and Lee. I had seen them bickering with their kids on the phone, and for some reason, I'd had the impression they were 5 or 6, but one was 17 and the other 15. They were practically adults. They still sounded like they needed to be taken care for at least another 20 years.

Maybe this was why there's so much caution about having kids. Deep down, you know you'll have to hold their hands past 18, maybe into their 20s or 30s. Who wants that kind of commitment? A dog lasts about 15 years, and then it sucks when it dies, but you're free again, right?

"Do you think you will still be looking after your kids in the same way when they are adults?"

"I hope not," Antoine said." I have a brother, still lives at home, and he's 39. He doesn't want to do anything. Since I started supporting my parents, he thinks he can just coast."

"He can," Maribel said.

You can tell it was a sore subject for them.

"He can't," Antoine said.

"Then, just kick him out. You own the house," she said, her voice raising.

"You know Mom won't let that happen."

"It's your house. It's your money," she said.

"I can't kick out Boris, it will kill Mom, how many times do we have to talk about this?" The lovebirds were on the verge of an argument. That was the first time I heard them raising their voices at each other. My parents never fought. They probably did, but never in front of me. I didn't even know parents could fight until I was eighteen. My folks maintained an airtight propaganda that everything was good between them and I bought it. Antoine and Maribel had that sheen, that they were creating a facade of heavenly perfection for their children.

But I was not their children.

"Why do you say 'your money' whenever you get mad," he asked. "You know it's our money. You know if we got divorced, you'd get half or more."

"And I'd deserve it," she said.

"Then stop calling it your money when you know it's our money."

I'd love to have an argument with anyone about my money.

"You enable Boris, just like your parents. You can kick him out. You can. And you know that's the best thing for him."

Antoine was quiet.

Then, Maribel went quiet.

Soon, they started holding hands.

As if I wasn't even there.

The two were very much in love.

The things they said to excuse themselves from me were hilarious.

"You're supposed to send Lee that blog, remember?" Antoine said.

"Oh yeah," she added, "and I wanted to ask Michelle what color scarf she wanted."

I haven't seen a scarf on sale this entire trip. But, I didn't give them a hard time about it. You could tell they did it a lot, even though it was difficult to imagine. She was 5'2" and he was 6'7", which is challenging just to think about. But that's love, I guess. Maybe there's an advantage to that. Maybe you shouldn't be similar heights. Then, you don't have to confront each other's faces all the time.

I had a good time with Jake's friends. Though it would have been nicer to be hanging out with him and his friends, together, like we used to. The conversation about Antoine's brother, Boris, kept playing in my head. What kept replaying was that Antoine and his family were enabling Boris, a really weak dude, to be where he was in his life. Unemployed, shiftless, going nowhere. At one point, Maribel almost shouted, "His problem, he doesn't have a bully. You always need a bully in your life."

That was very interesting, with all the media about eliminating bullies today, and the fact that they had kids. I agreed with what she said. You did need a bully. In movies, bullies always push the hero to be stronger, bigger than him or herself. Without the bully pushing you, you're stagnant and lukewarm. Jake was my bully, even though, ironically, he was stagnant and lukewarm. He was pushing me into gazing at my life from different angles.

"Hi Natasha," I said. She was sitting in the lobby, staring at the ceiling, her face tilted sideways. She didn't really respond.

"Any spiders?" I added, as I waited an eternity for the elevator to show up.

"Where were you?" she asked me suddenly.

"I was with Maribel and Antoine," I answered, as the elevator door still refused to open. Like Natasha was controlling it.

"They've been back for a long time," she said.

"No, they've only been back for, like, an hour, I was with them."

"Where were you after?"

Mercifully, the door opened.

But it took forever to close now.

And Natasha was looking directly at me. And I felt guilty for some reason.

"I...I didn't go anywhere, I was just walking."

The door closed. And the clang of the metal had a dungeon feel to it.

Maybe Natasha was my bully.

THE LIFT

"YOU WERE HAVING DINNER WITH MEN."
"Maybe."
"What were you doing with them?"
"Eating dinner."
"And what else?"
"Are you actually jealous?"
"I'm curious, that is all," Jake said.

That's how our morning started. Somehow, he knew I had dinner with those married guys the other night. And he wouldn't even admit he was jealous about it. He kept saying he was concerned about me.

"Like you're concerned about Natasha. She's the one who told you, isn't she?"

"Savannah...I don't think you should drink anymore on this trip."

And then he said nothing. That was what you would categorize as a fight. But it wasn't a fight. I was scowling as he was putting on his jacket, which once upon a time was such a turn on. Still, I was semi-thrilled he was showing some emotion.

I even rode the bike with him. There was zero exchange. Nothing verbal. No texting. The wind caressing my face was calming. I leaned my head on his back as he we headed for the Sporthotel Panorama in Corvara, thinking about how it's more female to ride on the back of the bike. But shouldn't it be the other way around? The man is so vulnerable to his female passenger. She has her arms around his flank. He cannot see what she is doing behind him. She could tickle him, extract one of his organs, or write a "kick me" sign on his back. It's a very exposed position, if you think about it.

It had to be Natasha. Or was it Darcy? I was confused now. Who was leaking information about my life? I suddenly understood what it felt like to be a celebrity, a Kardashian or J-Lo or whoever. As I rode in the back, I studied Natasha and Darcy, even though they were both wearing sunglasses like the Chinese guys that win all the poker tournaments. So, I couldn't read their expressions. At all.

When we arrived at the Sporthotel, which was really a winter ski lodge, but somewhat of a beautiful ghost town while we were there, I heard Parker telling Colin that he was going to take the lift up and shoot some photos.

"I'll go with you!" I exclaimed.

Colin shrugged.

I found Jake over by the check-in counter and told him, "We're going up on the lift."

"Who's we?"

"The 'men'," I joked.

"I don't understand," he said, not getting it.

"Me and Parker. I assumed you wouldn't want to go."

"Well, I'd like to come. I want to make sure you're not drinking."

He was jealous. Score. I should have dinner with groups of men every night. Whoever leaked the event did me a fucking favor.

Unbelievable. He was practically a silent partner for what seemed like a week and he hears about me, what, cheating on him with piles of men...and he can't even admit he's pissed about it. What was wrong with this guy?

Hiding my shock, I acted like it was no big deal and shrugged. Meanwhile, I didn't take any chances. We dropped our stuff in the room and, before he could get too comfortable, I said, "OK, let's go!"

"Now?" he asked, incredulous.

Did he have a session with Natasha?

"Yes, now."

He followed me, sighing frequently. To his credit, we were going uphill a lot. I insisted he should go back to the room, if that's what he wanted. There was so much silent complaining that Jake's presence felt like pulling one fat wisdom tooth.

He was pretty out of breath when we arrived at the lift.

"Are you alright?"

He nodded. It was a little strange even having him outside with me.

It felt like I'd just run into him there, like the last time I actually saw him was at Starbucks on Wilshire across from his office. That felt like a like a long time ago.

"I said you didn't have to come up," I insisted.

"I understand. No need to repeat," Jake protested.

"You look like you're in agony."

"I want to be here. I want to make sure..."

I was really defensive about being "naggy." I didn't want to feel like "the men" thing was the reason why he'd made an effort, but that was likely the truth. It wasn't the drinking. He didn't want me to have any fun. Jake was on death's doorstep because he was jealous. Had to be. You couldn't get him off the goddamn mattress yesterday. Now, he's climbing mountains.

"This was a trap," I said.

"Here, the ski lift...a trap?" he said, stupefied, as we climbed into the lift.

"No, this trip. I shouldn't have come."

I could see the shrink machine inside his head turning. He usually stopped blinking when this happened. He was reviewing years of practice in human behavior; old case studies, prior patients, even fictional characters. His repertoire was deep.

He was probably thinking, "Savannah is acting like the Queen of England, Pat Bennetar, and this really fucked up patient I once had.'

"But, you are here, " he said, calmly, "so why should anything else matter?"

Here goes.

When he's on, he poses things in questions. They train shrinks for that. How to Pose Any Sentence into a Question 101. I'm sure Jake Rivers got an A+++.

"Just think of it like this...there's a dimension out there where you didn't come to Italy. Where you're in LA, but you wish you had been here. Consider that scenario."

He was referring to the multiverse.

Seriously? Axel's multiverse? It was true.

I tried to remember if I'd brought this up to him during one of our sessions.

"What about a scenario where I stay in LA and I don't regret not coming to Italy, where I feel really good about myself for not falling into temptation?"

"Temptation?"

That's really all he said.

"We both know I shouldn't have accepted your invitation. I'm not supposed to be here."

"You're feeling this way, Savannah, because..."

I couldn't wait to hear this.

"...you really don't have a lot to worry about. You're a forty-year-old woman. Beautiful, smart, talented, but you're a product of your generation. And you should be careful about your drinking."

"Do I have a drinking problem?"

I wasn't sure what he was getting at, but he had finally called me beautiful, albeit in a clinical way.

"I wouldn't say that," he answered.

"What are you getting at, Doc?"

"You fear invisible things. You worry about elements that are irrelevant. Look at the group you associate with...Darcy, Natasha..."

"Excuse me, I don't normally hang out with these people. These are your people."

"But you are in their company, aren't you?"

"I don't follow you."

"You have really nothing to worry about. Nothing tangible, don't you think?"

"I'm not scared of aliens, or worried about being photogenic. I'm pretty stable."

"You are stable, but still a product. You can't help that."

"A product?"

"You're on vacation. You're riding a bike across Italy. I don't see you embracing that. Do you?" He gazed out across the horizon and lit a smoke. We had taken the lift to the top of the mountain by now.

"We're not in your office, Doc. How about not phrasing everything into a question? Can you do that?"

"OK, I am not indulging in your dysfunction. I'm descending."

That was the first time he phrased a sentence in a non-question. Maybe it was a low blow for me to say "we're not in your office". It was pretty passive-aggressive. Maybe I'm good at that, after all.

Was I really like Natasha? Darcy?

And he jumped in the lift and descended.

I'm sure, to the people working in these hotels, we were all the same person. Interchangeable worried women of North America. Sure, if it wasn't aliens, it would be something else – the fear of not being photogenic, or in my situation, the fear of growing old and never finding true love. Was that a tangible fear? Maybe he was right.

I was now missing him. Kicking myself for being in attack mode. I had a great opportunity with this men thing. I couldn't have turned that into a great day.

"Fuck," I said.

That's when I noticed Parker watching me.

I actually just saw a plume of smoke, heaping from behind a pole. He was smoking a cigarette. I could see one eye. Which quickly darted away, once I caught his gaze. I said "hi" to him several times. Usually, he'd look away and mutter something incoherent. He seemed a little shy, but I would discover this was a misjudgment on my part.

After Jake bolted, it was just me and him, waiting for the lift.

When it arrived, we got on it together.

It was awkward for him but definitely not for me.

In an attempt to ignite a conversation, I decided to smoke.

"Can I have one?"

He gave me a cigarette, lit one up himself, and still said nothing.

I took a drag and took in the expansive view as my lungs filled up with overcast clouds of nicotine. It felt like I'd sucked on the tailpipe of a cool car.

"So, how is it that you wound up driving for Colin?"

"What a cunt," he said.

Wow. The first three words.

"I mean, yeah, he got a sheeyat deal. But he's still a cunt."

"Colin? Yeah, I guess he doesn't treat you well."

"He's nice inside. On the outside, he has too much to prove. He's like a porcupine."

Did this place just attract shrinks? He had his boss broken down like a Swiss watch. I guess "porcupine" was an improvement from...

"But that's Uncle Colin."

Uncle Colin? He just called his uncle a cunt? I don't think I've ever called any of my uncles cunts before... or my aunts, for that matter.

"Was he born like that, or..."

"A cunt. Yeah, even before the accident."

"Actually, I was asking about his wheelchair-bound state."

"His apartment building was on fire. He was helping people even as the place was burning to the fooking ground. He was saving a cat when a beam fell on his back. A fooking cat. In China, that cat would be a meal. Here, Uncle Colin was saving its life."

"Wow."

"Yeah, he always thinks he has to save everybody. Even now. He likes you."

"Because I need to be sav- agggh," I said as the cigarette burned my fingertips. Without realizing it, I had smoked it to a nub. He offered me another one. I waved it off, but I did narrate the boring tale of the self-nude. I was surprised at how captivated he was. For some reason, Parker's interest meant more to me than everybody else's in the group. Then a text message flew in from Jake:

Please do not come back drunk.

STATURE

"I'M SORRY," I pleaded to Jake. I really was, too. He didn't say anything. He was getting his stuff ready for the next destination.

Before you paint me prideless, you should know that I got badly shit-faced after the ski lift. I'm talking about reality blending into dreams shit-faced. Day into night. Dogs into cats. It was bad, as if a goat said, "baaa-aaaad". I got mentally disfigured. Seriously. Jake had a wall in front of his usual stonewall. His fortress was impregnable. Appropriate wording if you consider the attention I've been paying to his stomach.

When we got back to the hotel, Parker and I started with a glass of wine. I was still talking about Axel, and his obsession with the multiverse, and Parker asked again about the self-nude, so I elaborated. Parker was suddenly my shrink.

"You know, there's a version of your uncle who did not save the cat. He's still walking around somewhere."

"Doesn't matter how many versions there are of Uncle Colin. In every one, he's a cunt."

And then, something in my head connected the ski lift to the merry-go-round. Maybe all the unearthing of Axel memories made the connections. Synapses were firing like crazy. But then, I must have had three or four glasses of vino, dangerously braiding them with shots of something syrupy.

Vince was there, too. And Hugh, I think. Maybe not. Another man was there. I was dancing with one of them. At one point, I was on the dance floor with Darcy. I asked her why she stabbed me in the back.

"You want me to slather your back?" she asked, scowling, then continued, "With what? The sun is going down, dear."

I'm not really sure what was said next, but I know "our gallery" was brought up again. Things were getting real loud. Darcy saw another really old couple and mentioned how cute they were, but this time went further than usual.

"I want to be them. I hope to be them," she said, when I realized we were not at the hotel anymore. We were in the ladies room of a bar-slash-club or whatever the coolest place in town was.

"You hope to be what, Darcy? Cute and old? I'm sure that'll happen for you."

I realized another thing...I was talking to Natasha and not Darcy. She looked at me curiously, like I was speaking backwards.

"Natasha, you told on me, didn't you, didn't you?" I asked her.

"I'm not big on being accused of things."

"HOW OLD ARE YOU?" I know I was getting loud.

"Twenty-five." I know she said that, twenty-five.

"ARE YOU A LITTLE OLD TO BE TELLING ON PEOPLE?"

"I'm sorry," she said, almost crying. And bolted out.

I might have vomited for the first time, shortly after that. I had the wherewithal to clean myself up, even though I felt like I was walking on the ship in The Perfect Storm.

"DARCY, ARE YOU OK?" I asked.

She looked scared, as she stared down the window of the bar...which might have been in the hotel, I guess. Locals were gazing at us. Lights were spinning. Locals looked French. They looked like French peasants.

"We're up too high," she said. Her face was the mask of fear. Even as I was watching this very confident woman crack, I could hardly believe it. I mean, she's a fake, but she's a very good fake.

"WHAT'S UP TOO HIGH, DARCY!?"

It was really loud, where we were. Even though I couldn't hear her speak, I could still read her lips. I have strange powers when I'm drunk. Seriously. I can't operate an elevator, but I can hear through concrete walls. I should work for the CIA. Drunk.

"We are too high," she enunciated. "This whole hotel could collapse in rubbles."

"BULLSHIT. THAT'S BULLSHIT," I yelled.

"Please don't curse like that, Savvy. It's unladylike."

"MOIS, UNLADYLIKE?"

"Yes, this behavior. It is unbecoming of an artist of your stature."

In this age, she said "it is" instead of "it's". Weird. And she accused me of having stature. I'm like the Stature of Liberty.

"Darcy, what are you not telling me?"

"I just don't want you to talk this way around him, I think I see him," she said.

"Hugh?" I asked, puzzled.

"No, Rick."

"Rick...Steves?" I asked, incredulous.

"Let's talk tomorrow, I'm feeling nauseous."

"BECAUSE YOU THINK THIS HOTEL WILL TOPPLE LIKE A FUCKING HOUSE OF CARDS OR BECAUSE YOU THINK YOU'RE HALLUCINATING RICK CREEPY STEVES?!"

Darcy was, I think, weeping. She left without saying goodbye.

Hugh later explained to me, she's sensitive to altitude.

"I HEAR YOU CAN FENCE, HUGH?!"

"Yes, I do OK in fencing. Are you alright, Savannah?"

"She's just having a good time," Vince insisted.

"Savannah, are you having a good time?" asked Antoine. I think it was him.

"She might want to turn in soon," Hugh suggested. But he quickly vanished after that. Suddenly...Axel was sitting there. In a wheelchair. Talking about his nephew. He had an Irish accent.

"Parker is a little cunt," Axel said. But then, it was Colin. I had been drinking since afternoon by now.

"But he's a good lad," he added, then clarified, "He will be. One day."

"We should find another club," Vince suggested.

"I'm going back to the hotel," a woman said. Natasha?

I believe we changed locations. I was on another dance floor with Vince. The music was all 80s stuff. Depeche Mode. Heart. Cindy Lauper's "Time after Time" seemed to play interminably, like the song was two hours long. I vaguely remember Parker driving us. Colin might have told him, "You're a pretty fooking good drunk driver, Park. You should have whiskey in your oatmeal."

I think we were all sitting around at a ruin, the only sound in the vicinity when Vince started sobbing. Or did he?

This was maybe the fourth time I threw up. I noticed Colin had vomit on his shirt, but it couldn't have been his, because he looked very stable, like he had only been drinking water the whole night. Did I really throw up on a guy in a wheelchair?

"She won't sleep in the same room with me anymore. She's very suspicious. She stopped using her phone. Poor girl."

"YOU MEAN, YOU HAVE TO BOOK TWO ROOMS?!" I asked. I couldn't switch gears from the dance floor to dead silence. My volume was locked on maximum. I saw Colin clasp his ears. Parker was urinating; I couldn't see him, but I could hear him. I know that sound anywhere.

"This fear of extraterrestrial life is tearing the girl apart."

"WHO'S TO SAY THEY WOULD BE MEAN?"

Everyone was grimacing now, whenever I said anything.

"THE ALIENS, I MEAN, WHO'S TO SAY THEY WOULD BE MEAN? THAT IS...I MEAN...THEY COULD BE. BUT THEY COULD BE NICE. OR DUMB. THEY COULD BE DUMBER THAN US!"

The whole fucking town must have heard this theory, whether they liked it or not. But you have to admit, it's a pretty good one. Maybe we're the superior life form and the aliens are stupid. Why not?

Then, I heard another sound.

A snorting sound that was not human. Was Natasha the only sane person in our group? Did she know things we were too blind to see?

I smelled a musky scent that could not be human.

I'm not sure if I dreamt this or not...

I noticed a huge eye, a big nose, like a giant penis. Long hair. It was a horse. He was tied to a porch. He was probably startled by my decibels. He was beautiful. Scary, too. Always strange to me how we tamed animals so much bigger than us. This horse could trample all of us right now, but he was standing there, patiently, tied to a pole. He's all muscle. But his mind is owned. It occurred to me, that's what we do in relationships. We try to own each other. I couldn't tame Axel. Maybe not Jake, either.

BRAIN SURGEON

"I CAN'T TAME ANYONE," I kept saying to myself as I hugged Jake during our ride to Hotel Terme Mirano. Meanwhile, everyone looked at me differently. Even Darcy. Especially Darcy. I felt like I could say "boo" and everyone would recoil. What happened that I can't remember? I threw up so much, I could still taste the acid in my throat. It felt raw, like steak tartare. My stomach was sore. I felt like I didn't need to drink ever again.

When we arrived at the hotel, Jake had vanished. Usually he at least told me the room number. But I had to ask the concierge, and he didn't completely believe me that I was a guest. The room, 214, was on the third floor, because they have 0 stories in Europe. I presumed Jake was there. He had checked in. There was a room number. He just neglected to share it with me.

When I knocked, he didn't answer. But like in a film noir, the door creaked open, as it was unlocked. And there sat Natasha. On the bed. On my bed. Waiting for Jake? I didn't know.

"Are you having...a session here?" I asked.

"A session," she repeated.

"Are you waiting for Jake?" I asked.

"Yes," she said, as I put down my bags. She didn't say anything else. Her eyes barely moved. It was really weird to have her in my room. When she smiled at me, I had chills in the back of my neck.

"Thank you," she said, "for last night."

"What happened last night?"

She didn't answer. I looked in the bathroom for Jake. There was no evidence that he was ever here. Eventually, it was too awkward to engage in my ritual; you know, of setting toiletries and computer in a certain place. Hanging a few things in the closet. So, I just sat near her on the bed and waited for Jake too.

I found her strangely calming. Maybe because she was doing what I had been doing this entire trip. Waiting for Jake to show up.

"Do you like this hotel?" I asked.

Two minutes later, she would reply, "I don't disagree with this hotel at all. It's not too isolated. But at night, it's different."

"How is it different?"

Around two minutes later, she would say, "It depends how many lights are out. You can tell who's in on it, based on the lights."

To clarify, she meant the arrangement of the lights. She suspected that any of the hotels could arrange their lights like a landing strip for the UFOs. Don't ask why I understand this.

Later on, she told me it was too bad she couldn't take pictures.

"Why can't you take pictures, Natasha?"

About five minutes later, she whispered, "They're connected to my phone. I'll give up my location."

"I'll take pictures for you."

"NO! NO! Don't you do that. They'll know, they'll know!"

When Jake got back to the room, he was startled to see me, as if it was me who was in the wrong room. I felt like a fifth wheel in my own room.

"Can you leave us alone, Savannah?" he asked.

"Where would you like me to go?" I asked.

"Anywhere, like you usually do," he offered.

"I usually take a shower and chill...then, I find somewhere to eat, alone."

"Why don't you eat and come back and take your shower after?"

I didn't answer. Because I was gazing at Natasha now. She wouldn't look at me. She appeared...embarrassed? I didn't say anything to Jake.

"Bye Natasha," I said, as I left the room.

I didn't feel like wandering into another city alone.

I didn't feel like capturing memories for just my memory banks.

I hung out in the lobby, only to run into Antoine and Maribel, sharing a drink. They had one drink. Together. They were sipping with one glass. Much making-up had occurred since the Boris conversation. It was now my turn to feel embarrassed. Even though it was the hotel bar, I felt like I walked into their private room.

"Come sit down with us," said Antoine.

"Oh no, no, you guys look like you're doing great. I don't want to ruin the mood."

"Don't be silly," said Maribel.

They knew I was pissed. But they couldn't help being kissy-faced. They felt bad for me, anyway. They never brought up Jake, but he was like the elephant in the room. You didn't have to bring up Jake to bring up Jake.

"What do you want to eat tonight?" Maribel asked Antoine.

"Whatever you want, baby," answered Antoine.

It would have been disgusting, if they weren't so cute together.

"Why didn't anyone invite me to the party?" asked Vince, dressed like he was going to the prom. He was seriously ready to rock this town.

"Savanner, you're starting a little early," he said.

But I was just nursing a glass of water.

"Where's the doctor? I hardly seem him anymore," said Vince.

"He's in his room...with your wife," I said.

"Great," he said, gesticulating to the bartender, then added, "they can both avoid that wanker, Rick Steves."

Now, he got my interest.

"Your friend, Darcy, she sees Rick Steves."

"Like, in real life?" I asked, baffled by how the sentence was structured. He said "sees Rick Steves" as if Darcy were having a love affair with Rick Steves. I know that couldn't be possible, since Rick Steves was the most asexual TV personality in history. I would rank Big Bird as having more sex appeal. But that didn't stop me from asking further questions.

"She saw him at this hotel?" I asked.

I must have looked really surprised, because suddenly Antoine and Maribel both jerked back and said at the same time, "You haven't heard?"

Then, all three explained, with a little too much enthusiasm, that she's been seeing Rick Steves in every city we've gone to. I just wasn't paying enough attention to catch it. But since we reached a higher elevation, Darcy's visions had sort of multiplied.

"Yeah, everywhere we've gone, she'd say, 'isn't that him? You think that's him?'"

"We were getting gelato and she turned around and straightened out her dress nervously and asked me, is Rick looking this way?"

I couldn't believe this. Darcy had a Rick Steves fetish. Darcy was having psychosomatic Rick Steves hallucinations?

"Haven't you noticed, she has stopped giving us lectures on the cities?"

"I thought...she got bored doing that?"

"No, no," said Maribel, "she didn't want Rick to overhear her."

"What? I don't get it."

"She didn't," Antoine clarified," want Rick Steves to judge what she was saying."

I still didn't totally follow.

"In case Mr. Steves overheard her speak about a city incorrectly...this was not a risk Darcy was willing to take."

Wow. Shit. Everyone was gone. It was just me in the lobby, thinking about Darcy's mind, saturated in Rick Steves imagery. I was still pretty hung-over from the night of terror, so I couldn't bring myself to order a real drink. Even though, hearing what I just heard, hangover-free, I would have poured myself a glass of anything, even cold medicine.

What the hell was wrong with her? Hugh was in some ways, creepier than Rick Steves. But I knew him, so he wasn't creepy at all. And even Rick Steves himself probably wasn't the guy he projected on TV. Darcy once told me the Rick Steves Empire was worth over 20 million bucks. Does that explain her fetish? Mr. Steves had to know what he was doing. Yes, Mr. Steves was pandering to our group; mostly white, fairly wealthy Americans who wanted to see new places, as long as safety, comfort and of course, English-speaking was part of the package. The image projected by Steves couldn't be a real man, could it?

I watched some BBC news on the flat screen. Donald Trump looked diabolical, refugee stuff kept popping up, and there seemed to be another weird disease threat. I guess there was an immense amount to fear out there. Darcy and Natasha might have been saner than all of us. They knew something was wrong, that there were a lot of threats out there, they had just misplaced what that fear was. It wasn't aliens. It wasn't heights. It was, as JFK so aptly said, fear itself. I think he got it from FDR, but Kennedy was hotter, so he gets the cred.

When someone switched the TV to soccer, I thought it had just been done independently like in "Poltergeist", but someone, a human being, had switched it. I couldn't see. I look around. And just saw empty seats and really believed my mind was playing tricks on me. Rick Steves perhaps?

I couldn't even see the bartender. Everyone vanished. Except for the guy around Jake's age, I think, who looked doctorly. I couldn't even tell you how I know that. He sat at one of the coffee tables, wearing a designer suit. He had been checking me out for God knows how long. Like some dark magic had beckoned him.

"You like Real Madrid?" he asked me.

"I don't watch sports. Isn't that predictable," I said.

"It's not. My ex-wife watched football, basketball...everything, even bowling."

"She must have been desperate to watch bowling."

He laughed, more because I was throwing the charm darts at him than for anything I was saying. Before I realized it, I was sitting at his table. And guessing what he did for a living.

"Brain surgeon."

"Warm."

"Heart surgeon."

"Cold."

"Proctologist."

"Warm."

Ugh.

"Ear, nose and throat," I guessed again.

"You get one more guess," he said.

"I'm going to throw a Hail Mary...in honor of your ex-wife."

"There's no need to honor her," he said, as he sipped his drink. Just from the way his eyes wandered away, you could tell the divorce sucked ass.

"OBGYN," I ventured my last guess.

"Really close, gynecologist."

"Wow...I was really, really close."

"You still deserve a drink."

"No thanks...I'm not drinking tonight."

I explained to him all the boring details of the night before. He shrugged. I asked him what made him decide to be a gynecologist.

"It was just the most fascinating of the medical sciences. It's where we come from. It's where we direct aggression. It's the most misunderstood organ. Even women don't know much about their own vagina."

"Oh, I know mine pretty well," I said.

"Did you that your vagina is connected to your spinal cord?"

"Shit, seriously, that means..."

"Neurons from your brain are connected to your vagina."

I've never heard the word "vagina" spoken so many times and I wasn't embarrassed.

"I did not know that," I said.

"There are networks of neurons connected to your vagina," he insisted.

"So, what does that mean?"

"It means your vagina is intelligent."

"It is? Wow. That's two things I've never heard."

He was a nice guy. If I was traveling alone, this would certainly have gone further. At least a long European talk. But I wasn't traveling alone. This meeting was a one-time thing. I didn't even want to know his name.

"What's your name?" he asked.

"We shouldn't know each other's names," I said.

"Why, you're married?"

"No, I traveled here with someone, as you know from my story."

I was standing up already by then. I was headed back to the room. The gynecologist had enlightened me about my privates in a way no one ever had. I always thought it was creepy that a man would want to be a gynecologist. But it made sense now why when I said "brain surgeon" he said "warm". All the discussion about vaginas was making me feel a little warm. I had fantasies about Jake as I headed back to the room. These fantasies were borrowed from the last time we enjoyed each other. I thought he could just grab me from the moment I entered the room. Throw me on the floor. The rest is pretty much what happened...you know with the handcuffs.

But when I got there, he was passed out. At least Natasha wasn't there anymore. It wasn't even nine o' clock yet. So, what did I do? I watched a bunch of Rick

Steves stuff on YouTube. Had I actually seen much of this TV personality, aside from a few snippets here and there? Never this much. Never in a marathon session. My mind was numb by three o'clock in the morning, around the time I stopped. I think my jet lag was finally worn out. And Rick Steves helped break that dam.

So, the guy just goes around to different cities, talks about the culture like he's reading it off his iPhone, barely talks about the food, and whenever food or drink is in front of him, he rarely actually eats it. As opposed to say, Anthony Bourdain, who ate the beating heart of a cobra. Steves just reaches for a glass of beer, strudel or whatever and then they cut to the next scene. My gay-dar is on for this dude, too.

The next morning Jake was a block of cement. Inanimate. An appliance. I had the impulse to recharge him in the socket like you do your iPhone. He felt very betrayed. Did I really drink like a frat brother just because he warned me not to? But shouldn't he have known the power of reverse psychology? As well as the powerful need to drink in the Italian countryside? I already apologized. What the hell else did the guy want?

I was sort of stuck with him too, because Darcy was a little freaked out by me after the night of the living dead. So, I couldn't complete the painting yet. Her Rick Steves visions were becoming Natasha-like. I'll get into that later. Hugh might have been cautious about me too. When I waved to them, they avoided eye contact. The entire group gave me the black sheep treatment, even Colin and his nephew. Antoine and Maribel, they were drunk on themselves. And Vince, he might as well have been traveling on his own.

I learned later that I was telling everyone the financial system is about to collapse and if they had money, prepare to kiss it goodbye. I was regurgitating what Hallenbeck had said to me on the plane, that the Fed was printing a Niagara Falls of money, even though I'm still not sure what that means. Hmm, in hindsight, probably the last thing rich people want to hear. And none of these folks weren't well off, I promise you. I must have sounded like the Grim Reaper.

Only Natasha was applying social lubricant on me. She talked to me, she smiled at me, she found me enchanting...I think. She liked me, precisely because I was a black sheep. She also liked that I freaked out everyone. It evened the playing field, even if she should be more concerned about her finances than extra-terrestrials. Her insanity had descended to murkier waters. Savannah's Waters, if I may be so bold. No, I had nothing to do with it. The girl was just teetering away from the normal, fast. Jake was probably pissed at me and stressed that he couldn't do it anything for her. After that moment in the room, I was relieved that it wasn't my job to set her straight.

But I started to feel bad for Jake. I understood a little more now why he was so reluctant to help her. I couldn't be a hard ass, I was just pushing him further and further away. There was no way to turn Jake around through argument. I had to drop the Cleopatra bomb on his ass. Cleopatra seduced Caesar by rolling out of a carpet and creating fantasy worlds for him. If Jake didn't want to see beauty outside of his hotel room, I had to bring the beauty inside.

ALIENS

THE HOTEL CENTRALE was our next location. I made sure to call ahead and plan certain elements. Flowers. A snack tray with cheese, prosciutto, fruits, and wine. The room was sweet and I made it unbearably romantic. I lit candles, played soft music from my iPhone...Serge Gainsbourg anyone? I sprinkled a trail of rose petals that led to the bed, with the main prize, me, in lingerie. It was perfect. I was ready to fuck myself.

You might wonder how I managed to arrange such an event in such a short time. This is where Darcy's altitude sickness played a huge role. Since Savannah's night of terror, the lady's condition only worsened. We were ascending to greater heights. You could see her expression of dread on the back of Hugh's bike. She held on to him like she had capsized in the middle of the ocean and he was keeping her afloat. Her eyelids were superglued shut. She could not look out at the vast expanse below. The drops were so deep, you could spit into it and not hear it splatter for a whole minute. The mountains were otherworldly. We were up high, swirls of wind pushing us to the brink.

Whenever we stopped, Darcy would sit by herself, a couple of feet from the bike, as if the vehicle might take off and abandon her, and trembled. This is when Rick Steves visions would come to fruition. She would mutter to herself. It sounded like she was speaking in tongues, like Robert DeNiro at the end of "Cape Fear" when he was sinking into the water. Once in a while, we would hear "Rick" or even "Mr. Steves" but it was hard to decipher what else was up with her.

As if I were talking to a child who was sure their imaginary friend was there, I would play along and say, "Oh yeah, there's Rick, he's waving to you?"

But that would only make her startled. She would say, "Where? Where?"

We all tried to talk to her, but only Jake actually could. Though, even The Beast Master had limits. He gave her some of his magic dope. Still, she would hyperventilate. She kept saying she was fine, but she never told him to leave. She would be in a squatting position to prevent the high altitude winds from pushing her over the precipice. "Is that him?" she would ask, referring to Rick, I guess. Long story short, her mind began to fall. Natasha seemed pleased, her face looking almost smug, as if she was telling us, see, it happens to the best of us. Some fear aliens, others heights. It's not a big deal.

Now, Jake had to put on his work clothes for two women.

I should have considered this as I sat on the bed for hours. And sat, and sat. Eventually, I uncorked the bottle of Chianti. I drank three glasses. I wasn't even hungry, and the platter was looking soggy and sad. I packed it all up, shoved it in the mini-fridge and blew out the candles. I planned on another attempt at the next hotel.

When Jake arrived, he looked like a stockbroker on the day the market crashed in 1929. His hair was disheveled. His posture, defeated. I could imagine how dealing with Natasha and Darcy could shatter all the nerves and fibers in your being.

"It smells lovely in here," Jake said, smiling thinly, then, "What a beautiful room."

There was no trace of anything and I sort of regretted pulling the plug, but I was depleted. From waiting. Cleopatra did not wait three hours to roll out of the carpet. She would have suffocated.

"How's Darcy?" I asked the next morning.

He looked at me hopelessly, and lit up a cigarette.

"She'll be fine today, maybe tomorrow too, but the next day, who knows?"

"Is it just fear of heights?"

"That's how it started, but now, symptoms are manifesting in ugly ways."

"Like what?"

"She's afraid of water, horses, and mirrors."

"Water? Mirrors?"

"But she's OK right now...for a couple of days. She might have to extract herself from the group."

"What? Wow, OK."

"Also, she thinks Rick Steves is following her."

"Hmmm, she might leave the group?" I asked again.

That wasn't such a bad idea, except that I was hoping I would still be compensated for that painting, my only exit strategy. Jake and I stood outside the hotel on a little sidewalk strip, waiting for the others. They were taking forever. Maybe because half the group had a neurotic mess for a wife. The sidewalks here were almost nonexistent...the width of a foot stool, and thus pedestrians and vehicles had a tendency to share the road. When a huge truck sped down the narrow street, the fight for space was between Jake and the truck. The driver did not see The Beast Master. But I could. I grabbed Jake by his jacket, jerked him, lifted him towards me, and held him in a tight embrace as the rig blew by us. He could have been roadkill. It was really that close. He held on to me.

He kissed me on the forehead.

It was nice.

A tiny strike into his armor.

During the ride, Darcy opened her eyes but rarely blinked. She looked lobotomized. But hey, she was riding again. Natasha was a different story. She was looking like her old self again, if you know what I mean.

The Hotel Valebella Inn was our next stop. This place was about as close to paradise as you could get. I had a good feeling about striking gold here. You know, seduction gold. Again, I ordered up a spread. In the middle of our ride, Jake said, "Did you have the complimentary cold cuts and cheese in the fridge? Incredible hotel. It was great to come back to that." I felt like slapping him. He didn't realize I ordered those snacks. But why would he?

Tonight, that would not be the case. I didn't just have a spread that would blow away all the guys in Goodfellas, I also drew up a bubble bath and I had dark chocolates out and a few bottles of wine uncorked and music and candlelight.

He again repeated that Darcy would be fine for 48 hours. Whatever he gave her would keep her from losing her mind for that duration of time. So, no one was going to get in my way, right? Wrong. Despite how temporary it was, Darcy's stability unbalanced Natasha. Her alien fears suddenly rushed back like a locomotive.

It was as if her neurotic fears wanted to duel Darcy's.

"The aliens are closing in on her," Jake said. "She thinks...she saw one."

"What about Darcy and her...sightings?"

"She hasn't mentioned Rick today," Jake said, as if he knew Rick. Then, he went directly to Natasha's room. He didn't even change. Our room would have made Marie Antoinette come in her panties. That's how awesome it was. But Jake would never see it. I went to the room alone. I didn't even unpack. I called Darcy. I just felt like talking to her. I asked for her room from the concierge desk.

"Savvy?" she said.

"Yep, the one and only."

I could tell she was wondering if I had been drinking. I wondered if she saw herself as having failed the mission. You know, the long forgotten one. She was here to watch me. And she failed. I got fucked up again. I alienated people again. I drank my way into a very dark place.

"Are you OK?" she asked me. Wow. I couldn't believe she asked me if I was OK. I was not hallucinating a TV personality or aliens, or was I? Now, I began to wonder. Was this that movie where the protagonist is looking for the bad guy the entire movie and realizes he's batshit crazy?

"I'm just watching some Rick Steves on YouTube," I said, matter-of-factly.

She paused. There was a really long silence this time. I heard rummaging, like she was passing the phone to someone else. And finally she said, "Isn't he amazing?"

"Sure he is," I said.

"What's your favorite episode? I love when he goes to Croatia."

"Have you seen the Istanbul one?"

"You know what, I don't think I have," she said, lying through her teeth.

"That's the best one," I said.

She strangely said nothing about having seen Rick in real life. I even said stuff like, "It would be great to meet him one day," but she never took the bait. She didn't sound like herself, to my credit. I got bored and ended the conversation.

By ten o' clock, I heard Natasha screaming from the room.

"No, no, no, no, no..."

I had chugged two bottles of vino by 21:30.

I heard a very loud noise outside. A ruckus. It sounded like it was on the rooftop, and there were huge lights beaming through the window. The whole place was vibrating. Wow. Maybe they really were coming for her. Good for her. At least one of us is getting some tonight.

I didn't even bother to clean up this time.

I probably passed out around midnight.

I woke up at 3 AM to the sound of Jake nibbling on cured meat. At least something in this hotel was cured.

"This is delicious salami," he moaned, displaying the most pleasure I had seen on his face, I think ever. The guy was making me hungry. "These snacks are better than at the last hotel," he added.

Two minutes later, we were both eating from the spread. It was almost as good as sex, seriously, unless I had just forgotten how good sex was. A sad probability. But on the positive side, eating smoked meats and local cheese and chocolate in the mountains of Switzerland, with someone you want to care about...it's not so bad.

I had to ask, "So how's Natasha?"

"We had to have her helicoptered out of here," he said, out of breath.

That explained the sounds and lights, I thought.

"I went with her to make sure she was OK," he explained, "and I just returned."

Natasha had had a full-scale nervous breakdown.

"Vince is a mess. He really loves her, you know."

"Sure."

I didn't think it even mattered to Vince. But it mattered to me. Poor Natasha. She was kind of growing on me. I had no bully now. What was I going to do? I felt like I didn't get that grand finale with her. That *womano a womano* moment. She'd probably massacre me, but I wanted it. I wanted the Natasha Hurricane Crescendo Twister Tsunami.

"She'll be fine," Jake assured me. Touching my leg. The first time in a while. I'm talking leg, vagina, elbow, anything. I forgot what it felt like to be touched by him. His fingertips noticed how soft my skin was. And later, that I was wearing his favorite lingerie. He was caressing my leg slowly...

I know he didn't fuck Darcy and Natasha, but it kind of felt like he did...and I just didn't want to be with him at the moment. I just wanted things to be more simple.

"There's another dimension where you came in at seven o' clock and we ate cheese and chocolate, and drank wine and made love all night. This is not that dimension," I said, as I turned over on the bed. It was a little bitchy, but sometimes power is better than sex. Not better than food, of course.

"How much wine did you drink?"

"Jake, you're not my shrink anymore."

"But I still care about you."

I was nearing the door when he said the "A" word.

"You're still getting over Axel, and I know it's not easy," he said.

He hadn't said Axel's name since we were in sessions together. It felt a little spooky, like Axel was hiding in the closet, listening to our conversation. I had no response for this…in any dimension.

I scowled at him.

My eyebrows really hit those upside-down Vs.

He didn't say anything back.

He looked a little vulnerable.

At the time, I made nothing out of it, except that I was somehow scaring him.

I just knew, I needed to get this painting done, with or without Darcy.

I was on a sinking ship. For whatever reason, I was near France, the country that held my self-nude hostage. I had to go there. The sensation of leaving this mental hospital of vacationers rushed through me…and the need to extract myself from this group became immediate. In other words, I gave up on Jake.

I grabbed my canvas and easel, and worked on my painting in the lobby in the middle of the night. The sense of urgency hadn't been this feverish for me since I was in my early twenties. The picture was dictating to me how it should look.

Night became dawn, when one of the bellhops asked me to stop because the fumes made people sick. He kindly offered me another room in the hotel. It was really small, containing the fumes even more aggressively. But you could see the sunrise from there.

It was fucking gorgeous.

Everything.

I was starting to get a headache from paint. But I didn't care.

I was freezing, too. But I didn't care.

I only had on a jacket with my lingerie underneath. I could hear birds, bees, the gentle breeze in the trees, a babbling brook nearby. Mother nature in glorious heat. The vision of that fucking sunrise. It was like the sun had a mouth and that mouth swallowed me whole.

I wished I had some of that salami and cheese with me. And more wine. It would have been perfect.

THE PORTRAIT

HELP ME, Natasha was texting me. A lot. I had breakfast with Vince, Antoine, and Maribel, and the topic was revolving around Natasha. Everyone was stupefied, except for Vince.

"Oh, she's a big girl," he kept saying.

"How is the big girl...doing, though?" I kept asking, not revealing that his wife was sending desperate texts. I kept replying that everything would be OK, but she painted the world of aliens so vividly, I almost believed she had been abducted.

"She's doing great," Vince said, sipping on espresso and chewing on eggs.

"When did you last hear from her?" I asked, while eating gelato. Yeah, it was early, but one of our members had been abducted by aliens.

"Savanner, don't worry about Natasha. She dealt with communists. This is nothing."

She dealt with communists? OK, I shrugged, finishing my gelato. It was fucking good. Seriously. I had one ball of chocolate, the other of lemon.

Antoine and Maribel glared at both of us like we were aliens. They, of course, were barely touching their breakfast.

"I just can't believe it was so bad, you had to fly her out of here," said Maribel.

"She's just being dramatic," Vince said, "and what's the worst case scenario?"

Although Vince was nonchalant, and maybe I was, too, the basketball player and his wife acted like we were at a funeral.

"What do you mean, worst case scenario?" asked Antoine.

But, Jake already had Vincent huddled off, probably planning their next motorcycle adventure.

Meanwhile, I was still receiving numerous texts from Natasha, saying I was the only one who could help her. She said they were going to probe every orifice in her body and insert devices inside her. After that, there would be no hope. They would know where she would be at all times.

I really didn't know how to respond to this. Who knows, maybe she was right?

While riding to the next location, I thought about her lying in a foreign hospital, with German-speaking aliens hovering around her. How petrified she must be. Poor Natasha.

Darcy's altitude sickness was also getting serious. When she came down to meet us, she looked exhausted and ashen, pale and colorless. Natasha's vanishing act had really taken a toll on her. Darcy no longer wanted to ride on a motorcycle, so she opted to ride with Colin. You could tell, Colin was not comfortable with this. We were all scared for him and Parker. Darcy no longer had a neurotic partner. She was going solo.

Jake warned Colin, "If she has an outburst, just stop the car and call me."

An outburst. Jesus.

Hanging around these sick women inspired feelings of pity and sadness. As if we were at war and soldiers were getting traumatized or taken out. Except we weren't at war. Like the Doc said, there really wasn't much to worry about.

But I did flirt with something totally dangerous that could have killed both of us. In retrospect, I shouldn't have done it. But before we got on the bike, he gave me that look that boyfriends give, that says, "We're going to fuck later, right? Right?" You know that look. I'm not against that look. Usually. In fact, this was probably the only time in the history of Savannah that I found that look irritating. I couldn't explain it, but Natasha's disappearance made him want me again - yet, it turned me off. His sexual energy got diverted to Natasha, and now it was free again.

You could see his penis piercing through his jeans like he'd shoplifted a candy bar. A big one, like a Toblerone. I sort of was enjoying that power.

I responded with a look that said, "Maybe, maybe not." I was getting off on torturing him a little, the way I had felt tortured the past few nights. I'm not a consolation prize. My vagina has intelligence.

But, I couldn't deny my attraction. So, while he biked us to the Hotel Forni Airolo, a truly shitty little hotel, I played with him. It started out by accident. I had my hand on his stomach, we hit a speed bump, and I accidentally touched him...down there...and felt the Toblerone. I may have gotten a little out of control. We were riding behind everyone, except for Colin; but we were dealing with very windy roads. I rubbed and tugged at his jeans for a little while...when he removed the Toblerone. We arrived at the hotel and he darted to our room, pulling my hand.

Colin was calling for Jake, but he ignored him and stayed focused. It appeared that Darcy was having a serious attack. Parker was also out of the car, and he and his uncle looked spooked, like they had just escaped a haunted house. I gazed at the car, which appropriately had tinted windows, like it was possessed, like there was an evil spirit inside that could control it to run over people.

"She kept asking us to stop. Saying she saw Rick Steves. We did at first, but then she saw him everywhere. It was relentless."

Ultimately, Jake changed course, let go of my hand with a look that said "sorry", and disappeared inside the car. That was courageous of him. I began to really admire his Florence Nightingale-ish need to help others.

I spent most of the afternoon completing my painting. I was determined to get it to the end. I even forgot to eat dinner. At about 9 p.m., Jake walked in the small room I had requested to work in and told me I could not sleep there. The fumes were toxic, he warned me. He touched my face and said I was getting pale. I looked in the mirror and saw a third sick woman. My face was discolored, and my eyes red-rimmed. My head felt like it was splitting in two. But I wasn't far from finishing.

"You don't have to do this. It won't bring Axel back."

"I'm not really sure what Axel has to do with this. And why are you bringing his name up so much lately?"

"Because I know he's at the heart of your problems."

"You're at the heart of my problems, Jake," I said calmly. "Now, let me finish this. Get out of here."

"You're going to get sick, breathing this stuff," he cautioned, as I shoved him out and shut the door.

I was coughing regularly at this point, but I had to get it done. I was a like a racehorse that could smell the finish line. Natasha sent me a shockwave of texts. It was hard to ignore them. I felt like her mother. It was very weird.

By midnight, I completed the portrait. A relief. I hadn't completed a painting in months; nothing since the self-nude. It was rather Sisyphus-like, a great feeling of pushing a boulder to the top. I felt pride in myself. I proved I could do it again.

I had to show it to Darcy and Hugh. But it needed to dry; at least a little. I laid my head down on the twin bed in the room…

"Shit!" I woke up and it was 2 a.m. I didn't care. I had to show them tonight. I carried the painting, still a little gummy, to their room.

It was heavy.

Hotel staff tried to help me, but I wouldn't let them.

I got it this far and I wanted to carry it, even though I was weak and sweaty. I must have looked pretty bad, because even other guests offered to help me.

"Are you sure we can't help you carry...that?" a Latin South Beach-looking guy asked me. And then, I could have sworn a guy who looked like Rick Steves also asked me. I don't know, maybe it was him.

KNOCK KNOCK

Hugh opened the door, rubbing his eyes. I imagined he went to sleep at 8:30. I wasn't the kind of person who woke people in the middle of the night, but this was worth it. My greatest painting. I created their vision. Sure, much of it based on Darcy's vision, but her vision is their vision.

"Hello," Hugh said. He seemed slightly pleased to see me. Well, not me, but the painting I clutched in my arms. He couldn't see it, because it was covered. Appropriately. The element of surprise and all that.

"Is that the...?"

He couldn't say "portrait", so I said it for him.

"...Yes, the portrait."

Hugh had clearly forgotten about it. It hadn't been that many days, but when you're traveling, when you see new places, your mind loses track of time. Two days can feel like months. I don't even remember the last time Darcy and Hugh modeled for me. But it felt like eons ago.

"Can I show it to her?" I asked.

He sighed, "I'm not sure, she's not feeling well, Savannah."

"Oh, let me show her. It'll make her feel better, I swear."

He didn't say anything. He led me into the hotel room. Their bags sat in darkness, unzipped. The TV was on. CNN. Stock market. Announcements in red. Like stocks weren't doing well. I don't know. Hugh made a gesture like he wanted me to wait there. He went to the bedroom. The door was ajar. I heard Darcy's voice. The two were muttering. Finally, he turned to me and gestured for me to advance.

Earlier I felt like a mother, but now I felt like a child. She was about to show off a picture she drew on Thanksgiving, in front of the whole family. They were all going to say how great it was no matter what, because it is a child we're talking about. How cute. You did that. That is adorable. Those are the kind of compliments I expected. Darcy was about to be blown away. Literally.

"Evening Darcy," I said.

Her head barely peeked from the blanket, like a possum or otter. Her hair was matted from sweat. Her pupils were dilated from drugs. Her fingers hung on to the blanket like she was keeping herself from falling off the edge of a building. I was thrilled that I had in my arms the very thing that would inspire her to re-emerge from her isolation.

"Hello Savvy," Darcy said, her voice raspy, like she'd been screaming or crying a lot, but trying to sound positive. "Is that the...?"

She wouldn't say "portrait" either. But her voice sounded full of hope, like I had springtime underneath the covering. There I was, like Vanna White, about to present my Darcy with the greatest of presents. Hugh reached for the sheet covering the painting. Revealed it. Not much light in here, so neither reacted yet. But I was thrilled, studying their facial expressions. The overzealous daughter thought, "So, do you like it?"

Hugh reacted first, blinked really hard, as if he wished the image would change once he opened his eyes again. It did not.

"You hate it?" I asked, but he still didn't say anything.

Darcy reached for her glasses. And peered at the painting with greater focus. She looked at me, then at the painting, then me again, then the painting...this occurred several times. I thought she was beaming, but when I leaned in, I could see she was just tilting her head and scowling. That's when I had a coughing fit. I couldn't stop. It was like I swallowed an ashtray.

"Are you alright, Savvy?" she asked.

"It's the paint smell," Hugh said. "You should go see a doctor. The hotel will certainly assist you."

My face was pale and haggard-looking, the last time I saw it. But for some reason, I felt good when I noticed my own reflection. My expression was sacrificial. I was hurting myself to create something.

"Move out of the way, Hugh," Darcy said. "I can't see it."

Hugh was obscuring the painting, I realized later, intentionally. Darcy leapt out of the bed to pull the frame towards her, towards light, but Hugh pulled it back toward him. They were both pulling the frame in different directions.

By now, you could see two devastated expressions. You really only see spouses look like this when one of their children has died. Honestly, I've never seen a woman's face shatter like that. How bad was it? Like an expensive piece of china bursting on the floor into shards. That was Darcy's face. Or what was left of it.

Then, the conversation about her being photogenic rushed back to me. Oh shit, I thought, grimacing. I don't know what it was, the rebel in me, or my insistence that I didn't want to do another portrait? Was this an act of aggression?

"I think this is my best, I'm sorry you dislike it," I said.

But Darcy was struggling to breathe. Hugh was completely blocking the painting now. She clawed at his shirt, twisting into it, pulling towards her. She was hugging him in a tight embrace. The woman started bawling. I can say, my work has never had that kind of effect on people.

"Oh no, I'm...sorry," I said, unconvincingly, because I still thought this was my best work. Then, Darcy fell to the ground. Hugh and I looked down at the fallen debutante, bewildered. I was holding my last portrait, the last one I would ever do, like the guy in the Subway uniform, dressed like a giant sandwich, on a traffic corner, dancing like an imbecile.

After all that talk about how cute old couples were, about how she wished she could be like them, I granted her, Darcy, her secret wish...I painted her and Hugh as an old couple, a couple beyond 100, the oldest couple in the world, full of beautiful wrinkles, emaciated from excessive age, wrinkled like the flesh of an accordion, a hunchbacked couple Darcy would point to in the streets and say, "aren't they the cutest?" That was not her reaction about herself in the oldest state I could create her. She was living her own personal version of "The Picture of Dorian Gray".

I felt bad because she was, you know, having problems already. The Rick Steves issue, etc. The painting visibly hurt her. Her face twisted. Her eyes blackened. Her unconscious claimed her. And she passed out. Hugh looked at me like he would pay me double to burn it.

FEMME FATALE

I WAS ON MY BED, in the toxic room. Chugging from a bottle of rosé. My gums were dry from dehydration. My lips were chapped like bacon bits. My mental state was in tatters from everything. I definitely should not have been drinking. I did not need a doctor to tell me that.

I felt guilty about everything. I coughed. I was drunk, high and broke. I was messaging with Chuck DeGoal about my painting. I told him, one way or the other, I was coming to get her. But for the first time, I started not to care. In a world where Jennifer Lawrence and Kate Upton's privates were out there, what did it matter? I wasn't famous. And if I was lucky enough to be that successful, the story of that painting would amplify my coolness even more. I'd pretend like I was uncomfortable. I'd pretend like it was inappropriate. The legend would be even bigger. But most likely, no one would ever care. I just wanted to go see it now. With my own eyes. And maybe talk this guy into giving it back to me. But if he said "non", which was the most common word uttered by a French person, I could live with it. Probably.

I felt bad about Darcy. I called her. From the hotel phone.

"Yes?" she answered. You could hear Hugh snoring in the background.

"Hi, it's me."

"Hi," she said, almost seductively.

"I'm sorry you don't like the portrait," I reiterated.

"You think I'm rich and stupid, don't you?"

"I think you're rich," I admitted, "and I think we're all stupid."

"So you do think I'm stupid."

"Darcy, what are you asking me?"

"I wanted to be an artist when I was young. Really young. At eight years old, I told my parents, I wanted to sculpt and paint and do all the things you see at museums. I was a straight-A student. I had a 4.0. But art class, that was what I most looked forward to. My parents were supportive. They wanted me to be an artist. I was praised a lot, all the way into high school. Mrs. Camien, my 10th Grade art teacher, once...we were supposed to do a painting of a brand of our favorite candy. I did one of Big League Chews. You know, those big pouches that looked like chewing tobacco? I did a painting of that. And it looked really good. And everyone in class thought it was amazing. But Mrs. Camien didn't think a girl should paint that. She gave me a B-. Something about that...hurt me deeply. I asked her why and she said, 'A girl shouldn't paint Big League Chews.' And that was it. That was her reasoning. Not only had I never received anything below an A-, but I had done my best artwork and I knew it. That was it...I was pregnant less than a year later."

"But, Darcy, you did some great work with me," I offered, while trying to compute how young she must have been to have a child.

"It's not the same, Savvy. You will see when you get to be my age. Seeing that portrait was just a reminder…I love looking at old couples because they make me feel young and full of possibility… but, the reality is, well, I am not.

My parents, they were supportive of whatever I was doing. My dad said, 'Whatever you want to do, we're behind you.' They were so supportive. So supportive. They really got along with my first husband."

Huh? I guess it makes sense that Hugh would be her second husband…maybe third. I just drank my rosé and listened as she poured her heart out to me.

"My mother loved him. I was jealous even. She looked great for her age, Mother did. When I was really young, when I had birthday parties and boys came over, they were transfixed by my mother. She was very, very beautiful. Most of my adult life, people thought we were sisters. I won't age that well. No one will. She drank a pitcher from the Fountain of Youth. I don't know, I thought my husband had a crush on her. I mean, I had a crush on my mom. The psychoanalysts think you're supposed to have a crush on your opposite-sex parent, but I didn't. I saw her naked once when I was four. I walked in and she was changing the sheets, naked. I saw her pussy, buttocks and everything."

Did Darcy just say "pussy'? Maybe I remembered that part wrong. Maybe I was really high and drunk.

"When you think of grandmothers, you think of old ladies on canes. But my mom wasn't like that. She was like a femme fatale. Even my kids were quiet around her. She had a face that was just…transcendent in its beauty. I would look at her face for hours when I was young. I'd comb her hair too, if she'd let me."

Wow, Darcy was really hung up on her mom. I had to meet this smoking hot grandma. I didn't want to ask if she was still alive.

"She died three years ago. She died beautiful. Like Jim Morrison, like JFK, like Curt Cobain. Her crypt was erotic, the way she laid there. Reminded me of Anne Rice's Sleeping Beauty books. My mom was Sleeping Beauty. I miss her." Darcy started sobbing.

She said little about her dad, though. She didn't talk about him much, except for this nugget.

"My dad was an ugly man. He was very kind. His face was just scary, almost deformed in how ugly he was. He was hairy too. He had the nicest voice, though. He was afraid to travel but loved to read about traveling. He knew everything about every country. He had all the books. Of every country. Brazil, Germany, Egypt, the Philippines, Russia. He collected all the guides. Frommer's, Fodor's, Rick Steves'. I probably look more like my dad than I do my mom…"

I started coughing, really hard. Additionally, I was having a hard time concentrating on what she was saying.

"Darcy, I've got to go. I'm sorry, and I'm sorry about the painting."

"Stay young for as long as you can," she said. And hung up.

GOD'S BOSOMS

IT WAS MY TURN TO BE SICK. My head felt like a stove top that had been left on while everyone went on vacation. My nasal cavity hurt like I'd snorted toothpicks. And, I looked like I felt (like shit). So it was really odd to have the good doctor telling me how beautiful I was. I honestly was pale, sickly, and sort of ghoulish-looking, and I couldn't stop coughing.

"You look radiant, don't worry," Jake said. "But, I don't think it's a good idea for you to ride on the bike today." I was forced to ride with Colin, who most definitely preferred a sick person in his car over Darcy. I was very quiet most of the ride. The things Darcy said couldn't escape me. Natasha was texting me less, but I was still getting them. I didn't read all of them; they all said the same thing – you know, aliens, orifices, etc. Colin did ask me, "Your prophecy about the end of money, what was that based on?"

He was referring to the night of terror when, I guess, I talked about the end of money and how the government was printing too much, you know, all that crap Hallenbeck was talking about. It's a good thing I met the gynecologist afterwards.

"I was really drunk, Colin. I was just..."

"But it must originate from somewhere."

He kept pushing and pushing. And I had no energy to fight it. So, I told him about Hallenbeck. And maybe the fact that Hallenbeck was a stockbroker, or former stockbroker, seemed to spook Colin. I guess he had his fortune in stocks. This conversation was pretty dull for me, and I was blowing my nose a lot, but to Colin, I might as well have been translating the book of Revelations.

"The stock market has been plummeting," he said to me in a disquieting tone.

"Yeah, you know," I said, "that's going to happen."

I don't think I made him feel better. I just wanted the conversation to end. My throat was hurting. My vocal cords felt stretched like a bungee cord.

I could see Jake biking ahead. Sometimes he would let the car pass, so he could take a peek at me, and he would wave. Who was this guy?

Then suddenly, I understood what it was like to be Natasha and Darcy. I was sick, and he had a thing for sick people. He'd offered me some drugs back at the hotel, but I was in the mood for my body to confront me. I also did not want to be a zombie like Darcy, or nuts like Natasha. Even though I actually really missed both of them.

Yes, Darcy left the party.

I'd seen her one last time this morning. She was smiling, but it was a mask, like the real her was locked inside, screaming. There was a numbness I did not want to share.

"It was fun, Savvy," she greeted me. "I'll see you back in Los Angeles."

I hugged her and Hugh. He had the painting rolled up in his hand. They'd asked for it. I'm not sure if it was the result of whatever she was on or because she wanted to burn it...but she paid for it. She could wipe her ass with it or whatever, because she owned it. The reward has always been in the journey. I never get to keep my paintings. Jake exchanged pleasantries with them, told them it was very nice to meet them, etc. And then, they hopped into a van and disappeared. There were other tourists inside, heading home with them. I hoped for their sake that her sanity was in check. Anyway, her exodus meant it was Jake and I, Antoine and Mirabel, and Colin and Parker...and Vince. We were down to seven. For whatever reason, Vince kept insisting I could ride with him, even though he was very aware of my condition, and that I really couldn't ride with anyone. Maybe he knew about the Toblerone?

Hugh had his assistant PayPal me $2,000, which is now how much I whored myself for. After two nights of decadent room service spreads and God knows how many bottles of wine, I was up to my neck on the Capital One Visa. I was in the part of the swimming pool where I could stand on my toes...but any further and I would drown. When I had a problem, my solution wasn't money or meds, like the group I was with, and I could see how having that ability could get abusive. The two grand provided my opportunity to exit the group. I would have to break it to Jake that night. I shouldn't have felt guilty, but I did.

When we arrived at Hotel Aspen, Jake walked me from the car to the room. He had his arm around me, almost as if he could sense my impending exit. The Eiger and

Wesserhorn mountains loomed behind this gorgeous hotel like God's bosoms. It was so painfully gorgeous that you felt it in all your senses. You couldn't just see it, you could smell and taste it. Beauty entered your pores, and became a part of your being. There was an outdoor spa you could see from the window. It was five stories, cloaked with glass and wood. I could imagine Christians, Muslims, and Jews frolicking in it, enjoying each other's company. If peace on Earth were ever negotiated, it would probably be at the Hotel Aspen in Grindelwald.

    The antique bed was dressed in linens you could die on. Willingly. The sheets felt like they were made out of virgins' skin. Even the toilet paper was out of this world. Once wiping your own ass reaches a state of bliss, you know you've entered uncharted waters. No pun intended.

    Jake opened the window to allow in the freshest breeze that this planet could exhale. He did not smoke. He didn't have to. He didn't want to. His lungs were filled with heaven.

    Jake did not leave me, constantly complimenting me and asking me if I needed anything. It was difficult to resist him. He was poetic, as if his texting personality had possessed his flesh and blood personality. I didn't want to resist him. I was lying on the bed, totally exhausted, but I could feel his eyes on me. I was aroused just by the presence of his stare.

    "I remember how wet you were the first time I touched you," he said matter-of-factly.

    "What about now?" I asked, hypnotized by the window.

    The sight was picturesque...a periwinkle blue sky framed by a floating wooden shutter, and right in the center...a mountain peak, haloed by clouds. Nothing moved. Except his hand on my thigh. I quivered a little, but did not turn to face him, as he ventured up to my nethers. I was breathing heavily, and my pussy was pleading for him to touch it. Which he did, softly, and over my panties at first.

"Getting there."

His breath was now on my neck. I could not move my gaze from the window as my body turned into a volcano beneath me. He continued to tease me. My head was buzzing, every part of me radiating from his touch. He started rubbing with slight pressure, until finally he slipped a finger inside the front of my panties. I yelped like Heidi. I was pudding now as he kissed me. Everything seemed wet, melted, liquefied. He put his hands all over me and fingers inside of me, and his mouth, and his cock, and every orifice was explored with ease as I clung to him and kissed him every chance I got.

And this time, I fell asleep first.

TORNADO

WE WOKE UP REALLY EARLY the next morning, and I was already feeling mostly healed, but I did not want to give up this rare attention. I begged him to take me for one more ride, since I had missed such a spectacular one the previous day. Jake didn't think it was a good idea, but I kept insisting it would make me feel better.

He finally said "OK", and we slowly took his bike up the mountain; purple laced with snowcaps, some peaking right through the clouds, they were like the doorway to heaven. And really, you began to understand why people believed there was such a thing, a heaven. A cloudy place of eternity with harps and wings and shit. This was why. The authors of the Bible must have vacationed here. The air was crisp. It reminded me of the perfect ecosystem we are so fortunate to live in. The only planet that can host us for millions of miles on each side. The right temperature. Atmosphere. Animals and plants we can convert into delicious food. I felt the miracle as I held Jake tight.

We stopped to enjoy the view. There was a little stream with fog suspended just above it like an empty thought bubble. The water glistened like it flowed with diamonds. We took off our helmets and kissed. His lips were so soft and warm.

Every fiber in my body was mousse. You could scoop me up with a spoon and put whipped cream on top. Jake had finally transformed into the man I had fantasized about. A man who touched my arm throughout the day, caressed my face, my hair, told me how beautiful I was, and shared experiences with me. It's all I'd ever wanted from him.

We drove back to the hotel and I hugged him tightly from behind. When we arrived at the room, he looked at me, grabbed the back of my neck and kissed my forehead before laying me down on the bed and making love to me again. At last, a Hollywood sequel I couldn't get enough of. This was one superhero I would always root for. Then we showered, put on our robes, and headed out for the spa. He was actually taking me to the spa.

We arrived. It was built entirely of cedar. The whole place emitted a sweet perfume that caressed your nose. You were not allowed to enter with any clothes on. There was no one else there, as if this place existed only for us. We explored all the levels, scrubbing each other down with salts, running in and out of steam rooms that we purposefully made too hot, and finally making our way to the rooftop, where there was a glorious sundeck and a cold plunge pool.

"You first!" he exclaimed.

"I'll go," I said smugly, and ripped off my robe.

But, suddenly childlike and pretty adorable, he leapt out of his robe and into the arctic bath, beating me to it. I followed suit. We both laughed and scrambled out of the tub with the same intention; to lie down on our two personal lounge chairs and drink in that glorious sun. Our naked bodies lay there, side by side, glistening from droplets of water illuminated by the rays, with little hairs still standing on end, excited from the extreme temperatures they had endured. The air was crisp and cool and the sun was just warm enough. I looked over at the Doc, who looked so peaceful with his eyes closed and a semi-smile on his parted lips.

"Savannah?"

"Yes?"

"I have something to tell you."

I was still looking at him, but he kept his face to the sun.

"Axel was... my patient."

You could see outside, the sky, the sun, but where were the dark clouds? The lightning storm? The fucking tornado to wipe up this gorgeousness into oblivion? They hadn't been cued. All the beautiful shit around me still thought he was going to say he loved me, or express something more profound, something that would bind us further together. And now, what Colin had told me in the car began to make sense.

"Would you care to know which country in World War II you are, Savannah?"

"OK," my mouth quivered. I could barely breathe, but I could listen.

"This is the country most pivotal in the first war. This country was badly invaded, and should have been dominated. Yet, she somehow held it together and came out victorious. But she paid a terrible price. Half of her population died. It was a pyrrhic victory."

Similarly, I dumped Axel, and felt great about myself for making a mature decision, but paid the price.

"In the second war, she did everything she could to avoid fighting again. No matter how dangerous the enemy got, she would avoid it. This time, she was invaded, and completely dominated. Only through exile and through being totally occupied by the enemy, was she able to once again recover and win."

I became intimate with Jake despite what my intuition warned me. He knew more about me than he let on. Only through leaving for Italy, and exiling myself from California, have I been able to find myself. But win? I don't know. Survive, maybe.

"The country is France. Rapidly invaded by the Germans. Occupied almost totally, with only the voice of Charles de Gaulle, who had fled to London, using the BBC radio to urge his countrymen to fight and take back his country. They were The Resistance."

It was surreal. I needed to take charge of myself again. This had gone far enough.

"You knew this whole time?" I asked Jake, astonished. "Wait, that was you… at the funeral… the cigarette… the hands."

"I failed him," Jake said sorrowfully, "he was my only patient who...died."

"Why didn't you tell me?" I felt my facial muscles beginning to function again.

"I didn't know how," he whispered, and I realized he was in as much pain as I was.

He grabbed my hand, keeping his face to the sun, and when he squeezed it, I saw a little tear trickle down the side of his face. I looked up at the imperfect clouds that lingered around the sun, letting in just enough light, and suddenly, the most beautiful sound filled the air... church bells. They kept getting stronger and deeper, and they echoed all over the sky. They were beautiful and haunting. They were never-ending. I can still close my eyes and hear them.

He wouldn't look at me. But I could hear him sniffling.

"Maybe I was an act of salvation," I suggested. I doubt I ever used the word "salvation" before.

"You were...someone I wanted to help," he whispered through his tears.

"And fuck," I added.

"Not at first. Well, you looked great in my office that day. What I mean was, I didn't intend to be attracted to you. I'm sorry, Savannah."

My skin was getting warm from the sun. The church bells persisted.

I was lying on the chaise, in the most beautiful place on Earth, totally naked, while memories since the night of my opening replayed in my head at high speed, like how you fast-forward a DVD x32, x64, x144. So fast in my mind, I couldn't make sense out of them. The hand paintings, the funeral, Axel's mom, the graffiti, the court grandma, cleaning the graffiti, meeting the Doc, Fourth of July, turning Italy down, accepting Italy, dinner with Joy, the first night when I waited for him, aliens, altitude sickness, World War II, France, Axel, Unicorns, Jake, old couples, Axel, horses, merry-go-rounds, wine, cheese, salami, Natasha, Germanic aliens, I love you Jake, I was Axel's doctor, WTF, purple mountains, The Sound of Music, Ethan Hawke and Julie Delpy, hand jobs on Harleys, fireworks, fat cat at AA meeting, the nude painting, France...

"I'm going to France," I announced.

UNICORN

JAKE HELD ME ALL NIGHT while we slept. And I let him. I wasn't angry; I was actually relieved in a way. It was cathartic. It was like that feeling after you had a really good cry as a kid. We both slept deeply. We woke up just when the sun did. And although neither of us wanted to, we began the deeply sad process of packing our stuff. We had packed after every hotel stay, but there's nothing like the sound of fastening and zippers when the trip is about to end. It feels like death.

When we finished, neither of us could find the ability to leave. We sat on the bed together, holding hands. My doctor was more fucked up than I was.

"When I was on drugs, I dreamt about a black horse every night. Fantasy and reality blurred a lot. Sometimes, I thought I saw this beast while I was conscious. He never harmed me, but he made sounds that were very frightening. His snort, it was like nothing I ever heard...when I went clean, joined NA, the beast slowly vanished from view. It was replaced by something else. A white unicorn. It had a beautiful mane, sparkling eyes, it looked healthy, it galloped with force, like it could never be tamed."

"You hallucinated this unicorn?"

"I dreamt about the unicorn. I dream about it every night. This creature is how I know I'm clean."

"Did you ever see this thing in real life?"

He looked at me like I should know the answer.

"I have seen her, yes," he said, his eyes caressing me.

We all had an early lunch outdoors together before parting ways. Fresh breads, salad with mountain goat cheese and herbs from the garden, smoked trout from the river... As it turned out, this was the end of the trip for everyone. Antoine and Maribel were next to leave. They were visiting Istanbul. They were very concerned about me going off on my own, and even invited me to come along. I declined, of course, and gave them a tearful goodbye.

"Stay out of trouble, young lady," Antoine said to me.

"You know me," I said.

"If you need anything, call us," said Maribel. It was kind to say that, but I'm always wondering what would happen if I ever called in this favor whenever someone said it. Hey, you said to call you if I needed anything, I was wondering if...I just wonder what Maribel would do. Has anyone ever actually claimed this promise? Maybe their brother Boris called in that favor. Look at what happened.

The group was decimated. Vince, Colin, Parker, Jake, and me – the only girl left, it dawned on me later. The fantastic five. No, it was more like the fatalistic five. I kept asking Vince about Natasha and he kept shrugging. The texts were still coming. She was in a hospital in Paris. And now, Darcy was re-emerging, texting me about the gallery. Joy was asking me when I was coming back. She had been "concerned" when Darcy returned without me.

I was thrilled to hear from her. It seemed like an eternity since we last spoke, but I turned the phone off.

We were sitting in a garden after lunch, now poking at some lovely pastries and petits fours, and ordering another round of espressos, just to buy more time. But, the end was imminent. The elephant in the garden.

Vince would be flying to Paris to pick up Natasha from the hospital, but first he would meet Pierce in Zurich. So, he did exist. Jake was going back to LA. The uncle and his nephew would actually keep me company for a little longer. But eventually, I would be flying solo.

At the airport, I hugged Jake like he was going to war and I was never going to see him again.

"Thanks for inviting me, Doc. It was a healing journey."

He pinched my left cheek like you do a child, before you say "she's so cute".

"Thank you for coming along," he smiled, then added, "my unicorn."

We searched each other's eyes for a clue of what was going to happen next. This is when you realize how limited language is. We both had more to say, but couldn't formulate the proper syllables.

"Axel loved you."

I might have loved him, too. I don't know. But I didn't share this with the doctor.

"According to Axel, there's a dimension where he's not dead. Do you think, you and I would have met anyway?"

"Yes," Jake said confidently, "we definitely would have met."

I looked right into his eyes. I loved him, in a way. He kissed my forehead.

Vince stared at me with kind eyes from just a few feet away, his arms outstretched. He was really the one to thank for the whole experience. He kept this humbly to himself. But, I knew.

"I don't know what to say," I was suddenly sobbing, as I walked towards him.

"Don't say anything, then!" he exclaimed cheerfully and embraced me.

Colin and Parker drove me to the train station in the next town. I had a whole arrangement to get from Italy to northern France. The old man who had my painting was on an island called Brêhat. There were no cars on this island. There weren't even addresses.

"There's no address?" Parker asked.

"I'm supposed to go to an area of the island called Pharon Sur Point. It's like the third house. I'm supposed to ask the neighbors, I guess."

"Would you like us to accompany you?" asked Colin.

"Oh no, please."

"You prefer to be on your own," Colin announced.

I didn't answer right away, but eventually said, "Yes, gentlemen. But it's very nice of you to offer."

"Do you think this old geezer will give you your painting back?"

"I don't know. But if I could at least see it. See where he's hanging it, even if I can't get it back...I don't know, we'll see."

I had coffee again with Colin and Parker before my train took off. They both seemed friendly with each other, as if the cruelty had been an act just for the group, but now that everyone was gone, they were their normal selves again. Colin kept asking Parker if he wanted something else to eat. I was really high on coffee by now.

"What was in that painting that freaked out Darcy?" asked Parker.

"I don't know," I said, "it was my best painting though. I would take that over the one I'm after. It's the last portrait I'll ever do."

Colin was watching the TV at the train station. The news was continuing to show evidence of the stock market descending. The headlines were all in red. A stock was in ruins. Another was devastated. Was what Hallenbeck predicted happening as we sat there?

"Gentlemen," I asked, "did either of you know that the vagina is connected to the spinal cord?"

They both looked at me like I was crazier than Natasha and Darcy. Then they cracked up. They were both in tears. Their skin was swelling, they were cackling so hard. It sort of irritated me, but I probably wouldn't see either of them again.

"I'm serious," I protested, "we're talking about a membrane with intelligence."

They laughed uproariously. Others were gazing at us.

When I hugged them, I had tears in my eyes. Not from laughter, but sadness.

They waved to me from the train platform. That was the last of the group. No more aliens, WWII theories, prescription drugs, spas, and motorcycles. Just me and my brilliant pussy. I already missed the gang.

PURE EVE

I WAS IN A TRANCE all the way to France. Natasha's eye daggers, Darcy's old people fetish (or so I thought), her traumatic reaction to my painting, Jake's extreme texts then extreme celibacy, the group of men I dined with, the gynecologist I should have had drinks with, the heart-shaped pizza, the Countach, the night of terror, Boris the mooch, Darcy and Antoine's trip to Cambodia, Colin's theories, Parker's assertion that Colin was a cunt, the aliens hovering above poor Natasha, Hugh's silence, all the food we ate (God, I'll probably never eat that well again, and I never need to), Hallenbeck's stock market predictions, Axel, my show, the funeral, Joy who was now texting me relentlessly...

"Hi Joy," I called her finally.
"How are you?" Joy asked cautiously.
"How should I be?"
"You should be great."
"How are you?"

"Good. When are you coming back? You want me to pick you up?"

"I'm not coming back. Not yet."

"Savvy, what do you mean, you're not coming back?"

"I mean, I have to go visit a friend in Paris, then do something else."

"But the...bike thing is over, isn't it?"

"Joy, I'm going to retrieve my painting."

"Which...painting?"

"The one where I'm naked."

"The pervert who bought it, you're dealing with him? That's it, Savvy, tell me where you're at, I'm coming."

"No, you're not. I'm fine. I can't wait to see you again. But I'm fine and I'm going to go get it."

"Darcy said you're losing it."

"Darcy said I'm losing it? That is hilarious."

"Are you?"

"I have to go, Joy."

"No, no, no, don't hang up."

"What...what's up?"

"Good luck."

"Thanks, Joy."

When I got to Paris, I had about five hours before my next train from Garre d'Austerlitz. I wandered aimlessly, smiling at no one in particular, feeling like I just escaped prison, feeling free for the first time.

I hadn't felt this sensation since I first arrived in Europe, but now it was different. I wasn't waiting on Jake. Yes, I was meeting Natasha, but I wanted to meet her. OK, maybe her texting had bullied me into it, but it was on my way to Brêhat, my final destination. I didn't have my phone on that much, but when I fired it up, I saw the messages pile up and shut it off again. Joy was sending me more messages than Natasha, if you could believe. But I stopped answering a while ago.

The Saltepriere was a very old hospital, hundreds of years old, where tons of diseases were discovered. Darcy normally would be the person to give me the guide book run-down on the place. But this time it was Natasha. This was her favorite hospital. When her mother had tuberculosis, this is where she was treated. Natasha didn't see her mom for three months, but it felt like a year. When she visited, she would frequently spend time in the Charcot Museum, this being the guy who discovered the endless diseases we love today. Freud studied here. At this very hospital. I guess we can't escape penis envy, even with vaginas of 150 I.Q. Like Darcy, she didn't speak about her dad much. In the back of my mind, I still wondered if what Darcy said to me was just a hallucination. Can I really compare their mother fixations?
"I was very big on my mother," said Natasha.
Up to this point, I'd only heard her say what she was NOT big on, so this was big. I didn't get this mother stuff. She actually appeared the healthiest she'd ever looked. To me. In the limited time we knew each other. Her eye daggers had vanished. She had this childlike, virginal glow to her. Constantly smiling. I wondered if being away from Vince had something to do with it.
"I miss Vincent," she said. Then, "You know, I'm 35."
Wow. She looked like she was about 21. And, I could have sworn she said she was 25. Guess my intoxicated ears are not bionic. It was crazy that she was that old. Not that 35 is old, but if you could see this woman, you just wouldn't think 35. You would card her, except that she's

pretty cute, so you probably wouldn't because of her charm. Why was she telling me how old she was?

"Since I was little, I wanted to be a mother. And now, I know I won't be."

"You're not that old," I said.

"It has nothing to do with age. I can't have children. But being 35, it reminds me of that. My body disagrees with my desires. That's just the way it is."

She paused for a while, then continued.

"Thank you for coming. For visiting me. It's very kind of you."

I don't know if it was necessarily kind. She was on the way to the island I was heading to. But I didn't say that. I shrugged and said, "Yeah, sure, anytime."

I was also wondering if she would talk as long as Darcy, since I only had a limited time before catching the train.

"What time is your train?"

"Don't worry about that," I said.

"Which train station is it?"

"Austerlitz."

"There's an amazing library near there. It's four stories. Buffon Library. I used to go there and borrow books and records and DVDs. It's beautiful. It overlooks Jardin de Plantes. I spent so much time there. Afterwards, I would wander through Jardin de Plants. In the summer, there would be a piano there. Music students would play Chopin, Beethoven, even Tchaikovsky. I thought these moments would last forever. They don't. Time doesn't agree with me. You know, I didn't lose my virginity until I was 25. I never told anyone that. Not any of my numerous shrinks. Not any of the doctors from Eastern and Western schools. Maybe I should have. Maybe that was the key."

"What...took you so long?" I asked curiously, really pitying her at this point.

"I was just shy. I learned later that shyness and timidity is a narcissistic impulse. You're thinking more about yourself than the other person. That's what they said."

"It makes sense, yeah."

"But maybe I was just afraid of men."

"Who did you finally lose your virginity to?"

It suddenly dawned on me how it's phrased. That you're losing something. When, in my book, you're, you know, gaining something. I was 16, in case anyone wonders. But I didn't tell Natasha that. Didn't want to give the girl a friggin' heart attack.

"Ernest. He was 11 years older than me. He wrote me letters. He liked me a lot. I just didn't like him. Not that way. But I wanted to get rid of it. I wasn't big on having my innocence anymore. It was choking me. It was choking my life. We were together for two years. When I broke up with him, he said it was like his skin was ripped from mine. I felt the same, but I just didn't care for him that way. Do you know what 'Freud' means in German?"

"No, what does Freud mean?"

"Joy. To anyone outside Germany, Dr. Freud was Dr. Joy."

"Dr. Joy would profess penis envy. Wow."

"And the Oedipus Complex. And dream interpretation."

"So, these things were positive."

"The German language has many double meanings, triple meanings. One word can mean all sorts of things. The translation does not always surface."

I couldn't wait to tell Joy that she was named after Sigmund Freud.

"Did you enjoy our trip, Natasha?"

"I don't like trips. I don't like traveling anymore. I lose too much control. I like being in one place. When I was a kid, I was in many places. I don't need to see any more places. I like where my friends are, where my habits are. When you go somewhere else, you go outside yourself too. That's why people do things they normally wouldn't do on vacation. It's a license to act outside their normal selves."

She was suddenly sounding like a shrink. Like a good one, too.

"You and Dr. Rivers, how is that coming along?"

"It's not. He's not my doctor anymore," I said defensively.

"He's not your lover anymore," she said matter-of-factly.

"Is he still *your* doctor?" My tone was snarky. I didn't want any tension between us, I mean we were having such a nice chat, but I couldn't help myself.

"He is everyone's doctor. He can't help it. And he struggles with it – the conflict of working with those he knows personally. It's his own battle. He had the same battle with you, but you were too close to see it."

I thought about this for a second, and then decided to keep it light.

"It's OK. I had a good time anyway. I'd always wanted to go to Italy."

"Did you know in Italy, divorce was illegal until 1975?"

"Incredible."

"Can you imagine the women waiting in line on that day?"

"Yeah, totally. The gelato place and the divorce office must have been packed."

"I would love some lemon gelato right now."

"What are your favorite gelato places in Paris?"

Her eyes lit up like the spaceship that brought her here.

"Let's see, I love Grom's, I know it's popular, but with their crème fraîche, it's quite delightful. Berthillon is very good of course. Their pear ice cream is better than pear itself. The only time humans have created something better than the original," she said, as she giggled and blushed. You wanted to pinch her cheeks, seriously. She even looked around to make sure no one heard her. Her adorable meter was through the roof.

"But you know, the best ice cream place in all of Europe is in Budapest. Fagoly. It's amazing. They have different flavors every day. In August, when it is baking, they have raspberry, cherry, olive."

"Olive?"

"Oh yes. It's quite good. Quite."

"What about chocolate?"

"Hot chocolate?"

"Hot, cold."

I didn't realize the girl liked desserts so much. It was fun to talk about.

"Well, in Paris, all the tourists go to Angelina's, but it's pretty gross now. And too sweet. It tastes like powder. I think it's like the Big Mac now, their African hot chocolate. There's a place in the Cartier Latin, Café Viennoise. The ladies there have been there since forever. They give you a hot chocolate with crème fraîche and sugar on the side. I never put sugar in it. I just drink the raw chocolate, but can I tell you a secret?"

Wow, Natasha was about to tell me a secret.

"Sometimes, I purchase a pain au chocolat with my hot chocolate. I find a private spot in Jardin du Luxembourg, and I dip it in the hot chocolate. And I eat it. Piece by piece."

"Bad girl."

"I know, it's so evil. But I love it so much."
"Well, your secret is safe with me."
"Your secret is safe with me, too."

I wasn't sure what she meant. I presumed, the nude painting. I didn't care anymore. I didn't want to know what she knew about me. I was just enjoying this moment with Natasha. I didn't want to get into defensive subjects. Also, I liked that she thought we both possessed each other's secrets.

When I left the Salteprier, I entered a nearby subway, where sounds of various languages echoed in the corridors, where the human ant farm of Paris erupted through every corridor. I ended up at Le Marais, where I sat at a random place for a café crème and baguette. Everything tasted delicious and my senses were alive. The bread was crusty and fleshy, soft and hard simultaneously. I gagged on the warmness and the tenderness. The café crème mixed in perfect textures with the bread. It was an intense moment. I watched traffic and pedestrians and the cloud formations. The sound of the subway cars burrowing through tunnels, arriving, the signal, the doors slamming shut; they were all music to my ears. I don't know if it was a coincidence, but I found "Grom's" the gelato place in question. And in honor of Natasha, I enjoyed a lemon sorbet with crème fraîche, which was indeed quite good. Quite.

My senses were hungry for more. Taste, sound and sight were taken care of, now the two others were begging for participation.

Smell was next. I found a place called Nose, where you sniff through a series of notes until they narrow it down to your perfect perfume. Between every enrapturing scent, I had to sniff ground coffee beans to keep my nose sharp and focused.

"Your scent is called Pure Eve," the Frenchman said, who presented me with my scent in a bottle. I don't know if he was full of shit, but I purchased the bottle. I had one more sense to attend to. I ended up at Jardin de Plantes, where smell again filled my nostrils with unequalled rapture. But I found a tree, crooked, disfigured and Elephant Man in every way, and I touched it, my fingers feeling its bark, and I shut my eyes, so I could just see it with my fingertips; its harsh, yet gentle texture, its jagged yet smooth timber. I felt like the tree knew I was connecting to it, like I wanted to feel what the tree was feeling. And I could tell, this tree had been around for a while, before World War II, maybe even into World War I, and its solidness exerted into my fingertips and I could see its memories and understand how it could just stand there and see human history and stay calm, because time moved amazingly fast for this tree. It was hot outside, but cool beside it. The cold breath of the tree told many stories.

Before the train, I somehow found the time (and appetite) for a place aptly called L'Éclair– it was like a gallery of éclairs, almost too good to eat, too deep to eat. Almost. I devoured a Madagascan vanilla éclair, that made my taste buds beg for fucking mercy. I was shocked into the memory of Jake handcuffing me. That's how good this phallic symbol shaped desert was. Jesus.

Then, Montpellier train station. There, I would purchase my ticket for Paimpol. The station was crowded. Filled with young women traveling alone and some in groups and some in couples. There were not as many dude groups, like you'd see in the US, for some reason. Not trying necessarily to paint a feminist picture, though never against it. Just reporting it like I saw it; the men were outnumbered.

By the time I got there, I missed the latest train. The next one was not for another hour, so I bought the ticket and explored the station, cavity and all. Train stations are so romantic, so nostalgic, no matter where they are situated. If there's one in hell, I bet it's quite good. Quite.

On the second level, there was a champagne bar overlooking all of the action, and light beamed in from a giant, arched window like God was pissing into it. I took a seat at the bar, basked in the dusty rays of sunlight, and ordered a glass of champagne.

"Would you like to see a menu?" the bartender asked suggestively. He was holding one out, sort of offering it to me.

Was I hungry? Did I need to be hungry in France? The sensation of pork rillettes was oddly tempting. Yes, I accepted the menu and ordered said rillettes.

"I'll have the pork rillettes. Merci."

But the way I said it sounded more like mercy. The rillettes came to me in a glass jar with crusty bread and cornichons, and it was just as decadently delicious as I had hoped. More food for a woman my size, but my heart was in the right place and I killed the rillettes and thought about the beautiful pig who gave his/ her life for me to enjoy this near-religious meal.

France, oh France, oh food bon vivant! I felt like screaming.

I was savoring a second round of bubbles, and finger-licking the remnants of rillettes, when I realized the time. Five minutes until my train.

"Shit! Garcon!"

I sucked down what was left in my crystal flute and scurried to the train. I was hauling my luggage like Matt Damon in a Bourne Movie, but I had luggage to carry and Damon had, like, five passports and that's it.

My car was full, so I sat upright, squeezed between two French women with my leather jacket draped over my lap and my luggage between my knees. I still wore my biker boots. They were too cumbersome to carry in my sac.

We zipped through several little towns along the way. I saw cows grazing in pastures, and vast fields of grassy land and thought about all the delicious Brie they produced and suddenly desired Brie or Camembert or something soft and cheesy.

Perched atop a rolling hill with a dirt path leading to the front, a bucolic home stood alone, made of stone with an A-frame roof and a bright red door. I wondered who lived there, what they did all day, what they ate, and if they made love in that little home with miles of vacant land on either side. And also, if they were currently eating Brie and cornichons and chugging Cabernet.

KISSING DISTANCE

GUINGAMP. I HAD EXACTLY eleven minutes for my train exchange to Paimpol, where I would catch the ferry to Brêhat. Good thing it was a tiny little station with only two tracks. Still, I felt the incessant need to ask for directions. I found a properly-dressed conductor, whistle and all.

"Sir, where is the train to Paimpol?"

The wind was blowing. Two American girls in front of me were buying tickets and their Euros flew away like seagulls. I rushed across the bridge to retrieve the money for them. They thanked me. I think. It was loud.

I returned to the conductory-looking dude and asked again where the train to Paimpol was, and with the bravado of a Broadway actor, he bellowed, "Madame... Paimpol!" He gestured with his arm theatrically, and pointed to the train...right across the track, of course. Wind blew my hair around like flames. It was very Gone with the Wind. Literally.

This train was tinier, and it really made me feel like I was getting off the grid. I was honestly sick of the grid. The train to Paimpol would only be another hour and a half, and then I would be just across the water from Isle de Brêhat...and thus my painting, ladies and gentlemen.

When I arrived in Paimpol, I needed to dig deep for my high school level French. I managed to hitch a ride with another family traveling to the ferry. They were French, and did not speak a lick of English; a refreshing attitude, after meeting almost exclusively Europeans who spoke only English to you in Italy, Austria and Switzerland, where they all juggled five languages.

We zigzagged along a windy little street, with boulangeries and patisseries, and hills with more fairytale homes and horses grazing about. There were one or two cars in the street, and a man dressed in his Sunday best marched up the street gripping a fresh baguette in one arm, which sort of embodied the essence of this sweet little place on Earth. Finally, we arrived at the ferry station to Isle de Brêhat. There wasn't much there, besides the ticket counter, and a little convenience store where I purchased a bottle of water and a Toblerone. I thought of Jake. He was texting me from LA. So were Joy and Darcy. Natasha was also still communicating with me, but no longer about aliens. She asked me to visit her and Vince. They were in Bordeaux. I considered it.

I took the ferry, which contained mostly French tourists. They were thrilled to visit Brêhat, "the island of flowers". They looked out at the volatile ocean with wonder, like they had never been on a boat before. The sky was ominous, I will attest to that.

There was a fat guy with a camera who took a million pictures. There was a little girl glued to the window, transfixed by the cobalt blue of the water. The wind whipped around the boat and the waves were rough and frothy. A light drizzle began, then it became more forceful, until finally it was a full-on rainstorm complete with deep grunts of thunder. I didn't mind. In fact, it seemed that everything was exactly the way it should be. Twenty minutes later, like on the show Fantasy Island, we marched from the boat and traversed Brêhat.

The rain stopped, and the sun peeked out. I felt like Dorothy when she landed on the yellow brick road. The rock formations looked prehistoric. The water was neither blue or green, but somehow both. The sheen of the Mediterranean was incandescent. There really were no cars here. The only way around was to rent a bicycle. So, that's what I did.

I pedaled through a maze of flowers: canary yellow, fuchsia, crimson. The sun was shining brightly now and the sky was periwinkle blue. It was like being sucked from one end of a rainbow to the other end, then ricocheting back. The air was fresh and calming, reminiscent of Hotel Aspen. The houses were right out of a fairytale, surrounded by lambent flowers with colors so potent, you had to wear your sunglasses to look at them for very long.

I stopped to visit a lighthouse on the edge of the island. I walked on the rocks, which had oysters and clams attached to them. I nearly tripped several times, hopscotching there when I realized seagulls were flying dangerously close to my head. Well, one of them was.
They were shrieking in panic.

I was getting too close to the lighthouse. They must have had a nest there. They didn't like that I was trespassing. I hurried back to my bicycle.

The island was a small world. Maybe a few miles wide. I thought if the world ended, if Hallenbeck was right, these Brêhat citizens may never know and just continue what they were doing. And maybe I should join them and never leave.

It wasn't difficult to find "Pharon sur Point". It was on the edge. Of the world, it seemed. At one point, the tribes living here may have thought that.

I passed two houses, and it appeared as if the third was attached, but I wasn't sure. I got off the bicycle, out of breath, and walked inside the coral-colored gate. I noticed there was another bike leaning against an apple tree. Although this was the front door, it felt like a back entrance.

The sun was pretty low now, silhouetting the person standing in front of me in his yard.

"Bonjour, hello...I'm Savannah...Waters," I greeted the old man.

He stepped toward me and seemed to emerge from his silhouette as if it was a cloak, as if he was squeezing out of the masquerade. And out came out, not an old man, but a younger man. In fact, as I computed his eyes, ears, nose, I realized that I knew him.

"Hello Ms. Waters," he greeted, taking my hand and kissing it.

"Oh my God," I couldn't help saying, "you're the guy from my opening."

"The hands, yes," he held out texty hands, "like a T-Rex."

I chuckled in disbelief, but then acted upset, slapping his shoulder. "You bought my painting on eBay?"

"Of course I buy it! It's incredible."

"You made me come all the way over here to get it back?"

"I told you in LA, you will be imprisoned here, to paint as I wish."

"Like the movie about the writer and the fat girl?"

"Precisely."

As I was absorbing the reality that Gaspar DeVillier was the man who had the painting I had given to Axel, he gave me a tour of his house. He didn't live there the whole year, he assured me. He would get sucked into a fantasy world. But this is where he kept most of my paintings.

There were two hand paintings he purchased from the show. There were some abstracts I did in the 90s, one portrait of a couple I don't recall doing. No idea how he found this one – there was one I did with Darcy, with both of our names signed. Courtesy of the contents of her purse...lipstick, eye shadow, American Express card, some cash...Darcy's driver's license, though her face was obscured. She didn't look 100 in this one.

And finally, he led me to the pièce de résistance.

Behold, the self-nude.

I hadn't seen it since I left it in Axel's apartment.

The light beamed on it perfectly, illuminating one half and leaving the other half in shadows.

"There she is," Gaspar presented, then said in whispery voice, "my pride and joy. I wake up every morning to her."

She was in the bedroom.

I stared at myself, sitting on a chair, my head tilted, my eyes melancholy...it wasn't as raw as I remembered. I was not obscenely nude. You saw boobs, you saw genitalia, but it was an OK posture. An honest depiction. My genitalia even looked kind of smart.

"I just wanted to see her," I whispered.

"Your greatest work," Gaspar said, admiring the painting in kissing distance, sort of caressing the frame, as if touching the painting itself was forbidden.

"I just wanted to see if she was in a good place," I clarified, "and she is."

"So, what's next?" Gaspar asked.

"She can stay here. For now."

FIN

Made in the USA
Middletown, DE
29 April 2021